CONSUMED

COLLIDE SERIES BOOK 2

J.C. HANNIGAN

T his is a work of fiction. Names, characters, places, and incidents either are the product of the author's imagination or used fictitiously. Any resemblance to actual persons, living or dead, events, or locales is entirely coincidental.

Copyright © 2014 by J.C. Hannigan

Cover Design by Yosbe Design
Edited by Nikki Colligan
Formatted by J.C. Hannigan

ISBN 978-0-9951911-8-1 (paperback)
ISBN 978-0-9951911-2-9 (ebook)

CONSUMED

Collide Series Book 2

J.C. Hannigan

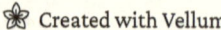 Created with Vellum

PROLOGUE

I had never been the typical female teenager. While I did keep a journal throughout my adolescence, I didn't fill it's pages with useless chatter about high school crushes and petty drama. Probably because the drama in my life was *far* from petty. My journal pages mostly detailed the dark musings of a suffering girl who's first sexual encounter hadn't been consensual, and who's only friend at the time died tragically in a car accident.

It wasn't until my final year in high school that the pages of my journal were filled with the whimsical musings of someone who thought she was in love. The stereotypical, almost nauseating story of how girl meets boy, girl falls for boy and thinks that boy is madly in love with her and would risk anything to be with her. Only...my story didn't end the typical way, either. We didn't remain together, which I suppose isn't much of a shocker...most high school romances do not last beyond the corridors lined with lockers and the smell of sweaty gym feet. Plus, the boy in question wasn't really a boy at all, he was a teacher. My teacher. Eleven years my senior, and he ended up in jail because of our relationship.

High school wasn't that long ago, in retrospect. Two years into University, two years into my Bachelor's of Art in English. I had one more year to finish up my Emphasis on Women's Studies, then I would be out in the real world trying to figure out exactly what I was to do with a BA in English with an Emphasis on Women's Studies.

In all that time, I hadn't heard a whisper from the person I'd foolishly fallen for. I knew he'd been released from jail, I knew that he definitely wasn't teaching again. I didn't know where he was though, and truthfully...I hadn't bothered to seek him out.

I did write him one letter, shortly after I learned of his incarceration. To this day, I still have no idea if he ever received it. He never replied. I told him where I was headed, and the silence on his end told me that things weren't *exactly* as I thought they'd been between us.

It was ridiculous to hope that after his release, he'd come to his home town and find me waiting patiently for him and we could resume exactly where we left off. Hope I did, for the first year...but as the seasons changed, and his silence stretched longer still...I knew we could never go back to the way that we were. I didn't know if jail changed him, but it had changed *me*.

I learned a hard lesson. Pursing the things that I wanted, when it came to matters of the heart, was dangerous and foolish. I'd only end up hurt.

My intention was to never let my heart do the thinking again. I never wanted to feel the way I felt in the wake of his silence. Or the guilt that twisted up my gut when I thought about how ruined his life was, all because I just *had* to act on that chemistry between us.

My roommate and best friend, Jenna, insisted that I wasn't to blame, that he should have known better. Maybe that's true, but I also knew I was playing with fire. I should have had the emotional maturity and clarity to wait to act. If I had merely waited a year, than everything could have been different.

CHAPTER
ONE

The first day of my third year of University was not off to a good start. I overslept my alarm, prompting me to have to rush my morning routine, my system void of coffee. I hated mornings to begin with, but mornings where I had to rush with zero caffeine in me were the absolute *worst*.

"Morning!" Jenna's chipper voice greeted me as I tore my room apart, looking for something to wear. She was paused in my doorway, peering in with just a towel wrapped around her body. I glared at her, resenting her early morning perkiness. Jenna laughed, shaking her head at me as she passed. She didn't take my crusty mood personally. After two years of living together in an apartment near our University, she'd long since accepted the fact that I wasn't and would never be a morning person.

I slapped on some makeup that artfully hid the bags under my eyes, and selected a semi-hot outfit from my wardrobe: a pair of well worn skinny jeans, a sleeveless black v-neck shirt, and a plaid black and blue button up blouse.

"Are you ready yet?" Jenna asked, standing in my doorway

again and watching me as I ran my fingers through my hair, teasing the slight curls.

Jenna was dressed in an expensive pair of Guess jeans and a A-line midnight blue shirt paired with a brown jacket. I used to complain about how much she spent on her clothes...until I tried a pair of her Guess jeans on. Even I had to admit they were almost worth the price tag, they were that comfortable.

"Yeah," I grumbled, still not awake yet. I threw on my black leather jacket, the same one I'd worn since high school. I couldn't remember a time I *hadn't* worn it. The leather had seen better days, but I still couldn't retire it to my closet. Jenna had been trying for years to get me to hang it up.

Jenna's thin blond eyebrows arched in question, but she didn't make a smart remark about the jacket. She knew I was ready to kill without my morning cup of coffee.

"Let's go to get coffee before class," Jenna suggested, speaking sweet promises of coffee straight to my soul. I nodded gratefully, grabbing my messenger bag and flicking off my bedroom light as I followed her.

Our apartment was rather small, but it suited us both well. We each had our own bedroom with large closets. The bathroom was a little cramped, but we managed. The living room and kitchen were open concept, with a flat screen TV and a couch, a coffee table and two end tables from Ikea...all second hand Kijiji finds found by me. Jenna had been completely wigged out over the idea of second hand furniture, until I mentioned we'd be depending less on her dad.

Jenna's parents paid for the apartment. They didn't want Jenna to have to worry about making ends meet while in school, they wanted her to focus on University. They allowed me to live there rent free as well, but I still insisted on giving Mr. Burke rent money each month, and working a part-time job. I was used to working, used to taking care of myself.

Mr. Burke allowed me the illusion of fending for myself, but I knew that he was not-so-secretly putting it all the money I gave him for rent in a separate bank account to give me after graduation. Jenna had spilled the beans one night, but insisted I keep the knowledge secret. I knew that her parents felt indebted to me.

I hadn't done a single thing to earn this kind of treatment from them. All I had done was stood by Jenna when she needed it. I didn't think I should get a free ride because of it. Besides, if anyone was indebted to anyone else...it was me to them. They lessened the headache and stress of living expenses, and got me out of my mom and Larry's house.

My mood darkened slightly at the thought of my mom and Larry. It'd been two years since I'd left home, and I was thankful every day that I was on my own. I still spoke to my mom often, but my trips back to North Bay were becoming less and less frequent. If it weren't for Jenna, I wouldn't return home at all. Unlike me, Jenna wasn't estranged from her parents and enjoyed spending holidays with them.

"I can't wait to graduate," Jenna remarked, sighing wistfully, thinking about the year ahead of us. We both had one more year left of classes before our undergraduate studies would be done. After that, it was a free for all. Jenna's goals tended to flip flop all over the place. She didn't really know what she wanted to do. She'd loaded up on a whole bunch of courses, taking several business ones.

Jenna always said she was envious of how solid I was in what I wanted to do, but the truth was...I hadn't the slightest idea of what was going to happen once I graduated. I knew I would always want to write, but I needed something a little more concrete than that to fall back on. It wasn't like they were dueling out jobs for writers. Still, I stuck to my goal. The last thing I wanted to hear from my

Mom and Larry was "I told you so". They both insisted I should pursue what they considered an "actual" career, like dental assisting.

"What's your first class?" I asked, my voice groggy from lack of use. We descended the stairs and pushed on the doors that led to the street. Our apartment was located in a beautifully renovated Victorian house near Sandy Hill, five minutes away from the University campus. I yawned as the chilly morning air hit my face. 8am was *way* too early for classes to start, in my opinion.

"Accounting, but not until 9," Jenna explained, giving me a sheepish smile. "I'm hoping to run into someone at *The Bean* though."

The little coffee shop between our apartment and campus, *The Bean*, was a quick seven minute walk from the stoop of our apartment, a mere five minutes away from campus. I'd managed to land a job there shortly after we moved to Ottawa. I absolutely loved working there, not only was the coffee and food *amazing*, but my bosses were really awesome. *The Bean* was run by Jamie Atwood and Mark Judge. Mark was the baker and chef, and Jamie ran all of the business end and scheduling. He also worked the front and was by far the customer's favourite to deal with.

Aside from Jamie, Mark and I, there was only one other employee, a guy that Jenna had a not-so-secret crush on. His name was Lucas, he was nice, from what I knew, which wasn't a lot as we worked on opposite shifts.

Lucas was cute enough, tall and lanky with jet black hair. His eyes were a hazel colour, and he wore black square framed glasses. He reminded me of what Harry Potter might look like in his early twenties, if Harry Potter was a hipster wizard. When Jenna had confessed her new crush to me, I couldn't help but burst out laughing.

"Were you obsessed with Harry Potter as a teen?" I had asked her, trying to control my laughter.

"No," she had glared, unimpressed with my analogy of his looks. Moments later, she could no longer hide the smile that revealed her true feelings. "Okay...maybe a little."

He was not my cup of tea, but Jenna was clearly into whatever he was serving...so much so that she could barely form the words to get her order out when he served her.

"Why don't you just ask him out?" I grumbled, questioning my friends sanity. If I had the option of sleeping in a little longer on Monday mornings, I'd definitely be taking it. Jenna shrugged, lifting her hand up to touch her short hair. She'd recently chopped off the length, going for a cute and trendy bob that resembled Victoria Beckham's hair. It suited her, but she was still unsure about it. I knew she was questioning her decision to chop off her hair again, especially with the looming possibility of seeing her crush. "You look fine," I added, rolling my eyes.

Jenna's insecurities were unfounded. She had that in your face, all-American-girl beauty. Blond hair, blue eyes, killer curves and a dimpled smile. She radiated a warmth that you couldn't help but be drawn to. She was a startling contrast from me. I had long dark hair, emerald green eyes, and a sarcastic bite that kept everyone at a safe distance. I had more curves than necessary, and I hadn't grown taller since high school while Jenna had shot up in height.

Our tastes were vastly different too. Jenna loved bright colours, she had a fashion taste that I couldn't understand. I liked nice clothes as much as the next girl, but I couldn't be tempted into splurging on anything. Jenna's look was considered expensive, professional and classy, while mine was more grunge...glam grunge, according to Jenna, and I certainly didn't mind thrift store finds.

Our walk took less than the predicted seven minutes, and soon we were waiting in the crowded line up of *The Bean*. It was a popular spot for college students, everybody loved the vibe of the shop and how personable Jamie and Mark were. I could hear their playful banter from the kitchen, even if I couldn't see them. It made me smile. Jamie and Mark were madly in love with each other, and it was refreshing to see.

Jenna grasped my upper arm, her nails digging in enough for me to almost wince, even through the leather sleeve of my jacket.

"It's him," she whispered, delicately nodding her head in the direction of the front cash. I rolled my eyes, exasperated with her.

"This time, try actually *saying* something to him," I muttered, gently tugging my arm away from Jenna's grasp. "Play it cool," I added.

Jenna looked nervous. My heart warmed a little for her. She'd had a rough go the last several years, a traumatic experience at the end of high school had left a sour taste in her mouth. She'd had a brief fling with a mutual friend of ours, Jake Patterson, but it hadn't worked out. They were just too different. The three of us were still friends, but more like distance friends that communicated by Facebook. The last I'd heard from Jake, he had cleaned up his act and was joining the military. It would be interesting to see how that played out; Jake hated authority figures, and had spent the majority of his high school career selling marijuana.

When it was our turn, I nodded at Lucas in greeting. He smiled back at us, his hazel eyes lingering on Jenna for a moment before he spoke. "What can I get you lovely ladies?" Jenna giggled in response, blushing.

"I'll take a coffee," I said, trying to hide my smile at my

friends discomfort, and allowing her a moment to collect herself.

"Green tea for me, please," she all but squeaked.

"Is that our Harlow I hear?" Jamie's sing song voice rang out, his blond head popping up over the kitchen door. "It is! Mark, Harlow's come to say hello!" Seconds later, he was walking purposely around the counter to embrace me in a hug. Mark came out with a tray of donuts, grinning his hello at me and winking warmly at Jenna.

Jamie was tall with shoulder length blond hair and a tan that he religiously kept up. He had forest green eyes and was very lean. Mark was night to Jamie's day. He had dark hair, dark eyes and a dusting of stubble across his chin. He was taller and broader. They were both friendly, warm, inviting and extremely fun. They'd all but adopted Lucas and I as their surrogate children, and what I knew about Lucas was from Jamie.

"You're not coming by to bail out of your shift tonight, are you?" Jamie joked.

"Of course, I already told you that I quit!" I joked back, grinning.

"Nobody else would hire you, you're too cold," Jamie shot back, winking at me.

"Oh please," I rolled my eyes. I knew he was kidding, but it still stung a little. I was a good employee, I did my job and I was warm to the customers, but I knew I wasn't fooling Jamie or Mark. Smiling and exchanging easy banter with customers did *not* come easily to me.

"Here's your change," Lucas interrupted, holding out the change. "Unless you want me to add it to my tip jar."

"Sure, go ahead. Buy yourself a haircut," I shot back, smirking. Jamie laughed.

"You wicked girl," he abolished. I shrugged, sparing a

glance at Jenna. She was biting her glossy lip, looking hopefully at Lucas. Jamie's intelligent eyes swept over her, noting the object of her attention, and grinned mischievously. "Hmm...looks like I have a lot of work to do today," he added thoughtfully. "I'll see you around 3, Harlow. Good luck today!"

Jenna and I stepped aside to wait for our orders. She looked down at her feet, disappointment marring her delicate features. She didn't see Lucas' eyes slide back to her after he finished taking the next order, or how his eyes lingered on her as we fixed our beverages at the sugar station.

"Gee, thanks for the help," Jenna muttered as we left *The Bean* and headed towards a cluster of the campus' many buildings. She took a sip of her Green tea, pouting at me with her wide eyes.

"Don't ask for my help," I warned her, laughing. "You won't like the method." I took a sip of my hot coffee, embracing the flavours as they danced across my taste buds. "Besides, I think maybe Jamie is adopting this cause."

"What?" Jenna exclaimed, looking behind us at the doors to *The Bean*. Jenna had heard stories about Jamie and how he loved to meddle and play matchmaker.

I grinned, happy that maybe Jamie would get off *my* back about dating if he had Lucas to focus on. Plus, Jenna needed the help. Of course, I'd thought about helping Jenna...maybe by mentioning her to Lucas...but I wasn't exactly known for my delicate approach of such matters. Jamie would be better at it. I was too blunt, through and through. Jamie was blunt too, but he was gentle about it. I was cold, and impersonal...as he pointed out.

"You're late, by the way," Jenna huffed, nodding her head in the direction of a large clock that hung on one of the campus building's towers. Talking with my co-workers had set us back.

"Crap," I muttered, glaring at her. She shrugged innocently

as she gave me a small wave and headed towards the building where her accounting class was.

I headed straight towards the lecture hall, trying to finish my coffee before I reached the doors. I shoved it into a nearby garbage pail, my anxiety rising with each step I took.

I hated being the last student in a classroom, and judging by the time on the clock tower, I was twenty minutes late. I would undoubtedly be the last student to arrive. I pushed opened the doors, wincing slightly as the creaked in announcement of my arrival.

A stern looking woman in her mid-thirties was standing at the podium, her pale hair pulled back in a tight bun and her piercing gray eyes narrowed in on me. She furrowed her brow, frowning as she showed her displeasure in my late arrival and disruption of her class.

"Sorry," I apologized, my voice barely above a whisper.

The lecture hall was massive, and it was full of students. My eyes widened as I searched the rows for a vacant seat. I started walking up the stairs, finally spotting one almost at the very back of the far left side.

"I do not like interruptions," the Professor, Professor Pedersen, said, her voice ringing out sharply against the silence of the hall. I gritted my teeth, feeling thousands of eyes upon me. "If you are late, don't bother coming in. I will be locking the doors. I do not wait around to start my lectures. You need to respect the hours allotted and be here on time."

My face burned with irritation and embarrassment. I kept my head down, allowing my dark hair to fall in my face. I didn't like being called out like that. Normally, I'd toss a smart ass remark at her...but I'd learned something about University teachers...they tolerated a lot less than high school teachers.

At the thought of high school teachers, my heart seized momentarily in my chest...as it did every time I thought of him. I absently fingered the necklace that rested on my collar-bone before I forced myself into the present: the task of finding that single free seat.

I made my way quickly, apologizing to the people whose legs I had to step over, and relief floored through me as I sat down in the free seat. The hall had been overwhelmingly silent, Professor Pedersen had refused to continue her lecture until I'd found my seat. Everyone was staring at me, including the Professor. Her stern gray eyes finally left my face as she resumed her lecture.

"What a bitch," the guy beside me said, his voice low and gruff. I looked at him, resisting the urge to raise my eyebrows in approval.

He was a good head taller than me, even while sitting down. He had long dark brown hair that reached just past his shoulders and brown eyes with an intense ring of gold encasing the pupils. He had a slight dusting of facial hair across his jaw, as if shaving hadn't been on his list of priorities. He extremely in shape, his prominent muscles showcased by the simple black t-shirt he wore.

I drank in his defined forearms, following the entire length of his body. Defined was definitely one way to describe him. I raised my green eyes to his face, pausing on his thick lips and sweeping across his strong features. He looked like a Viking, or a Barbarian, and I had to admit...I was impressed with what I saw, and I didn't normally like guys who had better hair than me.

The grin he was wearing as I studied him suggested that he knew what I was thinking. He extended a large hand, offering it to me. "My name is Jax."

"Harlow," I said, shaking his hand while I resisted the urge to smile.

"Pretty name," he remarked, his white teeth flashing as he smiled at me widely.

"If you two are done talking, I'd like to resume my lecture." Professor Pedersen' voice rang out across the lecture hall like a sharp whip, drawing the eyes of my peers back to me.

"Sorry about that," Jax grin was even wider. He waved his hand, motioning for her to continue. The Professor's lips were set in a thin line as she continued on.

It was hard to focus on anything that Professor Pedersen was saying. I knew that Jax was staring at me. The seats in the lecture hall were close to one another, separated by thin arm rests. Jax's arm rested on his arm rest, a mere inches away from my arm. I could feel tingles of his nearness, as if he was electrically charged and my own body was responding without my permission.

I bit into the inside of my lip, wanting to move away from this stranger that was evoking feelings of attraction in me. I didn't want to be attracted to anybody. I wasn't ready for anything. I absently touched the necklace at my collarbone again, a nervous gesture I had developed shortly after Iain.

My heart squeezed painfully at the mere thought of him. Iain Bentley was...well, Iain was a big deal to me...even still.

Iain had been my first love. We had met in my final year at high school. I still remember the first day I saw him, sitting at his desk. His dirty blonde hair and Caribbean blue eyes would stay etched in my mind, probably forever. Our relationship had been a whirlwind affair. I'd fallen quickly and hard for him, and it had been a relationship that was doomed from the start.

Iain Bentley had been my twelfth grade English teacher.

I know what you're thinking, that he took advantage of me and was deeply disturbed to even consider a relationship with a student. But it wasn't like that. Sometimes, life isn't black or white. It's complicated, it's messy, and it doesn't always fit into a perfect little category of right and wrong.

My final year of high school was dramatic and traumatic. I met Jenna then, and befriended her after she was sexually assaulted by a power hungry son of the town's Chief of Police. In fact, I'd tried to stop it from happening. When it was clear I was too late, I stepped into the role of best friend and helped Jenna seek justice from her attacker. Which she got. Thanks to my testimony, Andrew Cooper and his father faced legal repercussions for what they had done. Andrew Cooper got a slap on the wrist, really, but a smear on his permanent record was still a smear.

Carl Cooper, on the other hand, was serving time for dirty work. He'd covered up his son's illegal actions, as well as dealt in secret with some of the big drug dealers in town. When I exposed him for his part in keeping the law from touching Andrew, I exposed him in *all* his wrong doings. He would be in jail for a long time.

I'd also helped Jenna throughout her entire pregnancy. As if having her innocence stole from her when Andrew raped her wasn't enough, she'd ended up pregnant...like some kind of horrible Lifetime movie.

And Iain...he had been my rock through it all. Jenna's sexual assault brought up tormented memories of my own past, and if it weren't for Iain...well. I probably would have returned to a very dark and scary place. Iain had been the one to suggest adoption to me for Jenna, who couldn't stand the idea of an abortion, and struggled with the idea of raising a child conceived in that manner.

Unfortunately, just after the trial of Jenna Burke vs Andrew Cooper, photos of Iain and I together surfaced. Iain was charged with sexual exploitation of a minor, and had to serve one year in jail. Locals were outraged that one year was all he got, but I had been naive and optimistic that after that year, he would find me again.

He hadn't. I hadn't heard a word from him in the last two years. Not a whisper.

I missed him more than anything. I missed our casual conversations in his worn kitchen, the way he kissed me and the way he had known exactly what I needed when I needed it, often before I even knew I needed it.

"So...are you just going to sit here all day then?" Jax's voice rumbled, rosing me from my reverie. Startled, I looked around, noticing for the first time that the lecture hall was almost completely empty. I looked back at Jax. He was standing up, looking down at me with a delectable smile on his lips. I cleared my throat, forcing a smile, and all but jumped out of my chair.

"Nice meeting you," I said over my shoulder, weaving my way through the lingering students at the top of the aisle.

I didn't necessarily run away, but I wasn't exactly walking either. I pushed opened the doors to the lecture hall, carefully avoiding catching the eye of the professor that *really* didn't seem to like me.

I had three more classes that day before my shift at *The Bean*, and I couldn't concentrate in any of them. I was thankful that it was the first day of a new semester. Most professors weren't expecting us to focus, except Professor Pedersen, it would seem.

With fifteen minutes to spare, I made it back to *The Bean*, sneaking in the back to toss my uniform on and wrap my long dark hair in a sock bun. Mark greeted me with a cheerful hello, his hands completely covered in flour from preparing dough for the next days bread. Jamie was in the office, finishing up on inventory. I peeked my head inside while I tossed on my hairnet. "I'm here."

"Good," Jamie grinned. "I've been dying to ask you...you're pretty little friend, she has the hots for our Lucas, doesn't she?" he leaned back in his desk chair leisurely.

"Yes, she does," I shrugged. "I guess she likes Harry Potter more than I thought." I added, shrugging at him before I closed his office door to the sound of his laughter.

I joined Lucas out front. There was a few customers in line, but we handled them quickly. We had about ten minutes before the next rush of students came in. In an hour, Lucas would be off and it would be just me manning the front. Jamie and Mark would head out around 5, and I would close up the shop at 9 p.m. by myself.

"So, how was your day?" I asked, my lips in a thin line as I resisted the urge to smile at Lucas' bewildered expression. I didn't normally start conversation with anybody. Jamie was always able to get me to talk, although it had taken him a year, but I certainly wasn't friendly with Lucas.

He looked around, then pointed at his chest and mouthed 'me?', as if he couldn't believe that I was actually talking to him about non-work related things. I rolled my eyes, irritated. This was exactly why I didn't make a habit of talking to people.

"Okay, I'm just going to cut to the chase," I said, frowning. "My friend, the blond one? She thinks you're cute. Jamie noticed and he'll probably harass you into finding your balls and asking her out. You've been warned."

"The hot one?" Lucas' expression was even more bewildered. His eyes widened slightly, as if this information was new to him.

"Are you blind? Yes," I rolled my eyes dramatically. A huge smile broke out on Lucas' face.

"Huh, well go figure," he said thoughtfully.

"Excuse me," a voice that sounded vaguely familiar broke up the little pow-wow session Lucas and I were having by the coffee maker. Lucas chose that moment to go in the back to grab more coffee cups, leaving me to man the til. I turned my head, seeing the tall, dark and handsome guy from my Psychology lecture waiting in front of the cash.

"Oh, it's you again," I exhaled, approaching the cash. My lips curved in a small smile, in response to the infectious grin on his face.

"Yes, me again," he said, his eyes lingering on my face for a moment. I arched my eyebrow, alerting him that he was staring. He cleared his throat, shaking his head slightly. "Can I get a large coffee please?"

"Yes," I rang his order in, careful to avoid meeting his eyes. I wanted to look at him, and I found that a little...alarming. My body's reaction to just sitting beside him had been a warning in itself. I wasn't ready for anything, I didn't want anything. *I want Iain*, I thought stubbornly, but my body ignored me, tingling with anticipation and excitement.

Jax held out his money, forcing me to reach a little further than necessary. My eyes met his, and I was again struck by the gold rim around his pupils. The startling colour faded to a gentle brown, but it was still unlike anything I'd ever seen before. His eyes were captivating and mysterious.

He held onto the money, looking down briefly at my right forearm, at the tattoo of a quill and inkpot I'd gotten shortly before beginning 12th grade. "Love the tattoo, it's hot," he said, his eyes slowly roaming back up to my face.

I snatched it a little too roughly from his large hand, feeling vulnerable and exposed with his intense gaze upon my face. I handed him back his change, my mouth in a thin line. "Your coffee will be ready to the left of the cash," I told him, motioning with my head for him to move on.

"See you around," Jax said, winking at me.

I glared at his retreating back, at how muscular he looked

even from behind. The guy oozed sexual appeal in the most annoying way. I was left reeling and feeling guilty from the encounter.

"Oh my word," Jamie sighed, fanning himself and blinking dramatically. "Who was *that*!" My brows furrowed, I hadn't even noticed Jamie approach, I'd been so distracted with Jax.

"Some guy," I muttered, busying myself with wiping down the already spotless counter.

"I could practically *taste* the sexual tension rolling off you two. Snag that up honey, and hang on tight," Jamie winked. I rolled my eyes, trying not to let Jamie's comment get to me. Jamie predicted sexual tension at least a hundred times a day.

Lucas left at four, then Mark and Jamie left at 6, leaving me alone to manage the store until our close at 9pm.

Although I adored my bosses, and could tolerate Lucas...I preferred closing alone. It wasn't a difficult job, and I enjoyed watching the majority of the customers. They were the pretentious University type that thought they were rare intellectuals. Watching them interact with each other was amusing.

Closing the store was simple. I powered down all the machines, made sure everything that needed to be kept cool was in the refrigerator, threw out what food hadn't sold or took it home, because Mark's baked goods were too good to resist...not that there was ever enough left over. After that, I scrubbed down every surface until it shined, then activated the alarm and locked up. It took about an hour to ensure everything was done, and my walk home was quick.

I had never been fond of walking around at night, my past hadn't exactly eased my anxieties about it. But I also knew how to defend myself, or...at the very least, how to run fast and scream. I carried pepper spray with me, and made sure I walked down the brightly lit portion of the street. My heart still pounded erratically in my chest any time I had to pass an unfamiliar person, but I made it home safely, closing the door swiftly behind me.

The delicious scent of Chinese take-out greeted me, and my mouth started watering in response to the assault on my nose.

"Oh my God, that smells *amazing*," I said, practically drooling as I kicked my shoes off and made my way over to the island that separated our kitchen from the open concept living room. Several boxes from our favourite Chinese take-out spot were laid out, along with two plates. Jenna was leaning into the refrigerator, searching for something to drink.

Neither one of us was big on cooking. We lived off of take out and frozen dinners, which explained why I'd gained a couple of pounds. Every once in a while, one of us would go on a health kick and try to cook healthy for a while. It typically lasted a week, if that.

"You're just in time," Jenna told me, closing the refrigerator with two bottles of water in her hand. "The guy just delivered it."

My stomach rumbled, reminding me that I'd skipped out on almost all of my meals the whole day. I snagged a plate and started filling it with the delectable goodies from the cartons. Jenna followed suit. We didn't have a kitchen table, so we made our way over to our second hand couch and set our plates down on the coffee table.

"I'm *so* hungry," I whined, practically moaning as I shoveled a hot spoonful of Chow Mein.

"You should probably stop forgetting to eat," Jenna commented, eying me judgmentally as I scarfed down another bite. "Unless you want to ward off any potential love interests with your Neanderthal table manners."

I snorted, nearly choking on the mouthful I'd been trying to swallow. I grabbed the water bottle, drinking back to help move the clump of food down my esophagus. "Funny girl," I muttered.

Jenna smirked, pleased with herself. She grabbed the remote off of the coffee table and started flicking through the channels, looking for something to watch. She settled on reruns of *Jersey Shore*.

"Will you ever get tired of watching that?" I grumbled, irritated at her choice. I wrestled the remote off her, choosing an episode of *The Simpsons* to watch instead. At least re-runs of *The Simpsons* were slightly more tolerable.

"Old habits die hard," Jenna remarked, looking at my collarbone where the silver necklace Iain had given me still rested.

"I know," I sighed, rolling my eyes. She was right, of course. The mention of Iain prompted my thoughts to drift, only this time...it wasn't Iain's face I pictured.

"What's with that look?" Jenna inquired, taking a bit of an egg roll. She chewed, staring at me as she waited for me to explain.

Jenna and I had grown extremely close over the last several years. We were best friends, practically sisters. She tolerated my dark and brooding moods, and I tolerated her spells as well. Jenna, as happy and bubbly as she naturally was, still had her moments of falling into a deep depression.

Every once in a while, Jenna would think about the little baby girl she gave up for adoption. I knew it had been the hardest decision she had ever made, and would remain the hardest decision she would ever have to make. Jenna's virginity had been ripped from her. Prior to being raped by Andrew Cooper, she'd been a virgin, hoping to save it until marriage...or, at least until she found someone she really cared about. The first time she'd ever gotten pregnant, and it was with the guy who raped her. I could fully understand her moments of deep depression.

It was suffice to say that Jenna and I had bonded over having similar experiences. My first time wasn't exactly the story book picture of perfection either, I hadn't been willing either. I'd also had my virginity stolen from me as if I'd had no right to it to begin with. I had gone to a party with my boyfriend at the time, to celebrate his win in a silly little high school basketball game. Things had been new with Cole, and I tended to go along with whatever he said. I never expected him to slip a roofie into my drink, nor did I expect him and his basketball buddies on the team to take turns raping me.

I kept silent out of shame and embarrassment, I hadn't gone forward or reported it to anybody. In fact, I barely told anybody about it. Shortly after the incident, I switched schools and met a girl named Lauren. She had quickly become my best friend, and for the longest time, she'd been the only one to know about what *really* happened that night. The all of my peers thought I was just a whore who had wanted it to happen.

Our friendship had been dramatic and intense. Lauren had a taste for trouble, and I tended to go along with her absurd plans. Lauren just made everything sound like a good idea. I was rebelling a lot, trying to overcome what had happened to me at my old school, and I wanted to forget. Lauren's plans for fun always seemed...fun. She had a way of getting me to forget about all the crap of my past and let go. It was her zest for life, her hunger to just be. She was free-spirited and edgy.

Lauren introduced me to my second boyfriend ever, Rhys. He was best friends with her boyfriend, Alex. The two of them worked at a tattoo shop in Toronto. I'd met him when Lauren and I skipped school one day to get friendship tattoos. The six minimalist black birds in flight across my left collarbone was done by Rhys. It was a painful reminder of a painful past, but also a beautiful tribute to my friend. Lauren had gotten the same thing across her right collarbone, inked by Alex.

My relationship with Rhys had been one born out of convenience. At the time, it made sense to date him. His best friend was dating my best friend, he was cute, and he hooked me up with free tattoos. He'd done a gorgeous cherry blossom tree that crept up my right ribcage and cupped under my breast. But Rhys and I never connected, he never cared to hear about my day or get to know what happened inside my head. I was just convenient to him in the same way he was convenient to me.

Lauren died in a car crash during our eleventh grade year, on the way home from a Halloween party we'd attended with Rhys and Alex. Rhys had been driving the vehicle and lost control. He'd been completely messed up on cocaine, and my biggest regret was not knowing. Losing the first person I'd ever really felt a true and real connection to nearly ruined me. It was a big part of the reason why I'd relocated from Toronto to North Bay. I had desperately needed a change, plus my mom had remarried and the guy lived there.

"You gonna tell me?" Jenna asked, still patiently waiting for me to continue. I chewed on my lip thoughtfully. Jenna was always open and honest with me, while I didn't exactly enjoy divulging any of the heavy shit that went on in my mind...with her, I tried. She wanted to know, she wanted to be there. I guess that's what made her different from anyone else I knew. Aside from Iain, she was the only one who knew about my past, and about Lauren.

"I don't know," I shrugged, shifting uncomfortably under her intense stare down. "I sort of met someone today, kind of."

"How do you 'sort of meet someone, kind of'?" Jenna questioned, her lips curling with a slight amused smile. I shrugged, choosing to shove another spoonful of food in my mouth instead of answering her. She waited a beat before impatiently rolling her eyes. "Okay, so tell me about this person you sort of kind of met."

"I don't know," I said, my voice muffled with food. I swallowed. "He's hot, I guess."

"How hot?" Jenna grinned, loving that I was sharing this rather insignificant detail with her. I was going to just keep it to myself...but I felt the need to hear her opinion about the sudden attraction I'd felt, even though I knew what she would say. I knew she worried about me, and I wanted to give her a reason to let go of some of that worry. Maybe hearing that I'd actually been attracted to someone who *wasn't* Iain would help with that.

"Not Harry Potter hot," I admitted, smirking at her. "But...more like..." I paused, thinking about the different kind of actors I could compare Jax too. "Jason Momoa. But Conan The Barbarian Jason Momoa, not Baywatch."

"Oh, *nice!*" Jenna said, nodding with approval. "So, what's the problem?"

"I don't know. He just...stood out. He's hot."

"This is a big deal," Jenna declared, looking on at me proudly. "You haven't been attracted to anybody since *Iain*!"

"I know," I gritted my teeth, annoyed at the reminder. I had hoped that she wouldn't point it out. "But I'm honestly not ready for anything. Not that he asked."

If I was being completely honest with myself, I was afraid. I'd felt attraction before, I'd definitely felt it with Iain. I knew what it was like to be in lust, and in love. But my track record wasn't exactly good. Bad things seemed to happen when I dated. Take Cole and the basketball team, for example. Then there was Rhys, the very reason why I no longer had Lauren in my life.

Then there was Iain. Two years was a long time to reflect

upon ones choices, and I couldn't help but see the whole situation from an entirely different perspective, one marred with doubt and insecurity. Iain's silence since his arrest whispered that maybe he felt the same way I was feeling...wrong about it. When it was happening, it had felt *so right*. Iain had awoken things in me that I didn't know existed. But now...as I stood in the aftermath...I questioned it all. I wasn't looking through things with rose coloured glasses. I didn't doubt my feelings for Iain had been legitimate, I knew they had...but I didn't know if it was *right* anymore.

It didn't help that the psychologist I had seen at my mother's request had basically told me in more ways than one just how deviant the whole thing had been. It was easy to believe your love was real and raw and perfect when that person was there with you, reminding you just how true it was...but when they leave, you start to question things a little more.

I suppose it didn't matter, Iain's silence meant that he'd also had time to think...and the result wasn't a desire to be with me. If he had wanted that, I would know by now.

"You just met him, you felt an attraction," Jenna said wisely, her words coaxing me back to the present. "Don't read into it any more than that. Take things a day at a time. Just...don't close yourself off."

CHAPTER

TWO

Adjusting to my busy new schedule after a summer off from the worries of University was disorienting. It was difficult to get back into the groove of classes, work, and a meager social life...but I was determined to not let anything fall through the cracks.

I caught myself scanning each classroom for familiar faces...one in particular. I couldn't understand why he stood out in my mind, why my thoughts would occasionally drift to him with open curiosity. I suppose certain people just make lasting impressions.

I saw a few people I had shared classes with in previous years, but I didn't see Jax until our Psychology lecture that following Monday.

Not wanting a repeat of last week, I had shown up for the lecture early. Professor Pedersen was setting up the slideshow she had prepared on her laptop, and barely lifted her eyes at my arrival. I quietly made my way to a secluded section where I would still be able to see and hear Professor Pedersen's seminar.

I sat down, relishing in the emptiness of the hall. I flipped down the tray on the arm rest, setting my notebook down and opened it. I started to dig for a pen in the bottom of my messenger bag.

"Is this seat taken?" a voice asked, rousing me from my search for a pen. I looked up, feeling flustered at the wave of nervous anticipation and excitement that washed over me upon hearing his voice. Jax grinned down at me, and I was struck with how remarkably tall he was. His presence was commanding, you couldn't help but feel intimated by him.

The wave of guilt accompanying the pleasant sensation that rolled in my lower belly was perplexing. Attraction, lust, and guilt about it all. Perfect emotions to deal with on a Monday at an ungodly hour.

"No, but neither are *any* of the others," I replied, my brow furrowing in annoyance at my body's reaction. I gestured with my head to the near empty hall pointedly. Jax grinned, amused by my answer, and sat down in the seat behind me.

"I like the view from here," he answered, sending me an appreciative look. My frown increased in match to the tempo of my heartbeat. I took a deep, calming breath, closing my eyes as I tried to regain my composure and patience.

When I opened my eyes, Jax was still looking at me, his head tilted as if he was studying something incredibly complex and yet captivating.

"If you're going to be here, be quiet," I grumbled, forcing my eyes away from his intriguing eyes. The golden rings that danced around his pupils were borderline hypnotic.

"Yes ma'am," Jax said, saluting my command.

I tried to ignore him, but class wasn't due to start for another ten minutes. I resumed my quest for a pen, knowing I had ten of them, buried somewhere in the depths of my bag.

"Need a pen?" he asked, holding one out to me.

"No, thank you," I sighed in aggravation. He shrugged, drawing his arm away. A moment later, I found one. I pulled it out, testing it on the blank page of my notebook. Blue ink flowed from the tip of the pen. Satisfied, I wrote the date and rested the pen against the page.

I bit down on my lip, feeling Jax's gaze still upon my face. It was doing strange things to my blood, heating it. I felt myself blushing, an uncommon thing for me. He was unsettling me, and I didn't like it. "If you're going to stare at me the whole time, I'd rather you move to another seat. Preferably one further away."

Jax smiled, amusement dancing in his eyes, causing my annoyance to grow. "Who says I was staring at you?"

I rolled my eyes, shaking my head. "Whatever. Just...don't be distracting."

"I should be telling *you* to not be distracting," Jax argued, angling his body to me. His eyes light up something in me, something that had been sleeping for the last little while. Desire.

I didn't like it.

"How am I distracting you?" I narrowed my eyes. "I'm not stalker-staring at you."

Jax laughed, a rich, delightful sound that prompted my lips to curve up slightly in response. "Stalker-staring, huh?"

"Yup," I said, accenting the P with a pop of my lips. I sent him a challenging look.

"Actually, I was just trying to figure out a polite way of telling you..." he hesitated, looking deeply amused.

"Telling me what?" I frowned.

"You've got a little toothpaste, right here..." Jax said, using his thumb to wipe away what he claimed was toothpaste from the corner of my mouth. His thumb left tingles in it's wake, leaving me almost breathless. I frowned deeper, aggravated at the uninvited personal contact. I grabbed his hand, pushing it away from my face.

A strange torment of emotions took over me. On the one hand, I was mortified that I'd left my apartment with toothpaste on my face. Being mortified was a new first for me, I didn't embarrass easily. On the other hand, I *hated* being touched without permission, or at least me without me initiating it. Third, I found myself *not hating* that Jax had touched me, which both angered me and made me feel guilty.

"I don't like to be touched," I said, my voice wavering slightly. I hoped he couldn't sense what his simple, brief touch had done to me.

"Sorry," Jax's voice was sincere, but at the same time...it wasn't. "It's gone now," he assured me.

Before I could reply, the firm click of the lecture hall doors closing alerted me that class was about to start. I closed my mouth, watching Professor Pedersen's smart heels clicked against the floor as she returned to the podium.

Professor Pedersen was dressed in a conservative looking pencil skirt, brown in colour. Her plain brown heels blended in perfectly with her psychologist feel. She surveyed the now full hall, as her eyes swept from one side of the room to the other, silence fell in it's wake. The other students sensed the same thing I did...Professor Pedersen wasn't the kind of professor to take *any* shit.

Despite her calling me out on the first day, I couldn't help but respect that about her. I settled back in my seat comfortably, ready to focus.

Professor Pedersen's voice washed over me. At first, I listened with rapid attention, then Jax's arm accidentally brushed mine. I felt a sensation similar to that of an electric shock. My body responded with goosebumps and raised hair. I pulled my arm to my side, rattled. Jax seemed unbothered by the contact, he was listening to the lecture and writing down notes.

I tried to regain my focus, but all I could do was sit and analyze my own behavior.

I hadn't dated since the whole Iain thing. I hadn't had the slightest desire to. At first, I was just waiting for him to contact me. I'd be so sure that our love could withstand anything. As time wore on and as I realized that he wasn't going to reach out to me, well. I got angry.

My track record with guys has been *anything* but good. The one good relationship I'd thought I had was with Iain. I received no closure from him, so moving on had been difficult. I was stuck in a strange limbo, unable to move forward but also not wanting to. Not a single guy had sparked my interest since then. At least, no one until Jax.

I spared a glance at Jax, he was still writing, pen to paper, looking up every once in a while at Professor Pedersen. Occasionally, he'd tuck a strand of his hair behind his ear.

I sunk lower in my seat, pushing myself as far away from Jax as I could without drawing attention to myself. I saw him smile out of the corner of my eye, his gaze still facing the front of the classroom.

When class ended, I couldn't get away fast enough. I shoved my stuff into my bag quickly, wincing at the fact that I had not taken *any* notes and had scarcely paid attention.

MY THIRD CLASS of the day, Sociology, was canceled, leaving me with a three hour window of leisure before my shift. It was a beautiful day, warm with just a hint of coolness to the breeze. I decided to head to Tabaret Lawn to spread out under a tree and do some Psychology reading.

I pulled my books out, leaning against the trunk of the tree and shifting my weight, attempting to get comfortable. I was reading the first chapter, focusing all my attention on the words so that my thoughts wouldn't drift elsewhere.

When I realized I was just reading the same sentence over and over again, I closed my book and leaned my head back against the tree.

I breathed in the crisp September air, allowing the hint of fall to envelop me in a comfortable blanket of familiarity. I watched the breeze make the leaves, just beginning to change colour, dance in sync with one another. I felt peaceful for the first time in over a week.

"Do you mind if I join you?" I tore my eyes from the dancing leaves, in the direction the voice came from. A girl I vaguely recognized from my Sociology class stood in front of me, looking hopeful. She was a shy looking girl with wiry, curly red hair, thick rimed glasses and freckles dusting across her cheeks. She seemed harmless enough, although something about her was familiar.

I was bad with faces, and the familiarity might have just been that I had seen her somewhere before. Her red hair did stand out in a crowd.

I forced myself to smile, actively trying to look more inviting. I think I just scared her, though. She took a step tentative step back.

"Sorry, I'm still working on my friendly face," I said, wrinkling my nose at her discomfort. She laughed awkwardly, managing to sit down and cross her legs in one fluid movement. "My name is Harlow," I told her, raising my eyebrows in question. She stared intently at my lips as I spoke.

"Oh cool!" the girl's face lit up, her pale blue eyes sparkling. She leaned forward eagerly. "A unique name! It's very pretty! How did your parents come up with it?"

I blinked once, caught off guard by her response as my earlier assumption that she would be shy evaporated. "Um...my dad picked it. I think I'm named after Jean Harlow...he had a thing for old movies."

"Cool," she said, smiling, still looking at my lips. I arched my eyebrow again, waiting for her to answer my question. "Oh, sorry. My name is Crimson."

"Interesting," I gave her a small smile, feeling worn out from all the interacting I had been doing lately. I could count on one hand the amount of people I spoke to regularly. Making conversation wasn't something I'd been interested in, at least not since high school. Conversation seemed to cause me a lot of trouble if I wasn't careful.

"Yeah, believe it or not...it basically means red," the girl, Crimson, rolled her eyes, as if bonding with me over strange names. She didn't seem to notice my demeanour.

"I would have never guessed," I said dryly. Crimson winced, sensing the sarcasm. I felt bad, not wanting her to take it to heart, which was unusual for me. Usually, I didn't care if I offended someone. "I'm sorry. I'm naturally sarcastic and bitchy. I truly don't mean to offend."

"It's okay," Crimson blushed, thrown off by my apology. She dipped her head down. "It's just hard for me to tell with most girls what they mean by what they say...most people, for that matter."

The sentence may not have made sense to most, but I thought I understood where she was coming from. I had to agree with her. Girls were bitchy, most of them were two-faced and cruel...or at least, the majority of the ones I had come in contact with. My heart warmed slightly towards her. She looked lost, as if she was desperately trying to find a familiar face that wasn't cruel.

"I know what you mean," I said, nodding in agreement. "You're in my Sociology class, right?"

"Yes!" she exclaimed, seemingly excited that I had remembered her. "I mean, yeah. Totally. I can't believe class was canceled already, what luck is that?" the girl rambled on nervously. "I'm also in Psychology with you, only you probably didn't notice. I can't *believe* how massive that class is! I can't hear a damn thing!" Then she laughed with delight, shaking her head as if she'd just told a hilarious joke and couldn't believe how perfect the deliverance had been. She turned her head from side to side, gesturing to the small hearing aids she wore in her ears. "Get it? I'm partially deaf."

It made sense why she had been staring at my lips intently, she was lip-reading. Before I could respond, I saw Jax walking towards us and my words melted on the tip of my tongue. He was *just* the person I wanted to avoid, and there he was...sauntering up to me like he had no idea how much his presence irritated and confused me.

To be fair, he probably didn't.

"Fancy running into you here," he said, coming to a stop beside Crimson. He dropped his bag on the ground and sat down beside her, across from me. His eyes swept across my face, and I felt that annoying swell of attraction.

Crimson's jaw dropped as she drank him in, her eyes widening slightly before she shook her head, breaking herself out of the spell his attractive face cast upon anyone with ovaries.

"You again," my eyes narrowed. I couldn't help the nervous butterflies fluttering in my stomach, but I could be pissed about it. I didn't *do* butterflies, at least...not since Iain. "Please stop stalking me."

"You can stalk me," Crimson said, almost in a daze. Jax's laughter made her shake her head again, and she flushed deep red...as if she hadn't meant to say it aloud. I couldn't help but smile with amusement. She was endearing.

"You're both hilarious, you should consider doing stand up comedy," Jax said, shaking his head. I watched his beautiful hair flow with the movement, angry at how he kept captivating my attention with the smallest of actions.

"And you should consider getting a haircut," I retorted, bristling.

"We're not even dating yet and you're already telling me how to wear my hair?" Jax asked, arching his eyebrow at me. Conflicting emotions of anger and desire reared up, making me glower at him. "Kidding," he said, raising his hands in innocent surrender. My eyes were still locked on his, his annoyingly magnetic pull making me even more hostile.

Crimson's pale eyes bounced back and forth as she watched our heated exchange. I had almost completely forgotten about her, until her head moved slightly, the copper highlights in her hair catching the sunlight and reflecting it back to me.

"I'd love to say and chat, but I've got to go...see you around Crimson," I said, grabbing my things in one quick motion. I was on my feet in an instant hoping that nobody would follow me. I walked quickly, my feet digging in to the grass as I tried to give myself momentum to get away.

I barely knew the guy, and he was rattling my core. That, in my opinion, was *not* a good thing. I didn't want to be rattled.

"Hey, Harlow...wait up please!" Jax shouted, obviously not getting the hint. I didn't slow my movements for him. I didn't even turn to see if he was catching up. He was suddenly beside me, gently touching my arm. I stopped, freezing on the contact, his simple touch had sent an electrical shock coursing through my body.

"What is your deal?" I demanded, shaken at how out of

control I felt. I crossed my arms, trying to keep my expression from betraying the inner turmoil I felt. Jax seemed to know though, and he lowered himself slightly so we came eye to eye.

"I just want to get to know you a little, is that so wrong?" he asked. I frowned at the thrill his words evoked.

"Maybe I don't want to get to know you," I muttered, breaking his gaze so that I could figure out how to think again.

"I don't believe that," Jax said with confidence. I shot an angry look at him, and he grinned. "Come on, I know you feel it. I can't be the *only* one who feels this...connection." his voice grew deeper, almost husky, the rumbling low tones vibrating into my core, making my pulse do strange things.

"Easy Romeo," I backed away, heart pounding with anticipation, thrill and fear.

He smiled, a genuine, friendly smile. "Would you settle for being friends? Comrades in arms? You know we need each other. I heard from the grapevine that Professor Pedersen loves assigning group homework."

I chewed my lip, eying him suspiciously.

"Besides, I *think* you might want my notes," he added, winking. For the first time, I realized he was holding a couple of loose pages in his hand. I'd been so caught up in his mere presence and watching his face that I hadn't even noticed them. He held the pages out to me, a peace offering of sorts.

"Thanks..." I muttered, warily accepting them. I bit my lip when our fingers brushed.

"See you around, friend," Jax said, his eyes pausing to rest on my lips. His eyes raised, meeting mine, that captivating golden swirl aglow with the same lust I was feeling.

I watched him return to the tree, where he'd left his bag beside Crimson in his haste to follow me. I sighed deeply, realizing that I'd been appreciating the toned muscles of his back the entire time.

This was not going to end well.

I OPENED the door to our apartment, my head aching from the day I'd had. After leaving Tabaret Lawn, I'd worked a 4 hour shift at *The Bean,* hedging off a torrent of questions from Jamie about Jax.

It felt good to get home, finally. I knew I had a long night of studying to do. I had to copy out the notes Jax had loaned me, and actually absorb some of the information in them so that I would be prepared for the next seminar.

"OH MY GOD," Jenna squealed with excitement, rushing towards me in a blur of blond hair flailing arms. It was almost comical. "You'll *never* guess what happened to me today!"

"What?" I asked warily, pulling my shoes off and dropping my bag on the floor. I kicked it over to the corner, waiting for Jenna to spill the beans. I knew it likely had to do with her crush, from the way she was buzzing with happiness.

She stood in front of me, practically bouncing on her heels, her lips tight as she tried to reign in her excitement. Giving up, she screeched, "*LUCASASKEDMEOUT!*"

"Could you say that a little slower?" I frowned, rubbing my sore ear drum.

"Lucas asked me out!" Jenna tried again, this time speaking incredibly slow.

"That's great," I smiled, my words sincere. I wondered why Jamie hadn't spilled *that* little piece of gossip. "Details?"

Jenna followed me as I made my way into the kitchen to load up a plate with leftover Chinese food. I didn't even care if it was cold...cold Chinese food tasted even better than hot Chinese food. I headed to the couch, sinking down into the comfortable, worn cushions, Jenna following me the whole time like an excited puppy.

"Well, I went in to *The Bean* on my break...and he was there, only he wasn't working. He was hanging out with his friends or something...anyway, he saw me waiting in the line up and waited until I was at the station fixing my tea. Then he came up to me and asked me out!" Jenna said, practically dancing around the coffee table.

"That's awesome Jenna!" I smiled wider, happy for my friend. "When is the date?"

"Friday night," Jenna's smile wavered a bit. "Oh my God. I have *nothing* to wear! We need to go shopping, Har."

"Okay," I sighed, almost heavily. I placed my plate down, massaging my temples with my fingers. I felt a headache coming on.

"Hey...are you okay?" Jenna asked, frowning in concern as she sank down beside me.

"Yeah, I've just had...a day," I sighed again. Jenna crossed her arms and leaned back, tapping her foot impatiently as she waited for me to continue. I exhaled deeply, not wanting to make a big deal about anything...but also wanting Jenna's input on things. "Well. I saw Jax again."

"And?" Jenna arched her brow, shaking her head slightly as she urged me to continue.

I drew my legs up, hugging them to my chest as I stared at the cold food on my plate, my appetite diminishing. "I think I like him. Like, I'm attracted to him. He makes me feel...things."

"And that's bad because...?" Jenna wasn't following. I chewed on my lip, trying to put into words the complicated emotions I was feeling.

"For one, it makes me feel guilty...about Iain. I feel almost like I'm cheating on him," I confessed, feeling the pang of sadness in my heart.

"But you're not, because you aren't together," Jenna reminded me, her voice gentle and her eyes understanding. She hesitated.

"Go ahead, say it," I sighed, knowing I wasn't going to like what came out of her mouth.

"I know you really cared about him, and he cared about you too...but Harlow, he was our teacher. He knew better. 'Pull' or not, he knew better. If he truly wanted a future with you, he would have waited instead of jeopardizing everything."

I muttered a sound of displeasure. When Jenna had first found out about the relationship between Iain and I, she had thought that it was romantic. As she watched me suffer in silence when Iain didn't immediately reach out to me, she stopped seeing my relationship with him as a romantic version of Romeo and Juliet. Jenna never bashed Iain's character, but I knew she didn't see him in the same light that she once had. Her rose coloured glasses came off long before mine. She made it her personal goal to help me get over him and move on. She never made me feel bad about my feelings for Iain, but she made it clear that I deserved more, and that there was more out there for me.

Jenna sighed, as if this conversation was just as painful to her as it was to me. "Har," she said softly. "It's been a while since his release. Have you heard from him at all?"

"No," I said, miserably. I hated that I was letting everything affect me to the point that it had almost changed who I was. My 'don't care' attitude that I had worn for so long was ripped away by Iain's presence, and by his absence, it hadn't returned to me. I was left bare and exposed.

I was angry about it, angry that I let the pain of our relationship, of what happened, affect me at all. It wasn't like I sulked in my room, day in and day out. I still tried to live my life...but I let Iain's memory cloud everything that I did. I closed myself off from any opportunity at happiness with someone else. I shot down guys before they could even declare an interest, just to protect myself and my heart.

Before Iain, I didn't allow anybody the chance to get close enough to me, I was scared that I would get hurt. Letting Iain in, and then having him leave...it shredded my heart and I hated it. I knew that Iain's reasons probably made a lot of sense - hell, he went to jail for a year because of us, but it was the silence that followed...the wondering if he hated me for it. The guilt I felt for him losing *everything* in the process, all because I pursued what I wanted...I pursued him.

"You feel something for this...Jax guy, so go for it. Don't let a memory hold you back..." Jenna trailed off, consuming her own words. I looked up, knowing by the expression on her face and the darkness behind her all-American blue eyes that she was thinking about Andrew.

"Same goes for you," I said weakly, offering a small smile.

CHAPTER
THREE

The next day at school, I realized I had a lot more classes with Crimson than I originally thought. She was in pretty much all of them, and eagerly sat beside me in each one.

She stuck to my side the whole day, chattering my ear off about everything from what music she liked to what she hoped to do after University. Apparently, she wanted to be a social worker and work with kids who had special needs.

"Honestly, growing up with hearing aids was hard and isolating, I want to help kids so they don't feel held back by their differences," she was saying while we sat under a tree on the Tabaret Lawn during a break between classes.

"Wow, that's deep," I told her, impressed.

"What do you want to do after University?" Crimson asked, taking a bite of her pizza.

"I'm going to write," I shrugged. "But I'd also like to help women who have been through trauma." I had recently started looking into halfway houses for battered women. My emphasis on women's rights may help me a little, but I would also need to focus more on Psychology and Counseling. Next semester would be my heaviest course-load yet.

"Cool," Crimson smiled, before changing the subject to her favourite animals. I blinked, thrown off a little by her abrupt topic changing capability. It was almost as if she was on a quest to get to know me entirely before next week.

By the end of the day, I was ready to shell up in my bedroom and tune out everything. I liked Crimson, she was genuine and kind, but her chatty personality was a lot for me to handle. She was intense.

Unfortunately, I had to endure a night of shopping at the mall, at Jenna's request. She claimed she had *nothing* to wear on her date with Lucas.

I headed towards my apartment, putting in my headphones and listening to the album of my new favourite band...*July Talk*, relieved at finally being alone.

Since it was daylight, and I was still on campus, I wasn't paying close attention to my surroundings. I knew better than that, of course, but I was distracted, thinking about all the things Jenna and I had talked about last night.

I was heading away from the hall where my last class had been. I didn't notice anybody approaching me until a large hand reached out and gently touched my shoulder. I whipped around, my heartbeat jumping in fear.

In my haste to turn around, I rolled my ankle off of the sidewalk. I fell backwards, but before I could catch myself, Jax's strong arms encased me. He held me, almost in a dip, looking down at me with amusement and concern. My palms were splayed out across his chest, I could feel the muscles beneath them. He was even more impressive to touch than he was to just look at. His scent was intriguing and almost mouthwatering. He smelt like amber, with hints of sandalwood and spice and something that was just him.

"I knew you liked me, but I'll admit...I didn't expect you'd fall so quickly," Jax said, his voice oozing with the attraction I knew he felt. The air seemed to sizzle between us. My heart beat erratically, and I had a feeling it had more to do with him and less to do about being caught off guard. The scent that was all Jax overwhelmed my senses. It overpowered and intoxicated me, and the fact that he was looking down like he was about to kiss me didn't help.

I wasn't one for swooning, but it was kind of hard to not swoon with a guy like Jax holding me and looking at me like he wanted to devour me.

I shoved him away, frazzled. A part of me instantly missed the feel of him. Another part of me yelled obscenities.

"Don't sneak up on me," I grumbled, standing as tall as I could, despite feeling so shaken. Jax stepped back, giving me space. He still towered over me.

"Noted," he promised.

"What did you want?" I asked, searching his face.

"I wanted to know what you were doing tonight," Jax answered, still looking at me like he wanted to devour me. He put his hands in his jean pockets, giving me the space he knew I needed.

"I'm hanging out with my best friend," I said, resuming my walk. I didn't have time to just stand there exchanging starry eyes with some guy, even if he *was intoxicatedly* handsome. He was pretty much designed to make a girl's ovaries scream with desire.

"Oh," Jax sounded disappointed, but I didn't spare him a look as he kept up with my pace. "Well, how about tomorrow?"

"I work," I answered, trying not to smile. He was relentless, but I wasn't saying no either. I got the sense that if I shut him down, if I told him I wasn't interested and I meant it...he'd back off. Only...I wasn't sure if I *wanted* him to back off. I liked how he made me feel. I like the unwilling smile that came to my lips whenever he was around. I hated that I liked it, but the fact that I liked it had to have stood for something.

"When are you free then?" Jax spun in front of me, blocking my pathway. His hands gently grazed my arms before he remembered the rule I'd laid out for him. He let his hands fall to his sides.

"I don't know, Jax," I sighed, worrying my lip. I was afraid, and it all circled back to my complicated history and the fact that I wasn't entirely sure I'd ever get over Iain. Even in his absence, he had a hold on me. But Jax was slipping in through the cracks.

"I just want to get to know you, a harmless coffee date between friends is all I'm asking for..." he trailed off. I wanted to call bullshit, I knew he didn't just want to be my friend, but I went along with the charade.

"Okay, after Monday's Psychology lecture then," I gave in with a small smile, bowing my head as I skirted around him to resume my walk.

"Awesome," Jax said. I could hear the smile in his voice and feel his eyes on me as I turned onto the street where Jenna and I lived.

Jenna was waiting in our apartment, sitting on one of the island stools. She was ready to go, her purse swung around her shoulder and a light jacket on. She almost glared at me when I walked in.

"I'm like, five minutes later than I said I'd be," I rolled my eyes, dropping my messenger bag down on the ground. I fished my wallet out, grabbing my barely used purse from a hook by the door. I shoved my wallet inside. "Okay, let's go."

Even though Jenna and I lived together, we still tried to make a habit of getting out together as often as we could. Our schedules differed vastly from one another, Jenna was kept busy with volunteering for a crisis line. At first, it had been *incredibly* hard for her, but then she realized that she had more to give then her own fear and anxiety. She had empathy.

It was the same reason why I couldn't leave that door closed at that party and let Andrew Cooper destroy her.

"Where do you want to go?" I asked, rolling my head to work out kinks in my neck.

"The St. Laurent Centre works," Jenna answered. She had already called for a cab, it was waiting by the front door of our building. I should have known, two of Jenna's favourite stores could be found in that shopping centre...Le Chateau and Guess.

We caught up on the cab ride over, talking about our days.

"I thought I saw him today," she said. She tried to sound casual, but she couldn't keep the fear from making her voice waver.

"Who?" I asked. I had been trying to comb the tangles out of my hair with my fingers, but I froze upon hearing the tone in her voice.

"Andrew."

"You have a restraining order against him," I reminded her, trying to force my body to relax. "He's not supposed to be anywhere near you. I doubt he'd even try it." Besides, the last thing I had heard about the Coopers was that Carl, Andrew's father, was still in jail and that Andrew and his mom moved out of province to escape the shame.

"Yeah, I know," Jenna sighed deeply as the cab pulled into the parking lot of the St. Laurent Centre.

The vastness of the St. Laurent Centre wasn't lost on either of us. It rivaled shopping centres in Toronto, and made the North Gate Mall look like a small strip mall. The interior was magnificent, everything was gleaming and new even though the shopping centre opened in 1967.

"I saw Jax on my walk home," I told Jenna, trying to draw her away from the dark thoughts as we walked inside the main doors.

"Oh?" Jenna asked, raising an eyebrow coyly at me. "And?"

"And I tripped, and he caught me. And he smells *so damn delicious* and he feels amazing and I hate it," I summed up, frowning deeply. Jenna laughed, a rich, warm laugh that always made me feel relieved to hear.

My rant about Jax pulled Jenna away from her dark, worrisome mood. I told her about saying yes to a coffee date, and I swear she squealed so loudly that several people stopped to stare at us.

"It's good seeing you get worked up about someone," Jenna remarked, pawing through several outfits on the sales rack at Le Chateau. I rolled my eyes at her, resisting the urge to stick my tongue out as well.

It was true, though. I'd fallen into a ridiculous, self imposed numbness after Iain.

"Whatever," I said. "Can you just pick something? You're going to dinner and a movie, not some swanky release party with a celebrity." I paused thoughtfully. "Well, actually...you *are* going out with Harry Potter...maybe some new dress robes?"

"Shut up," Jenna laughed, rolling her eyes at me. She picked up a royal blue Jersey knit V-neck sleeveless dress and held it up to her thin body.

"Go try it on," I encouraged her.

While Jenna was in the change rooms, I drifted over to do a little shopping for myself. My eyes found a beautiful pair of fake leather lace-up boots. It had been a while since I splurged on myself, and I wanted a couple new outfits anyway. Just in case.

I ended up grabbing the boots as well as a soft gray knit

tiered top. I snagged another pair of black stretch slim leg jeans, and a checkered chiffon blouse before making my way over to the change rooms to try on my own selections.

As I waited for a spare change room, Jenna stepped out in the dress. She looked stunning, dressed up but not overdressed.

"Perfect," I told her, nodding my approval. "Harry Potter won't know what magical spell hit him."

Jenna rolled her eyes at my nickname for Lucas, but she couldn't hide the genuine smile of excitement.

Le Chateau dipped into my savings account, but it was hard to feel guilty about it with Jenna's good mood imprinting on my own. Plus, I'd scored some awesome new clothes...some of them were even on sale, which wasn't saying much, Le Chateau prices were ridiculously expensive even with the sales. I pacified myself with the reminder that I didn't often go on shopping sprees, it was practically over-needed.

Jenna called for a cab and was told it would take twenty minutes. Eyes wide, she looked at me with pleadingly.

"We *need* to stop at Cinnabun," she said, almost salivating at the idea.

"I concur," my stomach rumbled, craving the ooey goodness of a fresh cinnamon bun. She wasn't going to have to twist my arm for that one. With our shopping bags clenched in our hands, we made our way down the escalator to Cinnabun.

We sat at a table outside of Cinnabun after grabbing our orders, our shopping bags skewed about our feet, and started talking about random, nonsensical things.

"Have you heard from Jake lately?" Jenna asked, pausing before she took a dainty bite of her cinnamon bun.

"Nope," I shrugged, unaffected. "I heard he's in the military."

"How strange," Jenna smiled, shaking her head before she

voiced my original thought on the matter. "He never did get along with authority figures."

"I don't think anyone in that town did," I commented, shrugging. Jenna nodded, her smile wavering slightly.

"Oh my GOD! Hey Harlow!" an excited voice squealed before I was engulfed in a sea of red hair.

"Um, hi," I said, trying to distance myself from Crimson's excited embrace. She sank down into the free chair beside me, across from Jenna. "Jenna, this is Crimson. Crimson, Jenna."

"So awesome to see you here!" Crimson grinned, her coppery red hair bouncing. It was as if we hadn't spent practically the whole day together.

"What are you doing here?" I asked, raising an eyebrow.

"I work at Bed, Bath, and Body," Crimson shrugged, moving her arm so that we could see the embroidery on her shirt pocket.

Jenna was smiling with gentle amusement. She knew my dislike of making new friends first hand.

"So, how do you two know each other?" Crimson asked, breaking the beat of silence.

"We met in high school," Jenna answered. "We live together now."

"Oh, like, *live* together live together?" Crimson asked, looking between the two of us curiously. "Makes sense," she added, shrugging.

Jenna burst out laughing.

"No, we're friends," I corrected, amused by Crimson's behavior. "What makes sense?"

"Oh! Well, that's cool! I mean, it would have been cool if you guys were more than friends too. I guess I just wondered because you keep shutting down Jax, and, well...he's a God and he's totally into you!" Crimson blurted, blushing deeply.

"Well, I'm not a lesbian..." I frowned.

"I didn't mean it like that!" Crimson looked guilty. She absently tucked her hair behind her ear, adjusting the position of her hearing aid.

"How hot is he?" Jenna asked Crimson, leaning forward with a mischievous glint in her eyes.

"Totally hot, like, I would probably dump my boyfriend for him hot. Except I'm kidding, because I really like my boyfriend...but he's hot," Crimson answered, her words flowing out in a rush.

I wanted to get out of there. The topic of choice was making me fidget. "Our cab is probably here now..."

"Oh totally! I've got to get back to work anyway. My break is over. We should all hang out sometime, maybe go and catch a movie or get a mani-pedi!" Crimson declared, standing up quickly.

She bounced away, turning briefly to wave a final time before disappearing up the escalators.

I sighed dramatically, as if interacting with Crimson had taken a lot out of me...and it *had*. I didn't think it was possible to find someone more bubbly than Jenna. Jenna had certainly calmed down in the last few years, but Crimson's natural bubbly personality constantly seemed to over-boil.

"She seems...nice," Jenna said, standing up to throw her nearly empty plate in the garbage. I did the same before grabbing the shopping bags out from under the table.

"Yeah, she's nice...just a lot to handle," I answered.

"She seems almost lonely..."

"Still, I don't do spa days," I reminded her. I didn't mind painting my toenails, but I hated when total strangers touched my feet. It was not calming to me, it didn't relax me and it certainly didn't make me feel good. Jenna knew this, as she had once dragged me to a spa, kicking and screaming. She now refused to ask, I had embarrassed her so much.

The cab Jenna called for was parked out front of the mall, waiting for us.

ON FRIDAY EVENING, Jenna was a complete nervous wreck. She was dressed in the new royal blue dress, running her hands down invisible wrinkles and obsessing over her already perfect hair and makeup.

"You look amazing," I assured her as I lounged on top of her perfectly made up bed. My hair spilled off the bottom of her mattress, and I was looking at her upside down, but Jenna's obvious beauty and perfect was clear even with my upside down view. "Harry Potter will fall to his knees and be your man-slave!"

"Stop calling him that," Jenna frowned. "What if I slip up and call him that when we're out?"

I rolled over, resting my chin in my hands with a wicked grin. "Then I will love you forever and not stop laughing for the next 15 years."

"Hmmpf," Jenna reapplied her soft pink lip gloss again, making sure that it was as perfect as she could get it. I touched the embroidered deep purple flower on her comforter. Jenna had done up her entire room in beautiful grays and deep purples. Her bedroom was a testimony to her amazing tastes. I'd basically gotten myself one of those 50 dollar bed in a bags from Walmart and called it a day.

I hadn't set up any photos, aside from the one Jenna gave me at Christmas with a photo of us both from prom. Jenna's bedroom had collages of photos, beautiful paintings that her mother had given her, and textiles to make it appear warm and inviting. She even had a small, dark gray armchair with a deep purple pillow in the corner of her room. The room definitely did not reflect the fact that a college student lived in it, it was too neat and tidy.

"How do I look?" Jenna asked nervously, smoothing the nonexistent wrinkles in her dress again as she turned to face me. She had matched a pair of classic black pumps and a black clutch.

"You look great, as I've said a hundred times," I answered, as patiently as I could. Jenna had just cause to be nervous. It was her first date since, well, Jake. I knew she hadn't really been intimate with Jake. It had been too soon, her scars were too raw.

I could tell by looking at Jenna that she was ready to try now, that tonight was more than just a first date to her.

I went to open my mouth again, but a sudden knock on our apartment door had us both in a scramble.

"Can you get it?" Jenna hissed, obsessively checking her hair for the millionth time. I rolled my eyes, heaving myself off of her bed and walked down the narrow hallway. Jenna hadn't only been obsessed with *her* appearance, she also had scrubbed our apartment from ceiling to floor and purchased ridiculously trendy throw pillows for the couch. Whenever Jenna got nervous, *something* got a makeover. I was just glad it wasn't me this time.

I was still smiling, shaking my head slightly at all the cosmetic work she had done to our place in a span of a week. There was no doubt about it, she was freaking out about this date.

I opened the door to Lucas. His first was raised mid-knock. He'd styled his hair and was wearing a black Ramones t-shirt, skinny jeans, and construction boots. It was an odd combination for sure, but it worked for him.

I crossed my arms, leaning against the door frame, and studied him sternly.

"Is Jenna here?" he asked, nervously looking down at his feet.

"Ya, come in," I replied, dropping my stern parent act to stand aside. He was nervous enough as it was, they both were. Lucas came in, standing awkwardly near the front door, as if he didn't know where to stand or what to do.

"Wow, you look incredible!" Lucas said, his eyes widening as Jenna walked down the hall towards us.

"Thank you," she said, blushing demurely.

"Well, you kids go have fun now. Have her home by midnight, or whenever," I shrugged, clumsily trying to break the awkward silence that had fallen while Lucas and Jenna stared at each other with nervous, hesitant smiles.

"I'll see you later," Jenna told me, following Lucas out the door. I locked it behind them, shaking my head. Turning around, I surveyed the suddenly quiet apartment. It was so silent, it was almost loud. I didn't know what to do with myself. I had to turn the TV on, just for background noise.

I had been alone in our apartment before, of course. But there was something more profound about this. Normally, I would be enjoying the quiet, basking in the chance to just be in my own head for a bit without worrying about shutting Jenna out.

Maybe it was being exposed to the nervous anticipation of a first date, but I was feeling very lonely. I crossed my arms, trying to hold in the dull ache of my heart.

Missing Iain was complicated. On the one hand, I wanted more than anything for him to walk back into my life. But then...what would I say? How would we even recover from what happened between us, and what happened after? He had served jail time for our relationship. We never really broke up, but it was clear that we weren't together.

And then there was *Jax*. I couldn't get *him* out of my head either. I had tried to ignore it, but he was there, and I was having strong feelings of lust and attraction for someone that *wasn't* Iain. I didn't know how I was supposed to feel about that.

My relationship with Iain had been unconstitutional and complicated...but I had to wonder, was it so sizzling because of the forbidden factor? Was it possible that we could have had a long lasting, healthy relationship? There was a thrill factor, yes, and attraction so deep that it still made my blood heat when I thought about it...and he listened, he counseled, he cared...but still, his silence now spoke volumes.

I'd started to wonder if *maybe*, he had played me. What other explanation could there have been? I felt like an abandoned project that had felt fun at the time. Plus, there was the fact that I had inadvertently helped his sister adopt a baby by recommending the adoption agency she was with to Jenna. Of course, Jenna had unknowingly selected Iain's sister and brother-in-law, but still.

I had a lot of hurt and resentment twisting me up.

I found myself wanting something that was easy and mess free...something that was uncomplicated. Every other factor of my life had been complicated and messy.

And I was tired of waiting.

I HAD FALLEN asleep on the couch, waiting for Jenna to get in and tell me about her date. I awoke to our apartment door closing softly, and feet padding over to where I was laying. I shot up into a sitting position, my heart hammering in my chest with terror.

"Hey, it's just me," Jenna said softly, perching on the coffee table.

I nodded, trying to play off my terror, thankful that Jenna wouldn't push me for answers about it. Jenna didn't know *everything* about my past. I hadn't told her that my first step-father, Rodney, had a nasty habit of sneaking into my bedroom while I slept so he could watch me and masturbate. I was 8 years old at the time, and although he never actually touched me...the act itself had scared me and the fear of waking up to someone coming into my room had not dissipated in all that time.

"How was your date?" I asked, keeping my voice steady as I swung my legs off the couch.

"It was great," Jenna said. Even though our apartment was dark, the glow from the streetlights that poured in from our kitchen window made it easy to see her eyes shining with excitement. "He is so sweet, and he asked me out again! To some music concert at Major's Hill Park on Saturday. Apparently his best friend plays in one of the bands."

"Oh cool!" I was glad to hear Jenna's date had gone well. She deserved every bit of happiness she could get.

"You need to come!" Jenna begged, pleading me with her wide blue eyes. "I don't want to go alone."

"You won't be alone, Lucas will be there," I pointed out, yawning.

"You know what I mean..." Jenna trailed off. "Please come? You could always ask that Jax guy you've been crushing on to come," Jenna suggested, raising a dainty eye brow. I snorted, getting up off the couch to head to my bedroom without replying.

CHAPTER

FOUR

I spent the weekend catching up on the homework I'd neglected over the week. On Sunday evening, I sat on the couch, my laptop opened on my lap and the Word Document staring blankly at me for hours. My last assignment was a paper to write on Death, only I couldn't focus. It should have been easy - I was no stranger to saying goodbye to loved ones. I'd seen death, touched it's cold stiff hand.

I felt myself panicking whenever I tried to think of how to start my paper. I wanted to sound detached from the subject, but it was hard to be detached from death.

Needing a distraction, I clicked over to Facebook.

I hadn't stayed in touch with many of my high school classmates over the years. I tended to purge my list every so often, getting rid of the people that didn't do anything but bump up my "friends" number. Some people used Facebook to collect friends, I used it to stay connected to people I wanted to stay connected to. Which explained why I rarely used it and why it was so boring...Jenna and Jake were the only ones I spoke to outside of high school, and I lived with Jenna.

The only person I kept on my list from my life in Toronto was Lauren, and she was dead. I kept her on because I could still message her, even if she would never read the messages. I could still see the photos we took together, and the ones she took without me.

I went to her wall, scrolling through some of the things our classmates had written recently. People she didn't even like, claiming to miss her daily and think about her always. Lauren would have laughed at it, I knew she would have.

I stopped scrolling when I saw a familiar name, Alex, proclaiming an undying love for her. I clicked his profile. He was still tattooing, by the looks of things. He now sported a tragically beautiful portrait of Lauren on his chest.

I shook my head, bewildered. When Lauren was dating Alex, he never told her that he loved her. I knew he'd been crazy about her, unable to keep his hands off of her at any given time...but I didn't think it was *portrait over your heart* serious.

Just as I was about to close down Facebook, I received a friend request. I clicked on the notification, unable to hide the smile that lifted the corner of my lips as I saw the friend request from a Jax Walker.

I clicked accept, then went over to his profile. He looked extremely hot in his profile picture, his long hair was pulled back and he was wearing a leather riding jacket and holding a helmet, posing beside his black Harley.

"Oh my god, he has a *Harley*?" I jumped, caught off guard by Jenna's sudden appearance behind the couch. She was looking over my shoulder, at Jax's Facebook profile.

"I guess so," I shrugged. "I didn't know, he like...just added me."

"You're right, he's totally Jason Momoa from Conan the Barbarian hot. Are you nuts!" Jenna shoved the back of my shoulder. "Why haven't you climbed that delicious body like a spider monkey?"

I snorted, amused by that image. "I don't know, maybe because I'm not *ready* to."

"Damn," Jenna shook her head, resuming her quest to the kitchen for a drink. "I don't know how you've resisted so far, but you are one strong ass woman. My ovaries are demanding I lick his manly chest."

I rolled my eyes, amused at Jenna's commentary.

Shutting down Facebook, I decided to focus all of my attention on my paper. I wrote about death and social media, and how people now used social media to cope with their grief. I didn't finish editing until nearly two o'clock in the morning.

DESPITE THE LATE hour I got to bed, and a restless night of sleep...I found myself awaking before my alarm clock even went off. I felt nervous and excited, and I knew it had everything to do with the dream I had just woken up from...a dream involving Jax, a dream that left me breathless and very awake.

I kicked off my blankets and wandered down the hall to the bathroom. Jenna was still sleeping, so I grabbed a quick shower and went about my morning routine as quietly as I could. I dressed in my new outfit, the black stretch slim leg jeans, and the checkered chiffon blouse. I glanced at the time on my cell phone's clock as I slipped into my jacket and my boots.

I would be early, but if I walked slow, I wouldn't be *too* early.

I threw my messenger bag over my shoulder, pausing only to lock our apartment door behind me. I flew down the stairs and pushed open the doors to the crisp September air. It was a little chilly, but the fresh air felt good on my face.

At first, I tried to walk slowly...but I felt like someone was following me. I looked behind me, seeing a person walking with a backpack. I couldn't make out their face, as they had a hood pulled up over their head...but there was something about the person that unsettled me. The sensation of being followed wouldn't go away, so I picked up my speed. I would rather be early for class than feel that prickly anxious feeling.

I kept looking behind me, checking that the hooded person didn't get any closer. I was so preoccupied with checking that I walked into what I thought was a wall, until two large hands gently steadied me.

"Easy," Jax chuckled, quickly releasing his gentle hold on my arms. He looked at me curiously, tilting his head slightly. "What's the rush? Excited about our coffee date after class?"

I looked behind me again, and the hooded person was gone. My heart beat was still racing, my skin still prickled with anxiety.

"Yeah, sure. That's it," I said, my voice laced with sarcasm. I didn't want to admit to Jax that I was quite possibly the most paranoid person in the world and thought that someone had been following me. Now that I was away from the situation, it seemed likely that the person was a student at the University, on his or her way to class, and maybe they had their hood pulled up because it was chilly out. I also didn't particularly feel like telling Jax about the other issue clouding my mind...the steamy dream that I had had.

I rolled my shoulders to ease the tension.

"Shall we go to class then? Get this seminar over with so we can finally have that coffee date you've been agonizing over all weekend?" Jax asked, cocking an eyebrow at me.

I rolled my eyes, walking away from him, towards the lecture hall. "Sure thing, Fabio."

"Fabio? Like I haven't heard *that* before," Jax scoffed, keeping pace with me. I resisted the urge to smile.

I pushed open the doors to the lecture hall, finding it nearly empty. A few early students had snagged seats, including a bright mass of copper hair. Crimson waved at us frantically, motioning for us to join her.

Jax and I both stopped at Professor Pedersen's desk to drop off our papers before we walked up the stairs that let to where Crimson was sitting. I sat down beside her, and Jax chose the seat beside me.

"How was your weekend?" Crimson asked, looking at me briefly before she grinned widely at Jax.

"Boring, I did homework all weekend," I answered, yawning.

"Yeah, I played catch up too. What about you, Jax?"

"I worked, and did some homework. Mostly worked though," Jax answered.

"Where do you work?" Crimson asked.

I tried not to grit my teeth. Too much talking in the morning before I had my coffee was not ideal.

"A couple of places," Jax answered, amused. "This weekend I worked at the garage."

"So, you fix cars?" Crimson asked, needing clarification. I resisted the urge to roll my eyes at her as Jax nodded. "Good! I need a mechanic. My boyfriend is not good at car things. I have a weird tinking sound in my engine, and he says it's fine but I'm second guessing him because he doesn't even know how to change the oil!"

I tuned out, ignoring the conversation of possible things that the tinking in Crimson's engine could mean. Absently, I fingered the necklace on my collarbone.

I had no difficulty focusing on Professor Pedersen's lecture, but I may have groaned aloud when she told us she would be assigning our first group assignment. We had to write a Psychology thesis together. Each group would be assigned a different topic. She gave us 20 minutes to find a group of five.

"Looks like we just need two more people," Crimson said, glancing around. She leaned forward, tapping a girl on her shoulder. "Do you and your friend want to join our group?" she asked, gesturing first to herself, then to Jax and I.

The girl Crimson had tapped on the shoulder turned to look at us. Her eyes widened with approval as she studied Jax. She nudged her friend, smirking and raising her eyebrows in unspoken question. She looked too, her eyes falling to rest on Jax's face before she nodded eagerly.

"Hell yeah," the first girl said, grinning. I clenched my fists, irritated at Crimson's choice in group members. The first girl had dark hair that reached her shoulders and cold blue eyes, while the other girl had golden hair and brown eyes. They were both pretty, and the fact that they agreed to join our group after seeing Jax pissed me off. I didn't want to have to carry their workload because they were too busy hitting on him to do their part.

I sent Crimson an unimpressed eye roll, shaking my head at the girls' giddy attempts at flirting.

"I'm Brianna, and this is Alissa," the dark haired girl said, speaking mostly to Jax. She smiled appreciatively at him.

"I'm Crimson," Crimson smiled.

"I'm Jax," Jax added, an amused smile on his lips. He glanced at me, waiting for me to speak. When I didn't, his grin widened. "This is Harlow."

Brianna and Alissa eyed me suspiciously, as if sizing me up. Brianna's eyes narrowed as she saw how close Jax was sitting beside me.

"Are you two, like, a couple?" she asked Jax.

"No," I answered stiffly. Brianna and Alissa exchanged a look, one that I didn't like.

"If you've chosen your group members, please have *one person* come up and select a topic from the bowl," Professor Pedersen instructed, her voice ringing out sharply.

"I'll go," Brianna said, standing up and walking purposefully down to the podium to select a topic, her hips swinging far more than necessary. Professor Pedersen wrote down the topic, and our group number. Brianna sauntered back up to her seat, her hips swinging like she was on a run way. She handed the paper to Crimson.

"We've got *Child Abuse*," she said, almost coyly as she batted her lashes at Jax. His arm was so close to mine, we were practically touching. I was able to notice the stiffening of his muscles, although when I looked closer at him, he had purposely relaxed his muscles and was back to being his relaxed and collected self.

Since we were the first group to go up and get our topic, we had to wait quite some time for the rest of the groups to grab theres. Crimson used that time to try and create a schedule on when we could meet up.

"I'm busy a lot. I'm on the student board, I have a lot of important events to plan," Brianna said, her aura of self-importance nearly suffocating me.

"We could always divide into subgroups," Crimson suggested. "Then tackle individual sections and meet up every now and then to see how everything is meshing."

"That sounds good," Brianna agreed, cutting off my reply. Her eyes drifted to Jax, as if she hoped he would ask her to be in his subgroup. I held my breath, thinking he would...but he didn't. For some reason, this relieved me.

"Want to be in my subgroup?" I asked him, nudging his

shoulder with mine. I'll admit, it was a petty attempt at keeping him close to me. I didn't like the new comers, especially Brianna. There was something about her that rubbed me the wrong way. He grinned down at me.

"Sure," he said, drinking me in with those captivating eyes.

I could feel Brianna's angry gaze zeroing in on me. She wasn't pleased that Jax's attentions were on me.

"Now that all of you have a topic," Professor Pedersen's voice rang out, silencing any conversations the moment the first word fell from her lips. The class listened in earnest as she continued, very slowly looking from one side of the room to the other. "I will expect you to take this group assignment *very* seriously. It will be due at the end of the semester and worth 30% of your final grade. I will be grading you on how you work together, and your individual work as well."

Professor Pedersen waved her hand carelessly to dismiss us. Brianna and Alissa lingered, probably hoping that Jax would stop to talk to them some more. I stood up, stretching a little as I did so. I could feel Jax's eyes on the small portion of skin that showed when my shirt crept up with my movement. I pulled it down, sending him a warning look. He shrugged, unashamed at being caught.

"Let's go get that coffee," I told him.

"We'll catch you later," Jax said, peaking around me to say goodbye to Crimson, Brianna and Alissa. I felt all of their eyes on us as we left. Crimson looked delighted, but Brianna was scowling. Alissa seemed indifferent.

We left the lecture hall, instinctively heading towards *The Bean*. Jax's arm would occasionally brush against mine, setting my nerves on fire. I found myself enjoying and craving more than the casual contact. I couldn't help but remember the dream I had woken up from.

"So, group work," Jax said, making conversation as we

walked. He was smiling in a way that could melt panties. Not very helpful, given the state of my hormones.

"I know," I groaned, looking at him accusatory as I tried to bite back my attraction to him. This coffee date was both a very bad idea, and a very good one. I was already having difficulty focusing on conversation. "I was hoping you were joking about the group work."

"Nope," Jax tucked his hair behind his ear. The action carried over the enticing aroma of his shampoo, reminding me just how *appealing* everything about him was to me.

"Wish I could have had more of a say in our group members," I sighed, pushing open the doors to the *The Bean*. There wasn't a line up, and for that...I was thankful. I had already waited long enough for my morning coffee.

Lucas was working away with a bounce in his step and a grin on his face that said he had just as much fun as Jenna had the night before.

"Morning Harlow, coffee?" Lucas asked, his eyes bright with happiness. It actually almost made me feel hostile. How could people, myself included, get so muddled up over physical attraction? How could we so easily delude ourselves into thinking we connected with someone, just because that physical pull was there?

These are questions I had wondered aloud to my therapist for the last two years. After everything happened the way it did with Iain, I was left with a lot of hostility and resentment, and worst of all...I felt betrayed by myself. My physical feelings had tricked my mind into believing that I was in love, that he loved me and everything would work out fine in the end.

Jax nudged me, bringing me back into the present and away from my dark thoughts. "Oh, yeah. Coffee."

"For me as well, thanks. Large," Jax added, looking at me with intrigue. He waited until we fixed our coffees at the fixing station and found an empty table. He sat down across from me, looking at me with the open curiosity...as if I was a perplexing puzzle he wanted to figure out.

"Why are you looking at me like that?" I demanded, feeling unsettled. The gold that edged his pupils was flickering with interest. I had never felt so exposed by someone's eyes before, and had to physically stop myself from blurting out that his eyes were the most captivating, magical things I had ever seen.

That damn physical attraction, rearing it's God-like head of perfection right in my face.

"You're incredibly difficult to read," Jax laughed lightly, not breaking his gaze as he took a sip of his coffee. I was getting warmer, and I had a feeling it had very little to do with the temperature inside *The Bean*.

"I'm incredibly difficult, period," I sighed, shrugging out of my jacket.

"I like that," Jax's eyes didn't leave my face. I felt myself coming undone, and it was aggravating. A *stare* shouldn't be able to do that, not after I had spent a good solid year building back up the wall between myself and anyone else.

I had vowed to not let anyone in, but I knew I was in trouble with that. Jax's gaze was enough to destroy the walls I had carefully crafted, if I wasn't careful.

"Most girls seem so two-dimensional. They claim to be complex, but they're really just carbon copies of one another. Take Brittany and Alicia, for example. They're exactly the same, even if they look totally different. Their mannerisms are the same, hell...even the way they talk is the same."

"Brianna and Alissa," I corrected, trying not to smile at the fact that Jax hadn't remembered their names. It was silly, really, just how good it made me feel. "Besides, how do you know I'm not two-dimensional?"

"I just know," Jax shrugged, still looking at me. "I've got a good judge of character."

"Well, I'm fairly good at reading people...and I'd have to agree with your assessment on Brianna and Alissa. They are carbon copies of each other, the stereotypical University girls that are a dime a dozen. Crimson seems different. She's got more personality than the two of them combined. They should be great fun to work with, especially if they keep drooling all over your presence."

Jax's laughter was rich and warm, and it made me feel better. It warmed my blood and made me feel...lighter.

I didn't like that.

"You sound jealous," he remarked, the amusement evident on his face.

"Definitely not," I argued, frowning. "I just hate listening to girls giggle and act dim-witted in front of an attractive guy."

Jax smiled slowly. "You think I'm attractive?"

"Don't even," I rolled my eyes, embarrassed that he was focusing on that admission. Jax laughed again, shaking his head as if he was deeply amused by me .

"Tell me more about yourself," Jax said, that delicious smile still on his lips.

"What do you want to know?" I asked, arching an eyebrow inquisitively at him. I was thankful for the change of topic, but I was far from an open book. I didn't know how to respond, a lot of the subject matter in my past was not first coffee conversation. Nor was it first date conversation. I didn't often share bits and pieces of myself with strangers, even those trying to befriend me.

To be completely honest...nobody had tried to befriend me in the last two years, excluding Jamie and Mark. They had taken me under their wing, ignoring my attempts at maintaining a safe, bitchy distance from everyone I had to deal with. They had cracked through, yes, but nobody else had, at least not until this year...not until Crimson and Jax both decided to try and get to know me.

"Where are you from?" Jax questioned, giving me an encouraging, patient smile.

"Originally, Toronto," I answered. "You?"

"I'm from British Columbia, originally. I was born there. My mother came from Hawaii, actually. I moved to Ontario six years ago. My parents are still in British Columbia," Jax's answer made mine seem so vague and boring.

"Do you see them often?" I asked, sipping my coffee.

"No," Jax's jaw clenched slightly, but then he relaxed his features into another genuine smile. "What about you? Do you see yours often?"

"My dad is dead, has been since I was a little kid. I don't see my mom often. She lives in North Bay now, with her new husband."

"Do you like her new husband?" Jax inquired, titling his head slightly.

"Why do I feel like I'm in an interview?" I laughed, feeling uncomfortable, as if Jax was trying to peel back each and every one of my complicated layers.

"Well, technically...this kind of *is* an interview," Jax confessed, leaning back against his chair. He had a playful glint in his eyes, and a bemused smile teasing his thick, kissable lips upward.

"And what position is the interview for?"

"Multiple ones, if you're game," Jax grinned, unable to hide the boyish delight in having me walk right into his dirty joke. I shook my head and rolled my eyes, trying to resist the urge to smile back.

"Very funny. Okay, if this is an interview, I'm going to ask more in-depth questions. Where do you see yourself in five years?"

"Hopefully opening up my own Mixed Martial Arts gym for troubled youth," he answered easily. His answer threw me off guard. I wasn't expecting him to actually *know* where he'd be in five years. I was expecting him to stumble and give some awkward answer with a run of the mill job. "What about you?"

"I don't actually know," I said, almost laughing. My smile faded as I returned to my generic answer. "I want to be a writer, but I also want to help women who have been abused."

"That's heavy," Jax commented, looking at me with respect. I shrugged, feeling even more exposed. I ran my fingers through the tangles of my wavy hair, giving myself something to do with my shaking hands.

"Where abouts do you live?" I asked, trying to draw the conversation away from heavy topics and in to lighter ones.

"In a house, with a bunch of other students. It's about as horrible as it sounds," Jax laughed, shaking his head. "What about you?"

"With my best friend, Jenna," I answered. "In an apartment, kind of near here."

"Cool. And are you single?" Jax asked, raising his eyebrows at me.

I frowned. "I thought we were trying for friends here."

"I made it clear, we're interviewing for multiple positions...and I'll be honest," Jax said, leaning towards me. He kept his arms on his side of the table, but the way he was looking at me made it hard for me to breathe. "I like you. I would settle for being your friend, but I don't want to settle. I want to get to know you and I can't promise you that I won't try to kiss you."

"That's a problem," I told him, not at all sure that it *was* a problem. I didn't know what I wanted anymore.

"Probably," Jax grinned, unaffected. "Let me take you out on a couple of real dates, I promise I will try not to kiss you...unless you want me to."

I already do, I thought before I could stop myself. I sighed. "Fine. And what kind of 'real dates' are you planning on?"

"You'll see. I'll pick you up on Thursday, if you're free?"

"Sorry, I work," I smiled, trying to hide my nerves and the butterflies that exploded in my chest.

"When don't you work?" Jax inquired, raising an eyebrow at me.

"I'm only off on Tuesday," I shrugged. "And the occasional Saturday."

"I guess we'll have to have that date sooner than I planed. Tuesday it is. I'll pick you up at 8pm," Jax said, grinning.

CHAPTER
FIVE

A t 8:00 p.m. the next night, I paced my bedroom nervously, anxiously chewing on my lip and casting nervous looks towards the full-length mirror on my closet door.

I wasn't an insecure girl, I knew I was pretty. I knew men were drawn to me. I knew there was nothing wrong with my appearance. I had curves that made men stare, long dark hair that made other women envious, and a delicate yet strong facial structure that made me stand out. I had been told before that I could model, only I knew that was bogus. I wasn't thin enough to model. I had curves and I was okay with that.

I didn't hide my body, even after all it had been through. I wasn't ashamed of myself, I was confident in my skin...but I still found myself pacing, my nerves frazzled as I tried to detect any kind of outward flaw to fix. I knew it had less to do with my body and my appearance, and *everything* to do with the fact that my most insecure part was my mind.

I worried that, aside from my body and appearance, I would have nothing to offer.

Sure, I was smart. That didn't set me apart from any other girl who landed herself a spot in University. You needed brains to get in, and brains to stay in.

I suppose it had a lot to do with keeping people around. I wasn't very good at that. I didn't let people in, and when I did...they didn't tend to stick around. The only exceptions to that rule had been Lauren, and now Jenna. They weren't romantic relationships either.

I guess I was worried that Jax would get to know me, that he would take the time to peel back all the layers I surrounded myself in, and that he would find me lacking.

I had done my eyes in a smoky dramatic look and had left my hair fall free in thick, curly trestles around my shoulders. I chose a form fitting wrap dress that was pewter in colour and stopped just below my knees. I fretted that the dress wasn't me, as it wasn't a colour I would normally wear. I worried that Jax would think that I was trying too hard. I worried that I *was* trying too hard. It had long sleeves and dipped in the front and the back, revealing a touch of cleavage and almost all of my tattoos.

I had a quill and ink pot tattooed onto my right forearm, six minimalistic birds in flight across my left collarbone, a phoenix tattooed on my right calf, and a cherry blossom tree that crept up my right ribcage and cupped under my breast.

I didn't think about them often, but then and again...I often hide the majority of them with my clothes unintentionally. Each and every tattoo that I had was important to me...they told a story of my life, and for some reason, I found myself worrying that they would give away too much of me. I didn't know if I was ready for someone else to learn my story.

The quill and ink pot symbolized my love of writing. The minimalistic birds in flight was a friendship tattoo I'd gotten with Lauren. The cherry blossom was just a beautiful piece that I'd gotten to hopefully express inner beauty, and the phoenix...my most recent tattoo, represented rising from the ashes.

I frowned, worrying my lip as I searched out any and all flaws.

"You're over thinking, like, *everything*," Jenna pointed out, leaning against my bedroom doorway and giving me a sympathetic look. She'd been just as nervous about her date with Lucas. I could tell that's what she was remembering.

"I know," I sighed, dropping my shoulders in defeat. I chewed my bottom lip nervously.

Before Jenna could impart any words of wisdom on me, the sound of someone knocking on our apartment door broke the silence. Jenna's face transformed to one of excited delight. I knew she was ecstatic to meet the guy that had me so twisted up after so few encounters. Before I could stop her, she flew away from my doorway and down the hall. I heard her open it, heard Jax's deep voice saying hello and Jenna's bubbly tone introducing herself.

"I'll go let Harlow know you're here," I could hear Jenna say. I closed my eyes, willing myself to collect my nerves and become stoic and calm.

I opened my eyes, seeing Jenna in my doorway. "Jax is here."

I gave her a look that let her know I was perfectly aware of that. I slipped on a pair of simple black pumps and grabbed my clutch from the bottom of my unmade bed. My room was a stark contrast from Jenna's. It wasn't messy, per say...but I definitely wasn't religious about making my bed and matching accent pillows to the bed spread.

I walked past Jenna, and she gently reached out to squeeze my arm. "He's hot," she whispered, grinning. "And sweet."

I stepped into the hallway, seeing Jax standing completely

at ease by the island as if he wasn't nervous in the slightest. His confidence and self-assurance made me waver. He was holding a bouquet of flowers, pink cherry blossoms and white roses. My eyes dropped to the flowers and widened in surprise.

The sound of Jax releasing a gust of air brought my eyes away from the bouquet of flowers and up to his gold laced eyes. "You look incredible," he said, his eyes taking in my body like it was water and he was extremely parched.

"Thanks," I muttered, still shocked and unnerved by the flowers. I wasn't aware that guys still did that whole romance thing, and I hadn't exactly pegged Jax to be one of them.

"Too much?" Jax asked, gesturing to the flowers and appearing a little worried. I drank him in, noticing his casual outfit and pulled back hair. He had shaved the careless stumble he usually sported. I smiled, realizing that he had dressed up too. I suppose that was expected of dates.

"No, how did you know?" I asked him, tilting my head curiously. He held the flowers out to me, and I accepted them, drawing in their fragrance with my eyes closed slightly. Jax looked sheepishly at me.

"In Psychology, when you stretched, I saw your tattoo and figured you liked them," he shrugged, seeming a little uneasy with the confession. I smiled, touched that he had taken notice of a rather small detail, and relieved that he too seemed nervous.

"Well thank you," I said sincerely, heading into the kitchen to look for something to put them in. Jenna and I didn't exactly have a vase, so I ended up filling a juice jug with water and putting them in.

"Guess I should have thought of that," Jax laughed. "Not everyone has vases lying around."

"We've never had a reason to get one before," I shrugged. "But knowing Jenna, she'll buy twelve now," I added, casting a bemused look at Jenna, who was not-so-discreetly observing Jax and I from the living room. She grinned, nodding in agreement.

"Ready?" Jax asked, smiling at me. I followed him out of the apartment, glancing at Jenna once more. She gave me a thumbs up and nodded enthusiastically to show me her approval. I rolled my eyes, sticking my tongue at her childishly before I closed the door behind me.

We got out onto the street and Jax headed over to a huge black Chevy Silverado. He hit unlock on his remote, then opened the passenger door for me. The truck *screamed* Jax. It was massive, sleek and impressive and completely customized. There was no chrome anywhere, just mat black and huge rims.

"Do you like?" Jax asked, amused by my open-mouthed expression.

"You know what they say about guys with big, modified trucks..." I trailed off, climbing into the cab with some difficulty.

"What?"

"They're over compensating," I said, winking as I closed the door on him. He threw back his head and howled with laughter before walking over to the drivers side.

"You know, I've kicked girls out of my truck for less," he warned me, sliding into the cab effortlessly with his long legs. He put the key in the ignition, and the truck roared to life.

I rolled my eyes, shaking my head. I had to admit...I was definitely impressed.

"How old are you?" I asked, the question appearing to come from nowhere.

"I'm twenty-five," Jax answered, curiously looking at me. "You?"

"Twenty-one," I answered, narrowing my eyes as I looked at him. "I'll be twenty-two in January."

"I'll be twenty-six in June," Jax grinned.

"An older man," I joked, almost wincing after the words spilled from my mouth. Iain had been eleven years older than me, and Jax was six. Still, Jax seemed pleased by my comment.

"So, what's the plan tonight?" I demanded, eager to change the topic from age.

"We're going to do your stereotypical, run of the mill first date...a *movie*," Jax winked. "Something action packed or scary."

"Action packed," I answered, knowing that the only scary movie in theaters was one about a girl who gets kidnapped by a serial killer. That kind of thing didn't mesh well with me.

"Awesome! Looks like *Furious 6* it is," Jax drove to the movie theater, and I played with the stereo, selecting CD to see what his musical tastes were. I raised an eyebrow at him in question as Dierk Bentley's "I Hold On" blasted through the speakers.

"Country?" I asked, amused.

"Born and raised," Jax admitted shamelessly. He'd thrown his arm across the back of the seats while I was preoccupied.

"Interesting," I smiled. "I'm not one to criticize other peoples' choice in music, but I had you pegged for Heavy Metal."

"Really?" Jax asked, his eyebrows shooting up with amusement. "It's the hair, isn't it?"

"Of *course* it's the hair," I laughed.

Jax shook his head, smiling with amusement as he pulled into the theater. He found a parking spot and pulling in with ease. I didn't know how he did it. I certainly wouldn't have been able to. Than and again...I had never been behind the wheel of something so massive.

Before I had time to register his fluid movements, Jax was out of the truck and walking around to the passenger side. Jax moved fast and graceful. He opened the door and held out his hand for me to take. I took it, about to climb down. He tugged my arm gently, and I feel forward...into his arms. My hands rushed out in front of me, connecting with his chest.

He held me effortless, as if I weighed nothing. He held me close to his body, anchoring me to him with his large hands encasing my hips. My heart jumped madly in my chest, the sudden movement catching me completely off guard and awakening the potent desires I had for him. My lids felt heavy, and I half closed my eyes in response to the heated look in his.

"Harlow," Jax said, his voice deep and laced with the same desire and lust I was feeling. I thought he was going to kiss me...I found myself hoping he would, but the he slowly lowered me to the ground. When I opened my eyes, he was looking down at me with longing and restraint.

"Let's go, before all the good seats are taken," he finished, his eyes lingering on my face a moment longer than necessary. I hoped he couldn't read the disappointment I felt from not kissing him. My hips still tingled from his touch, long after he had released me. We walked towards the theater, not touching save for the occasionally brush of the back of his hand against the back of mine. Even that small contact ignited a fire in the pit of my belly.

It was cheap night, so the movie theater was crowded. We used the self-serve ticket booths to get our tickets. I made a feeble attempt to pay for my own ticket, but Jax was ahead of me in the lineup and beat me to the punch.

"I could have paid for my own ticket," I told him, crossing my arms as we waited in the concession stand line up.

"I thought this was a date," Jax said, sounding amused by my irritation.

"It is, I guess."

"Well that's typically how dates work...haven't you ever

been on one before?" Jax asked curiously. His question stung a little, although that hadn't been his intention.

During our relationship, Iain and I couldn't be seen out in public together. Obviously, date nights out on the town couldn't happen, and if they did...they happened out of North Bay. Iain took me on a few weekend getaways. He took me to Niagara Falls one weekend. I could still recall how foolishly hopeful I had felt.

Then there was the time I came out to Ottawa to meet with Jenna's lawyers. Iain followed, and we remained in town for another weekend escape. Iain took me out to dinner at a Thai place I had actively avoided since I moved to Ottawa. My experience on dates was definitely less than the average twenty-one year old.

It was strange to think that my decision to move to Ottawa was pretty much *for* Iain. This was his home town, his parents supposedly lived here. I had foolishly thought that after his release, he would find me here effortlessly and we could start over. I thought we could begin our lives together.

That hadn't happened. I don't know why I had been so blind as to think that we could just pick up where we left off. Iain's silence ensured I would never know, anyway. *No sense thinking about it*, I reminded myself.

I had built a life for myself here in Ottawa, a life that I liked. I had a job I was comfortable at, a home I felt safe in, and Jenna. Iain's choice to stay away was redundant. Sure, it had affected my happiness for a while...but only because I had let it. I was trying my hardest to change that.

"I've been on dates before," I said defensively, thinking about the weekend getaways and dinners with Iain. I questioned whether or not escaping for a weekend to hookup and hanging out with someone could even be considered a 'date'.

"Easy," Jax grinned. He was standing close to me, looking

at me in a way that made my knees weak. His scent was almost over-powering me. It chased away the lingering thoughts I had of Iain, leaving only enough room in my head for what was happening *now*, what I felt *now*.

I had lived in the past for so long that it was strange to break out of it.

"Can I help who's next please?" the cashier asked, breaking Jax's gaze. He stepped forward, gently stirring me with his hand on the small of my back.

"What do you want?" he asked, looking at me expectantly.

"Popcorn is fine, and a drink," I said, looking at the cashier. She was young, likely still in high school, and a little clumsy at her job. We patiently waited while she tried to type in the proper combo number for one large popcorn and two large drinks, and again when she accidentally dropped the popcorn bag on the floor and had to get a new one.

"First day?" Jax asked kindly, noting the *trainee* label under her name plate.

"Yeah," she blushed deeply, embarrassed.

"You're doing awesome," Jax grinned, accepting the bag of popcorn from her shaky hands. She smiled timidly at him, her blush increasing.

"You have an interesting way of making people feel good," I remarked, following Jax to the counter to grab straws for our drinks. Jax ran a hand through his hair, smiling sheepishly at me.

"Yeah...I like to make people feel good," he shrugged, looking a little guarded and embarrassed. I tilted my head, reading him. I could tell that he was hiding something, something that made him uncomfortable. I wanted to ask him what it was that he was hiding...but then I would have had to lay out *my* secrets. I definitely wasn't ready for that.

"The world needs more of that," I said instead, my tone a little clipped.

"Do I make you feel good?" Jax asked, his eyes penetrating right into my soul. I hesitated, my mouth opening and closing for a minute as I struggled to answer truthfully. Jax smiled, seeming to read me as easily as I had read him. "I do, but I also scare you and make you uncomfortable," he answered for me.

"You don't scare me," I scoffed, meeting Jax's gaze steadily. It was a lie, of course. He *did* scare me and made me more than a little uncomfortable. Mainly because he was evoking feelings in me that had been resting since Iain.

"Whatever you say," Jax smiled, nodding his head in the direction of theater 12. "Let's go get seats."

We started to walk, weaving around clusters of people. Jax was holding the large popcorn and his drink in his left hand, his right hand finding mine almost timidly. Our fingers wove together and I bit my lip, looking away from him. He didn't notice, intent on leading me safely through the group of jostling teenagers.

The simple act of holding Jax's hand was stirring emotions in me that had been in hibernation. I felt them coming back in waves. Desire, intrigue, warmth, giddiness. I frowned, frustrated with myself.

It wasn't that I hadn't realized that I had returned to what Jenna dubbed "the cold zone", I knew that I was numb and had been since my first letter to Iain was met with silence.

I didn't want to be the girl that needed a guy to come into her life to wake her up and help her feel alive, and it angered me that maybe...just maybe, I *was* that kind of girl.

"Where do you want to sit?" Jax asked me, pausing at the bottom of the stairs in theater 12. The theater was nearly empty.

"The top," I answered, pulling my hand free and walking

quickly up the stairs. I made my way down the back row of seats towards the middle. Jax followed, sinking down into the seat beside me.

"Really? You prefer the top? That doesn't surprise me," he joked, turning to face me. His eyes were heated and there was a smile on his face that suggested his comment had clearly meant to be an innuendo. I smirked, enjoying his flirtatious behavior, and the tingles of desire that shot up my spine at the thought of me on top of him.

"Subtle," I ran my fingers through my hair, pulling it over my right shoulder, and squinted towards the front of the theater. I needed to look anywhere but at him, otherwise...I risked the danger of climbing onto his lap.

The screen was displaying the typical pre-show trivia questions. The theater seats were starting to fill up quickly, the wave of people coming from the concession line up.

Jax took his finger and started tracing my spin. "I thought you would have a tattoo here as well," he said huskily, intrigued. Goosebumps erupted in response to his touch. I shivered with pleasure, then shrugged away from his hand. He grinned at me playfully.

"Nope, sorry to disappoint," I replied, trying to keep my tone unaffected. My body was serging with desire, but I didn't want him to know that.

I leaned back in my seat, feeling it rock slightly with the movement. It had recently been updated to allow for more comfortable seating. The arm rests went up too, I discovered after testing mine.

I caught Jax watching me, and I pursed my lips in annoyance. It was aggravating how undoing it felt to have just his eyes on me. I was beginning to regret my decision to go on a date with him, suffering through one of those times where I wasn't sure I *wanted* to wake up from the numbness.

In fact, I knew I didn't. I didn't want to feel anything that could potentially lead to pain, and this sort of thing always did. My emotions and desires were already running rampant.

But I knew that I *needed* to break out of the numbing reality I had fallen into over the past couple of years. I needed to force Iain from my mind, as he had done to me, and my body had gravitated towards Jax.

"You think a lot, don't you?" Jax remarked airily, leaning back in his own seat and using his own hands as a head rest. He didn't look at me again, but I knew he was watching me out of the corner of his eye, waiting for my response.

"I do," I admitted. There was no harm in that. My past decisions had been made without much thought. I had always been the kind of girl to just pursue what she wanted to have and do what she wanted to do. I had never really thought out consequences to my actions.

Needless to say, I had learned my lesson after the last time. Seeing someone you *really* cared about, someone that you loved, go to jail over simply being with you was enough to open my eyes. Actions equaled consequences.

In the past two years, I'd had *a lot* of time to think about those consequences, and although I truly believe that what I had felt for Iain was love...if I could do it over again, I would never have showed up on his doorstep that night demanding to know his feelings for me. I would have never entertained the thought of being with him, with my *teacher*. I wouldn't have opened the Pandora box, even if it had given me some of the happiest memories of my life so far. I wouldn't do it because I wouldn't have wanted to ruin someone's life like that.

Teenagers, and young people in general, think that bad things won't happen to them. I used to fool myself into thinking I was one of the wise ones. I *knew* bad things could happen, I knew reality was a stone cold bitch...but I honestly hadn't thought my happy ending with Iain could come to an end, especially one like that. I hadn't thought people would care enough to put up a stink about it, not quitting until the "evil teacher that prayed on little girls" was behind bars.

"I would love to know what was actually going on in that head of yours," Jax said, turning his head to truly look at me again. Like every time his eyes fell upon my face, I felt as if he could truly see me. It was unnerving. I offered him a tiny smile.

"Maybe one day, I'll let you in enough to," I replied, trying to keep my voice playful and light. Part of me didn't want that, part of me wanted to remain on my safe little island. But there was another part of me, and this part was growing rapidly, that wanted to invite him in with open arms and just *see* what would happen. After all, it wasn't like I could ruin *his* life.

"I would like that," Jax whispered, drawing his face closer to mine. His lips were several inches away from mine, I closed my eyes as the warmth of his minty breath flitted across them.

The movie trailers started to play, and suddenly the warmth of Jax's breath was gone. I opened my eyes, blinking once to clear my mind of the disorienting sensations his nearness had created. Jax was staring straight ahead, his lips lifted in a soft smile.

I turned to face the screen as well, moments before he placed his arm around my shoulders.

***

IT WAS difficult to pay attention to the movie with Jax's arm across my shoulders. It was a gesture that was so date-like and innocent, and yet it made me feel...well, a lot of different things.

When the credits finally rolled and the lights slowly started to turn on, I had to blink a view times to wake myself up from the daze Jax's closeness always seemed to put me in.

This was the part about movie theaters that I *hated,* the part when every single person in the theater tried to get out at once. A swarm of people, almost mob-like, pushing towards the exits as if staying behind was dangerous. The mentality to get out and get out fast caused anxiety in me. Usually, I was the first to leave, purposefully pushing my way out the doors, least I get trapped inside. I tried to stand up, but Jax's arm across my shoulders was anchoring to my seat.

It should have made me panic more, to be trapped under a heavy arm with this need to escape sitting heavily on my chest...but it somehow calmed me.

"What's the rush?" Jax asked, looking at me gently. "The exit doors will still be there in a minute or two, and they won't be so packed."

I exhaled, focusing on the sensation of his arm and the butterflies in my stomach. I looked up at him through my long lashes, blinking a few times. I licked my lips, feeling nervous energy. I was beginning to panic. I could feel it bubbling in my chest.

That's when Jax kissed me. I felt his lips touch mine, pausing the world around us and making all of the chaos and noise fade away to nothing. My heart stuttered in my chest, then frantically increased in tempo as he deepened the kiss. His tongue sought entrance, and I gave it without thinking, returning the kiss with the same intensity he had. The need to connect to him consumed me. His hands rose, getting lost in the mane of my hair and finding the nape of my neck. I grabbed his wrists with my own hands, clenching to them as I moaned.

Jax let out a primal growl, deepening the kiss even more. I hadn't thought it was possible to kiss him any deeper, any harder, but he channeled all of his desire and need into it, and I poured mine in. It was explosive. I saw stars, the bubble of lust and need in the pit of my stomach exploded, and I wanted him then and there. I could feel every ounce of control that I had melt away.

I pulled away from him, almost panting. My eyes were wide, panicked from everything I felt in that single kiss. Jax slowly dropped his hands, but not before he brushed my cheek with the pad of his thumb. I closed my eyes, breathing heavily and trying not to cry.

I felt like an emotional mess of hormones and heartbreak.

I stood up, so quickly that I almost stumbled. "Looks like the coast is clear," I said, my voice shaking slightly. Jax frowned, confused and concerned at my behavior. He ran his hands through his hair, exhaling deeply.

"What?" I asked, almost impatiently.

He grinned, completely unashamed. "Give me a minute, okay?"

"Oh," I snorted. It was obvious that our kiss had evoked strong feelings in Jax as well. My stomach rolled with desire again, and I sighed, tapping my foot against the floor as I tried to bite back a smile.

Grinning, Jax stood up and took my hand without asking, as if the simple act was natural to him. He led me down the stairs towards the theater 12 exit.

The hallway was still full of people coming for the next viewing, but it wasn't as congested as it would have been had I tried to escape right after the movie ended. With my hand in Jax's, we headed towards the parking lot, our arms swinging slightly with each step.

Jax pulled his keys out of his pocket with his free hand, hitting the unlock button on the remote. Up ahead, his truck headlights blinked. I dropped his hand, walking around the length of the truck to the passenger side, and reached my hand out to open the door. Jax had gone around the other way, the quicker way, and beat me to it.

"And they say chivalry is dead," I crossed my arms, smirking at him as he held the door open.

"Certainly not," he winked, offering me his hand. I took it, using it to push myself up into the truck. He watched me with appreciation before he closing the door once I was safely out of the way.

I was at war with myself. On the one hand, the kiss we had shared in the movie theater was making my head spin and causing me to want to run far away. On the other hand, I didn't want the night to end. I wanted to kiss Jax again and feel all that I was feeling amplified, just like it had been in the movie theater.

It was probably safer to just head home, so when Jax asked if I wanted to hit up a pub for a drink or two, I politely declined. "I need to get home, I have a lot of homework to do tonight. I work the rest of the week and won't have a chance to catch up on it."

Jax nodded, understanding and accepting my excuse. He knew how packed our one Psychology class together was. The rest of my course load was just as ridiculous.

He drove me home, respecting my need for silence. When he pulled to the curb out front of my apartment, he turned off the engine of his truck and hopped out before I had a chance to tell him I could walk myself up.

Sighing, I opened the passenger door, hopping out before Jax could assist me. I didn't resent his desire to help me, I just didn't need it. He had caught me off guard the first time, and I didn't particularly like being caught off guard. As amazing as his large hands had felt when he held me...I felt myself sliding into a dangerous zone that I wasn't ready to be anywhere near, let alone in.

We walked up the stairs side by side, neither of us talking. When we reached my door, I turned to face him.

"I had fun tonight," I told him, speaking the truth. I did have fun. Lots of fun...even if I wasn't comfortable with the things I was feeling. *Too much too soon.*

Jax gently tilted cupped my chin and tilted it up, looking into my eyes. "I did too, Harlow. Kissing you was my favourite part. I would like to do that again...and often."

"What a line," I remarked, smirking again. He brought it out in me.

Jax grinned, tilting my chin a little more so that his lips could easily find mine. He kissed me softly, gently exploring the curvatures of my lips with his. My heart thudded loudly, and I felt the familiar roll of desire snaking over my skin. "Fuck it," I muttered, grabbing the collar of his coat and pulling him towards me as I deepened the kiss. I gently bit down on his lip, pulling it slightly and purring in response to his moan.

His body pressed against mine, pinning me to the door. His hands roamed my waist, finding their way to my hips. He squeezed gently, causing my pelvis to thrust in response.

Suddenly, I felt myself falling backwards as the door opened. Jax caught me in an odd looking dip, the same kind of move he had pulled before outside when I had stumbled on the sidewalk. I tilted my head back to glare at Jenna, my head almost upside down and my long hair nearly touching the floor. She had her hand clasped over her mouth and was trying to stifle her giggles. I'm sure it looked like we were practicing some kind of dance move.

"I'm sorry," she snorted, trying to reign in her amusement. "I heard someone at the door and...well..."

Jax stood up, dragging me along with him, and laughed.

I huffed, stepping out of Jax's embrace. I put my hand on his chest, gently pushing him out the door. "I had a wonderful time, I'll see you around," I said, closing the door in his laughing face.

I turned around, glaring at Jenna before stomping to my room. I knew she would follow me, and she did, coming into my room behind me.

"I'm sorry for interrupting your goodbye..." she apologized, looking guilty.

"It's fine," I sighed, kicking my heels off. "It's probably better that you did."

"Why?" Jenna sat down on my unmade bed, drawing her legs up to her chest. She was wearing her pajama bottoms and a tank top.

"I was...I don't know," my brow furrowed as I tried to think of an explanation. The problem was...I couldn't think. My lips felt swollen from his kiss, and my nerves were on fire. I wanted to crawl out of my own skin to escape all the feelings of lust I was having. It was too much, too soon. I wasn't ready for that kind of thing. I didn't think I could handle it, in fact...I knew I couldn't.

Now that I was free from Jax's presence, Iain was slithering his way back into my memory, making me feel guilty for the entire night.

"You're feeling guilty," Jenna accused, reading my mind. "Don't feel guilty! You have nothing to feel guilty for!"

I turned my back on her, slipping out of the dress and pulling a large band t-shirt over my head. It was pretty much all I slept in.

"I know that," I said finally, sighing again. "And I didn't...while I was with him. It's all so confusing. My head feels messed up."

"Looks like somebody's a little love sick," Jenna grinned.

"I am *not* love sick," I stared her down. "I am...lust sick. And I can't be."

"Why not?"

"I'm not ready for it," I said softly, my fingers instantly going up to my collarbone to touch the necklace, my thoughts absorbed by Iain.

CHAPTER
SIX

I made it my mission over the next few days to stay as busy as possible. I picked up extra shifts at work, jammed more activities into my already jammed schedule so that I wouldn't have time to think about all the things I was actively avoiding thinking about. Jax texted me, and I replied back but skirted around seeing him again. Monday was too soon to see him, and it approaching fast.

Thursday night, I was working the close shift at *The Bean*. It had been a long, boring, uneventful shift. I had done so much cleaning that I was certain Jamie and Mark wouldn't recognize the place the next morning. I closed up shop without any incident. I was just throwing on my jacket and grabbing my purse when someone started knocking on the glass pane of the store door.

My heart jumped with fear as I whipped around to see who was knocking. Jax stood on the other side of the door. The dark stubble was back, dusting across his strong jawline. I wanted to run into his embrace, to touch and taste him.

I frowned, shaking my head to try and calm my raging hormones. I definitely was lusting after him, *badly*.

"I told you that I would see you on Monday," I said, trying to ignore my increased heartbeat. At first, it had jumped with fear...but the steady, speedy rhythm had everything to do with the man in front of me.

"I know," Jax had his hands in his pockets. He was wearing faded jeans and a brown leather jacket that I couldn't help but appreciate, his hair was down and mused from the wind. I found myself envisioning my hands tangling in it, pulling his head down toward me.

I knew that Jax couldn't read minds, but he definitely seemed to know the direction my thoughts had gone. He smiled at me, his eyes dropping down the length of my body slowly before rising to rest on my lips.

"Then why are you here?"

"I take it you haven't been paying attention to the news, lately?" Jax questioned, his smile fading and his expression growing serious.

"No..." I trailed off, my heart jumping with fear in my chest again. There could be a million things being reported in the news...a re-run of the scandal that rocked North Bay being one of them.

"There's someone attacking females at night in this area," Jax answered. "I didn't think you should walk home alone this late."

"I would be fine," I rolled my eyes, trying to not show him my fear. "I've got pepper spray and I'm pretty sure I could kick some serious ass if need be."

"Have you taken self-defense classes?" Jax asked me curiously, stepping towards me. I stepped backward in response.

"No," I answered, the off-handed humor fading from my voice. "But I-"

"Well, that doesn't make me feel better. How is Pepper spray going to help you if an attacker grabs your hair?"

"Gee, thanks. Really, make me feel strong and capable why don't you?" I said dryly, rolling my eyes in exasperation.

"Oh, I think you're strong and capable alright," Jax smirked. "I would be afraid for anyone who attempted it. I saw the look in your eyes that day when I caught you off guard."

"So then, *why* are you here?" I asked, shaking my head. "What makes you think I need a chaperon?"

"I just wanted to make sure you got home safely," Jax said, raising his hands in surrender. "And *maybe*, I wanted an excuse to walk you home and see you."

I remained silent as I flicked off the lights, leaving only the dim light over the display counter on. Jax waited outside for me as I went about my tasks. I punched in the alarm system code before pulling the door shut behind me. I locked it with the key Jamie had given me.

After I finished locking up the store securely, I turned to glare at Jax again. "I don't need anybody's help."

Jax studied me for a moment, his face lit up by the street lamps around us. "I don't believe that," he said, his voice gentle. I took a steadying breath, calming myself. I couldn't deny that the real reason why I was so annoyed was because I was *happy* he had shown up, happy that he was looking out for me.

I opened my eyes again. A movement behind Jax caught my eye, and I watched as a figure slide into the shadows of an alleyway. Paranoia crept up, Jax's words ringing all too true in my head.

"Fine, you can take me home then." I grumbled, trying to beat back the paranoia stubbornly. People walked at night, home from jobs and to friends houses, out for dinner and to the bars for a drink. It wasn't a crime. I was just unsettled from

Jax's words. I was also angry at myself for not paying attention to the local news. There was nothing more inexcusable than being ignorant to what was going on in your own backyard. I looked around, expecting to see Jax's truck.

"I actually parked it outside of your apartment," Jax explained, seeing my searching look. I raised an eyebrow at him in question. "I stopped in to see you, and Jenna said you were at work and would be walking home soon."

"So that's how you knew," I started walking, shaking my head slightly. I could hear him following me, his long strides catching up to me with ease.

"I could teach you, you know," Jax said a couple steps later. He looked at me, his expression serious and yet passionate.

"Teach me what?" I asked.

"How to defend yourself. I've been doing Mixed Martial Arts since I was a kid," Jax answered. "Everyone should know how to defend themselves." I didn't reply right away. I figured he was probably referring to his childhood. We walked in silence while I mulled over his words. My apartment building was several steps away when I finally reached a decision.

"Okay," I finally said, turning to face him. It would be good to know how to defend myself a little better. I mean, I knew the places to hit a man to cause some pain, but knowing a little more wouldn't hurt my case.

"Great, let me know when you want to start," Jax grinned.

"I will," I paused, looking up at my building and hesitating. "Did you want to come up and maybe have a drink or something? Of water? Jenna and I haven't really had a chance to go grocery shopping this week."

"Sure, that sounds great," Jax laughed. We walked up the stairs to my apartment. I opened the door, expecting to see Jenna alone...not entwined on the sofa with the Harry Potter look-a-like, Lucas.

"I guess he texted you back?" I remarked, closing the door behind Jax and I. Jenna quickly tried to disengage herself from Lucas' arms. Her face was beat red with embarrassment.

"I guess Jax found you?" Jenna shot back, crossing her arms. I smiled, walking over to the refrigerator to grab two bottles of water.

"I guess so," I said over my shoulder. "Did you two want anything to drink? Or...did you get enough of each other's saliva?"

Jenna knew I was joking, but she still flushed with embarrassment. By the time I handed Jax a water bottle, Jenna had put some distance between herself and Lucas. She smiled slowly at me, showing me that she was about to get me back for embarrassing her. I took a slow sip of water, challenging her with my steady gaze.

"Well, now that Jax is here, maybe you could *finally* ask him about Saturday?" she asked innocently, blinking at me.

"What's Saturday?" Jax asked.

"Some dorky music festival at Major's Hill Park," I shrugged.

"Hey! It's not dorky, my friend plays in one of the bands," Lucas protested, shooting me a wounded look. I smiled in apology, not really feeling sorry.

"Oh yeah, I was going to go to that with one of my roommates," Jax answered, surprising me. "I'll go with you, if you want," he added, looking at me. I almost choked on the water I was drinking. I swallowed hard.

"I wasn't even planning on going," I answered, shrugging my shoulders. "Besides Lucas, who's going to cover Saturday?"

"I already spoke to Jamie. He said we could both take the day off, that he and Mark would be fine without us," Lucas answered. I believed him, but I was still going to double check with Jamie about it.

"Well, fine," I sighed, feeling cornered.

"Cool, it's a date. Another one," Jax said, grinning at me.

———

TWO DAYS LATER, I dramatically flopped down on Jenna's bed and stared at her with solemn eyes while she put the finishing touches on her makeup. I was still angry at her for all but bullying me into this concert. I hadn't planned on going because I knew I wouldn't like it. I enjoyed music, I just didn't enjoy crowded, chaotic places. Plus, it was outside. I knew it would likely be cold, and I didn't like being cold.

"Stop sulking," Jenna ordered, frowning at me. "This will be fun!"

"Right, fun," I huffed, rolling my eyes at her. My stomach tingled with nerves, and I didn't know if I could blame it on the concert, or the looming fact that I was about to see Jax again.

Jenna was muttering under her breath, trying to find what she dubbed as 'concert appropriate attire'. She glared at me. "You look perfect!" she accused, gesturing to my black denim skinny jeans and faded black skull top. She returned to root through her closet. "I don't want to look like a snob!" She added, tossing a conservative button up blouse aside with disgust.

"Just wear blue jeans and that black v-neck top with your brown jacket," I said, rolling my eyes. "It's not a fashion show. You'll be fine. Nobody else will care."

This would be my first concert. Shocking, considering that my father, Randy Jones, had played in a metal band called "Screaming Dragons" in the eighties. That's how my mom had met him, at a smoky bar in Toronto during one of his performances.

I didn't know much about my dad, I didn't remember him.

I had been three years old when he overdosed on cocaine. All I had were the snippets my mom told me, the faded leather jacket I still wore everywhere, and old pictures. I knew that my mom had loved him desperately, blindly, and that he loved her. I knew that he was talented, I still had one of his demo tapes that mom passed on to me. I knew that he loved us, but that he had suffered from depression and addiction for years, even before he met my mom. He kept all of it a secret from her, and she'd been too lovestruck to figure it out until it was too late.

I didn't necessarily blame her for my father's death, but I still couldn't understand how blind she had been. Of course...I had been blinded by love too. Love messes with your perception. Love had you seeing only the things that you wanted to see, the good things.

"Hello? Harlow? Jogging down memory lane again?" Jenna's voice broke me from my reverie.

"No, I'm just tired," I lied, pulling myself up and swinging my legs over her the edge of her bed.

Before Jenna could call me out, a strong knock strapped against our apartment door. "I'll get it," I said, standing up with relief. I didn't want to get into it with Jenna right now, and I could tell by the look on her face that she was going to press for answers.

I walked down the hall, leaving Jenna to finish getting ready. I opened the door to Jax and Lucas. They were standing in the hallway, awkwardly not speaking to each other. Aside from a couple of brief encounters at *The Bean* and the other night in our apartment, Jax and Lucas had yet to actually meet each other.

I leaned against the doorway and crossed my arms, smiling. Jax towered over Lucas, and his defined muscles made Lucas look scrawny. Lucas seemed aware of it, and he straightened his spine, attempting to appear taller than he was.

"Good afternoon," Jax smiled a smile that could melt butter, his eyes sweeping down to take in my appearance with appreciation and desire. The heat of the look set my own blood on fire. I knew Lucas could feel the sexual tension between us. He shifted uncomfortably beside Jax.

"Is Jenna ready yet?" Lucas asked as I stepped aside to let them in.

"No, go hurry her along. She's primping like we're going to a beauty pageant, not a lame outdoor concert."

Lucas' eyes narrowed momentarily, I knew my comment about the lame outdoor concert bothered him a little.

I nodded my head in the direction of Jenna's room, and he took off to find her, leaving Jax and I alone in the living room.

Jax stepped towards me, his hands gently grabbing my upper arms. The touch awakened my own desires, and I bit my lip to stifle the gasp that threatened to spill from my lips as he pulled me closer. He lowered his head, his lips brushing gently against mine, almost questionably. My own hands lifted to the back of his neck, and I pulled him towards me hungrily.

I had done a lot of thinking since the last time I saw him, on Thursday night. I was tired of fighting my reactions to him, tired of being afraid of what would happen if I gave in. I was tired of letting someone I hadn't heard from in years hold me back.

Besides, I didn't sleep any easier denying myself. My dreams were just as charged as the tension between Jax and I. It didn't make for a restful nights sleep.

Jax's tongue teased my lips, silencing the thoughts in my head. All I could hear was the roaring of my blood. I kissed him back, allowing myself to fall into him.

"Um...are we ready to go or..." I reluctantly pulled away from Jax's arms, looking down the hallway at where Jenna's voice had come from. She was standing beside Lucas with a bemused smile on her face.

"Actually, if want...we could skip out?" I cocked an eyebrow at Jax. He laughed, but the desire was evident in his eyes...and in the way he used me to block his body's reaction to the kiss.

"You guys can't miss this," Jenna frowned, stomping towards us, Lucas trailing awkwardly behind her. "We've already got the tickets, and it's going to be fun!"

"Fine," I rolled my eyes at Jax. "Let's go then."

The four of us left the apartment, Jenna pausing to lock it up. She tucked her hair behind her ear and smiled shyly at Lucas as he took her hand. Jax and I lead the way down the stairs and to the street, where Jax's massive truck was parked against the curb.

"Your chariot awaits," Jax told us dramatically, gesturing to the truck and bowing slightly.

Lucas glanced towards the tiny Honda accord parked behind the truck, shrugged as he stepped forward to open the back quad cab door. He held it for Jenna with an excited grin.

I rolled my eyes, trying not to smile as I watched Lucas help Jenna climb into the back. I didn't wait for Jax to do the chivalrous thing, I didn't need his help. I climbed in to the truck with ease. Jax shrugged, grinning at my stubborn, silent declaration.

I pulled the door shut, giving Jax a wary smile. "Let's get this show on the road."

Jax grinned at me, nodding once as he merged his truck back onto the road. The drive to Major's Hill Park was a quick one, but we had to park a block over and walk. The city had shut down the roads surrounding Major's Hill Park for the concert. I stepped out of Jax's truck, zipping my dad's leather jacket up against the chill. I knew I would be thankful for it's warmth later on, when the sun faded, taking the warmth of day with it.

Jax was leaning into the truck bed, hoisting something out. I looked at him curiously, one eyebrow arched in question.

"I grabbed a couple blankets," Jax answered, shrugging. He tossed his arm around my shoulders, pulling me to his muscular body. My heart jumped in response, and I stiffened against the urge to melt into him.

Jenna and Lucas were in their own little world, walking ahead of us. Jenna's hand was entwined with Lucas', and he kept looking at her and smiling as they quietly conversed. The corners of my mouth turned up, an involuntary response to my best friend's happiness. It was good seeing Jenna like this.

"Oh look, a smile," Jax commented, almost gleefully. I rolled my eyes.

"I smile."

"Not often enough," Jax's voice was husky, his breath hot on my ear lobe. His heavy arm was still across my shoulders, and he somehow managed to pull me closer while we walked. I stumbled over the uneven ground, but Jax steadied me.

We followed a mob of other people, heading towards the stage set up. It was a lawn concert, and I was thankful that Jax had brought blankets. We found a spot a little ways away from the stage, and Jax spread out the blanket and motioned for us to sit. The blanket was large enough that we could all sit comfortably. I sat between Jenna and Jax, while Lucas sat on Jenna's other side.

I exhaled, my hair blowing outward with the gust of air from my lungs. This all felt so...*date like*. It was making me nervous. I pulled my legs up to my chest, staring straight ahead at the stage. There were people on stage setting up.

"This is a charity music festival," Lucas told us, leaning in front of Jenna so he could look at Jax and I. "Proceeds go towards the local food bank and soup kitchen. Last year we raised 5000 dollars."

"That's impressive," I remarked, easing up a little.

"Yeah," Lucas glanced at me, smiling slightly, as if to say *not so lame now, huh?*

Lucas started to talk to Jenna about something, I stopped paying attention after the first sentence. As nice as I thought Lucas was, and despite being extremely happy for Jenna's happiness...he bored me a little. Instead, I scanned the crowd.

The concert wasn't terrible, but it wasn't anything to write home about. Still, I had fun. An odd concept for me, lately. At one point, Jax ended up pulling me to rest against his chest, his long legs on either side of me. He brought out a second blanket and wrapped it around us. My heart beat frantically against my chest. I bit my lip, staring ahead at the stage the whole time.

"Can we go now?" I had to raise my voice and almost shout in Jenna's ear. She had been so occupied with Lucas, that she had barely said more than two words to me. Lucas' arm was around her waist, his hand resting on the ground beside her. She had been so starry eyed with him that she'd barely taken in anything around us. I didn't blame her, they did seem to have a connection...one I hadn't seen Jenna have with anyone as long as I'd known her. She was friendly with Jake, but she had never had that dopey, happy look on her face before.

"Yeah," Jenna nodded. "But I'm going to stick around. Lucas wants me to meet some of the guys from *Steamlined.*" Steamlined was the band that Lucas' friend played in.

"How will you get home?" I asked, frowning.

"We can call a cab," Jenna assured me, her eyes finally taking in the position Jax and I were in. She smiled. "Have fun, and...*be safe,*" she added. A pained look crossed her face momentarily, but it was gone before I could question her on it. I knew it likely had everything to do with...well, her past. Jenna smiled at me again before she turned to say something to Lucas.

"Do you want to go?" I asked Jax instead, looking up at him over my shoulder. He grinned at me, like he had been waiting for me to ask those words all night long.

We stood up, leaving the blanket on the ground with Jenna and Lucas so that they would still have somewhere to sit. Jax took my head, and we stepped over legs and bodies as we made our way away from the lawn.

We had to pass the beer tent where several people were waiting in the line up. Several more hung out around it, drinking beers and talking...socializing.

I thought I saw a head of dark curls, a head I wouldn't forget anywhere, but when I blinked again...the person that I had thought was Andrew Cooper was gone. I stopped walking, my heart pounding with adrenaline. *It couldn't have been him*, I told myself. *Andrew Cooper had moved with his mom.* Where, I wasn't exactly sure. I hadn't been privy to those details, but I'm sure if I did some sleuthing I could figure it out easily.

"Hey, are you okay?" Jax asked, looking at me curiously.

I shook my head. "Yeah, sorry...I thought I saw someone." I resumed walking, tugging gently on Jax's hand.

Jax drove us back to my apartment. I chewed on my lip as Jax parked his truck against the curb. I wanted to invite him up, but I was afraid of what would happen if I did. I knew the inevitable would happen, and although my body was certainly ready for it...I wasn't sure if my mind was. Plus, I wanted to do some sleuthing. I unbuckled my seat belt, intent on telling Jax I'd see him later.

"I -" before I could finish my sentence, Jax was pulling me across the cab, almost onto his lap. His lips crushed against mine in a passionate, burning kiss that seared me. All my previous worries and concerns flew out of my head, and I wanted to crawl into that moment, into those feelings, and just stay there.

Jax's hands roamed up my hips, squeezing gently. He fed upon my mouth, and I returned the assault, just as hungry for it as he was. Breathlessly, I pulled away. My head was spinning in an entirely delightful way.

"Sorry," Jax grinned mischievously, his eyes dancing. "I've been dying to do that again all night."

"Apology accepted," I said, hoping my voice didn't sound as breathless as I felt. I pulled away, my hand still on his chest. I needed to put some distance between us so I could think clearly again.

"You're running," Jax remarked, tilting his head and fixing me with a gaze I couldn't break even if I wanted to. The darkness made it hard to see the those hypnotic eyes boring into my face, but still they held me, captivated like a deer caught in the headlights of an on coming car. "Why do you run?" he asked softly, his right hand coming up to gently cup my chin.

I sighed heavily, biting down on my lip. "I'm not good at conversations," I warned him.

"That's okay," Jax told me, and I knew that it *was* okay. "Just try me."

I sighed again, my brows furrowed. I didn't want things to be complicated, but who was I kidding? They were already complicated. My feelings for Jax were strong and sudden, and they took over everything...even my fears and the fact that I didn't think I was emotionally ready for another relationship.

"I want to be with you, I want to do this with you...I just..." I trailed off, struggling to find words to verbalize my feelings.

"You're scared," Jax finished, the pad of his thumb brushing across my cheek. "That's okay Harlow, it's okay to be scared. We'll take this slow...at your pace."

"I'm not sure what my pace is," I confessed, looking back

up to meet his eyes. "Some times I want to run, far away from you...other times I want to drag you into bed with me."

"If you run, I'll just chase you," Jax said, his voice heated with desire and promise. I felt my heart skip a beat in response to his words and the look in his eyes.

"That sounds creepy," I remarked, trying to lighten the serious mood we had fallen into. Jax laughed richly, shaking his head. The truth was, his words scared me because I could actually see a future with this man.

They unnerved me because I could very easily fall in love with him.

There was a connection between us that even I couldn't ignore or push away, and it was different from anything I had ever felt before...even with Iain. And that stung, it felt like a betrayal to Iain and what I thought we had.

Jax grinned, his eyes sweeping across my face and settling on my lips. He could see through my comment, and know that I definitely didn't find anything about him creepy. "You're a challenge. I like a challenge. I like that you put up a fight. I like that you don't just fall into bed with me. I like that there are a thousand secrets in those beautiful green eyes. I like your sass, your spark, and I like you angry too."

"You haven't seen me angry yet," I warned him, my eyes narrowing. Jax laughed again.

"I'm sure I will," he shifted, adjusting his body so he was facing me more. His hand fell away from my chin, but before I could miss the contact, he gently tucked a strand of my hair behind my ear. "The thing is...I want to be with you. I want to learn everything I can about you, I want to explore this connection I feel to you and find out exactly what it is."

I gaped at him, unable to think of a single thing to say in response. His words literally took not only my breath away, but my ability to think. He was undeniably wooing me.

"What do you say, do you want to give this a go?" Jax asked, motioning between the two of us with his hand. I stared at him for a moment, already knowing my answer.

"Yes," I whispered. I *did* want to give this...whatever it was...a go. I felt like I owed it to myself to explore it, to see just what it all meant.

Jax seemed to know what my basic core was about, and it didn't seem to scare him. The thought of me running, of me not knowing what the hell I wanted, didn't intimate him. He knew I had secrets, and he wasn't put out or turned off by them. I got the sense that he wouldn't be, even if he knew them.

Then and again, it was hard to judge how a guy will take hearing that your heart may lay with someone else.

He smiled and leaned forward to kiss me again.

———

JAX DIDN'T COME up to the apartment that night. I didn't ask him, and he was respecting my wishes to take things slow.

Despite that, I didn't get in until nearly an hour after our conversation. We made out in his truck for a bit, getting dangerously close the point of no return before Jax put a stop to things.

"I have to work early tomorrow," he had whispered against my neck with regret. "But I promise you, we'll finish this very soon."

My skin still prickled with desire, my nerves were still on fire from him. But the moment I closed the door to the apartment, all the things that had flown from my mind as Jax kissed me returned. Seeing someone who looked *a lot* like Andrew at the concert had been at the front of my mind. I hadn't wanted to freak Jenna out, so I kept silent, convincing myself that it wasn't him.

All night long, I tossed and turned in my bed, unable to fall asleep. On Sunday morning, I came up with a plan. I searched around my room, tearing open boxes I hadn't yet unpacked, searching through desk drawers. Finally, I found what I was looking for in the bottom of my night stand drawer.

I held up the card, reading the name printed on the front. *Mike Turner.*

I chewed on my lip apprehensively. Mike Turner was a police officer in North Bay. He had been the one to help me during the Cooper ordeal, he had been just as eager to see Carl Cooper and his son behind bars. Carl Cooper had been the Chief of Police, but it had never sat well with Mike to turn a blind eye to his dirty cop ways.

If *anybody* would know where Andrew Cooper was, it was Mike Turner...only...Mike had also been the one to arrest Iain. He had been the one to question me about my relationship with Iain, and the last time I'd seen him he hadn't exactly held me in a high regard. He had been one of Iain's best friends, and I'm sure he blamed me for ruining Iain's life. *I* blamed myself, too.

I took a deep breath and pulled my cell phone out from my back pocket. I dialed the number on the business card. I sat on the end of my bed, chewing on my thumb nail as I waited for Mike to pick up.

"Officer Turner," his crisp, clipped tone was all business.

"Hi, Officer? It's...it's Harlow Jones...you probably remember me from a few years ago..." I trailed off awkwardly, the silence on the other end of the phone overwhelming me.

"Yes, I remember you," Officer Turner said, his voice turning cold.

"Ok...well. I was wondering if you knew -"

"I haven't seen him since I arrested him," Officer Turner interrupted, his annoyance as clear as daylight.

I bristled. "That's *not* why I'm calling."

"Why are you calling then?" Officer Turner demanded. I could practically feel his anger through the line.

"I was wondering if you knew where Andrew Cooper and his mom were," I took a steadying breath.

"They moved," Officer Turner answered. I could sense that he was frowning.

"I know that," I rolled my eyes. "Do you know where?"

"Why?"

"Because," I gritted my teeth, my own annoyance slapping out. "Jenna and I moved to Ottawa, and I...I get the impression I'm being followed, some time. And I thought I saw him yesterday, only when I looked again he was gone." I paused again, remembering Thursday night. "Plus, there's a man in the area attacking women."

"And you think it's him," Officer Turner didn't sound convinced.

"Do you know where he's living, or not?" I struggled to control my anger. This was pointless.

Officer Turner was silent for a moment, then he sighed heavily. "I'll look into it," he said, before hanging up on me.

I sat on the edge of my bed, staring at my phone and trying to process the conversation with Mike. So he hadn't heard from Iain either...not that it surprised me, he was the one that arrested him and declared that Iain was no friend of his.

I couldn't say that knowledge made me feel better about the whole situation. Vaguely, I wondered what Jenna would have to say about it...only I couldn't ask her, because I didn't want to scare her.

CHAPTER
SEVEN

Over two weeks had gone by, and I hadn't heard from Officer Mike Turner about where Andrew Cooper was living. I was on edge about it, although I hadn't seen anymore 'Andrew sightings' since the music festival. Something had me on edge though, and I couldn't pin point exactly what it was. I *thought* it had something to do with Andrew, and seeing someone that looked a lot like him at that concert, but I didn't have any concrete answers.

Ottawa was still being plagued by a sexual predator. Three women had come forth. All three women had been sexually harassed while on the street, walking home at night. All three of the women were young University students. Despite their statements, the police had no leads. Nobody had a solid description of what the rapist looked like, none of the women had seen his face.

I was on edge, and so was Jenna. Even though I still hadn't told her that I thought I saw Andrew, she was not at all happy to be living in the same part of town where all the occurrences were happening.

Even *Jamie* was on edge about the whole thing. He tried to switch all of my shifts to morning ones, and when my schedule didn't allow it...he made certain someone else was there with me. If it wasn't him, it was Lucas. I tried to argue that I could take care of myself, but Jamie refused to hear it.

"Not on my watch, sugar. It's too dangerous to have you walking at night," Jamie had insisted.

I suppose it was too dangerous, and a lawsuit waiting to happen that he didn't want to chance.

I walked to school with Jenna, mostly out of habit but also because she feared walking alone. I wasn't exactly *comfortable* with walking alone, but I was used to it. I had walked the streets of Toronto pretty much alone when I was fourteen.

On Monday morning, when Jenna and I parted ways, I saw Jax waiting outside of the lecture hall for me. He was leaning against the wall beside the entrance door, holding two paper coffee cups in his hands. He kissed me good morning and handed me my coffee while I admired him. He was dressed in his usual, understated style of dark denim jeans, and fitted thermal shirt. He had his brown leather jacket on.

"Figured you'd appreciate this," he commented, smiling as I took it from him. He had *no* idea how much I appreciated it, and not just the delicious coffee. The view was pretty nice, too.

I inhaled the delectable fragrance, closing my eyes a fraction and almost moaning. I had overslept, and hadn't had time to make a stop of my own.

"Thanks," I murmured, taking a slow sip. My eyelids fluttered open to rest upon his face. Jax looked incredible with a five-o-clock shadow. He was making my ovaries announce their presence. I could swoon under the heat of his gold rimmed eyes. I blinked, trying to clear my mind away from the lusty thoughts that enveloped it.

I opened my mouth, longing to clarify our conversation from the other night. We had talked about a lot of things, but we hadn't really clarified on what we were. Jax had said we would take things slow and at my pace...but I still didn't know exactly *what* that meant. Jax's morning coffee gesture seemed very relationship-like to me, and I didn't necessarily feel single.

I was feeling conflicting emotions. On the one hand, I was happy. I felt like this was the start of something new, something free. On the other hand, thoughts of Iain would sneak up on me to remind me that I wasn't completely over him. A part of me wondered if I would ever truly be free of Iain, or if he would always be a shadow in my happiness.

I sucked in my bottom lip, sinking my teeth into it to silence my buzzing, confused mind. This wasn't the time or the place to sift through my emotional baggage.

"Shall we go?" Jax asked, grinning at me as he held the door opened so we could walk in. The lecture hall was nearly full, with only five minutes to spare before class started. Crimson sat in the middle of the hall, waving frantically and gesturing to the two seats beside her with enthusiasm, her bright red hair impossible to miss.

I avoided making eye contact with Professor Pedersen as I climbed the stairs to our seats. I noticed with disdain that Brianna and Alissa were sitting in the same row, in the seats beside the vacant ones Crimson had saved for us. I sat down beside Crimson, and Jax ended up between Brianna and I. Brianna's eyes hungrily swept over his body, and she smiled coyly at him.

"How was your weekend, Jax?" she purred. I rolled my eyes, shaking my head at her shameless flirting. I was surprised to detect the undeniable swell of jealousy.

"Amazing," Jax answered, winking at me. His single worded reply, and the way he was looking at me, eased the jealous feelings back.

"That's good," Brianna said, drawing Jax's attention back to her by resting her hand on his bicep. She hadn't caught the heated look or the wink he had given me. "Listen, Alissa and I are having a party this weekend. You should come, it'll be at our house!"

"Oh! That sounds like fun!" Crimson interrupted gleefully. Brianna sent her an amused look. The invitation hadn't been to Crimson or I. Crimson didn't seem to know that though.

"It starts at 9 on Saturday, be there," Brianna finished, looking directly at Jax.

"Alright, I'll see if my girlfriend wants to come," Jax answered, looking at me with amusement. He knew my answer would be *not a chance in hell.* Still, my heart jumped at his words. It appeared that Jax had already defined our relationship - to himself, anyway, and I suppose to me as well. I could have argued with him, I could have told him that we weren't a couple...but I found myself not wanting to. I found myself wanting that status with him. Instead of sending him a dirty look, I smiled almost timidly at him.

"I didn't know you had a girlfriend," Brianna's eyes narrowed slightly, but I got the impression that she didn't really care.

"Yup, I do," Jax answered, not elaborating. He could sense that although I wanted the couple status, I wasn't ready for *public* status. Crimson shot me an inquisitive look. I shrugged, acting as if I had no idea what he was talking about.

"Oh, well, the more the merrier," Brianna said, looking as if she had swallowed something extremely sour.

"Could I bring my boyfriend too? He's dying to meet my new friends!" Crimson asked hopefully.

"Sure, sweetie," I didn't like the way Brianna's expression changed, or the way her voice dripped with false sweetness.

Before I could call her out on it, Professor Pedersen stepped up to the podium, demanding attention as her stern eyes swept across the room.

The coffee that Jax had supplied me with made it easier to focus, but the covert glances he sent me and the brush of our arms had me distracted.

I found myself entertaining the idea of skipping the rest of the day to just be with him. I had yet to skip a single university class, and there was something *wrong* about that, like I was missing out on a right of passage.

I had spent the last two years attending every single class, almost as if in a daze.

After my night of no sleep, I felt like I needed to wake up a little.

"Wanna skip with me?" I whispered at the end of our lecture, my eyes dancing with mischief.

"Of course," Jax grinned. We packed up our things and broke away from the group as quickly as we could. I knew I would likely face questioning from Crimson if I stuck around for our next class, and I honestly wanted to recharge before my shift at *The Bean*.

Plus, I was starving.

"Let's go get food, preferably the greasy kind of food," I suggested.

"Sounds like we need to make a trip to *Hintonburger*," Jax smiled. I looked at him curiously, having never heard of *Hintonburger* before. "It's only my most favourite place to go for burgers," he added, almost appalled that I had never heard of it before.

"Alright, where is it?"

"We'll drive. I brought my truck today," Jax gestured

towards the student parking lot. He took my right hand in his left one. I liked how big and strong even his hands were. Iain hadn't been a tiny guy, but he also hadn't been very large either.

Jax squeezed my hand with his, bringing me back to the enjoyable present. We started walking towards the parking lot.

"So, you have a girlfriend, huh?" I asked, blinking innocently up at him.

He smiled down at me, never faltering in his steps. "I hope so, I mean. I thought I made it clear the other night...and she made *no* arguments so..."

"Natural progression of things, I suppose," I sighed, pretending to be disappointed by this news. "She's a lucky girl, you're kind of hot. I mean, in that Barbarian, *throw-me-into-bed-right-now* kind of way."

"Um, what?" Jax laughed, shaking his head.

"Don't act like you don't know that you are undeniably sexy," I said flirtatiously, spinning around so that I was standing in front of him and walking backwards, still holding his hand. I was smiling, actually smiling. I felt free and light when I flirted with Jax. I didn't feel like I was doing something wrong or bad, like I had when I flirted with Iain.

I was surprised that that particular thought of Iain didn't sting as bad as it would have before.

I didn't want to spend all my time comparing two vastly different guys, but at the same time...it was comforting to feel the differences in them, and to not feel that sting of rejection and heartbreak. It still ached a little, a dull, barely there ache. I looked at Jax, still walking backwards. I almost tripped over a speed bump in the parking lot. Jax caught me, his other arm snaking around my waist to secure me before I could fall.

He pulled me against his chest, his face dangerously close to mine. Our lips were separated by mere inches. His warm breath washed across my face. "Do you want me to throw you into bed right now?" he asked deeply, the sound of his voice vibrating into my very being.

"Well, we're outside, in a parking lot. There are no beds around," I pointed out, trying to catch my breath and appear unaffected by his closeness. I was very aware of the feel of his heartbeat underneath the palm of my hand. It was pounding in his chest, the same racing intensity that mine was.

"There's the bed of my truck," Jax countered as he gestured to his truck with a playful grin on his face.

I shook my head, amused by him, by our effortless banter. "If it were summertime, maybe. But it's *kind* of cold out, and despite what you think, I'm really not that kind of girl. I like fun, but I definitely am not an exhibitionist."

"I can wait," Jax promised, gently leading me to the passenger door of his truck. I turned to face him, smiling.

"Who knows how long that will be?" I remarked, tilting my head. My hair spilled over my shoulder, and he caught a couple strands in his hand. He looked at it, stroking it gently before he raised his eyes to meet mine.

"I can wait," he repeated. Then a smile broke out on his face. "But...I can't wait to eat. I mean seriously, ever since you mentioned greasy food..."

I laughed, shoving him away from me so I could open the door.

"You've been doing more of that lately," Jax remarked, his hand on the inside of his passenger door.

"A lot of what?"

"Smiling, and laughing," Jax answered. "I like it." He closed the door, swiftly cutting off my reply.

EIGHT

We hadn't been an official couple for even four days yet, and already I was walking around in that infuriating "honeymoon" stage of a new relationship. It was easy to forget about all my reservations when I was around him. It was easy to get caught up in the feeling of newness and attraction. Jax made it easy to forget everything but him and I.

But when I wasn't around him, I couldn't help but want to punch myself in the face for feeling all that I was feeling. It was too soon, I felt as though I was hurtling towards an inevitable destruction.

Still, Jax made it incredibly easy to feel. He was sweet, he was attentive, and he thought up little ways to make me feel important. He courted me, something I had never experienced before. He hinted towards having planned something exciting for Friday afternoon, after my final class of the week ended around 1pm.

He told me to dress warmly and that he would pick me up around 2pm. All day long, I couldn't focus on my classes. I kept wondering what he had planned, warring with myself over being excited and being skeptical. I had a slight idea about where Jax was planning on taking me, and I couldn't decide if I was excited or nervous about it.

Jax wasn't into stereotypical dates, I knew that much about him. He could tolerate dinner and a movie, and had...but I could tell there was something more about him, something deeper. He'd been testing me the last few days, hinting towards something...asking what kind of things I liked to do. Was hiking on the list? Camping? Was I outdoorsy at all?

I wasn't completely outdoorsy. I didn't know how to gut a fresh or shoot a deer, but I enjoyed being outside. I loved walking, so I figured I would love hiking just as much. Unfortunately, my experience in all outdoorsy departments was next to null. Iain had taken me to a cabin once, and aside from a few skiing attempts...we had mostly remained inside, hiding from the cold. Iain had enjoyed winter sports, but it wasn't the outdoorsy type...

Aside from that, I'd never been camping, or fishing. I didn't have a father figure growing up, and the furthest thing from my mother's mind was a Sunday morning on the lake.

I followed his advice, dressing in a pair of my well-loved skinny jeans, and layering a thick wool gray sweater over my long sleeved shirt. I paired it with a black cowl scarf that Jenna had knitted for me a couple Christmases ago, during her "knitting hobby" stage. My long hair was French braided and resting across my right shoulder. I wore my warm black boots, not knowing what was on the agenda.

I paused by my doorway, hesitating for a moment as I touched gently the necklace that rested against my collarbone. I heaved a heavy sigh, unclasping it and laying it gently against the surface of my dresser. I couldn't keep carrying Iain around with me...mentally or symbolically. I touched it once more, my fingers brushing against the silver, still warm from my flesh.

When I came out to meet him, Jax was leaning against the passenger door of his truck, looking delicious in his ensemble of faded blue jeans, a long sleeved thermal black shirt and a thick tan work coat.

"Good afternoon beautiful," he said, grinning at me. I couldn't help but smile at the delighted expression on his face as I stepped into his embrace and kissed him gently on the lips.

Our innocent kiss quickly heated, as it often did. Kissing Jax was never boring. His hand came to rest at the small of my back, pulling me against him, and he kissed me as if he was starving for my touch.

I knew he probably was, hell...I knew *I* was. We had only known each other for a few short weeks, but the chemistry between us burned hot constantly. It was evident in the heat that always pooled in my lower belly at the mere thought of him.

A part of me was holding back, afraid of what would happen when we finally crossed that threshold. I was afraid that there would be absolutely no turning back, that I would be too far gone.

That was a terrifying thought for me to have, given what had happened the last time I had let myself fall.

Plus, any time prior when things would get heated between us, a well serviced interruption always happened. We hadn't really been able to spend any time alone together between our school and work schedules anyway. All that was about to change...our date today would undoubtedly lead to alone time at some point. My nerves jumped at that thought, torn between excitement and nervousness. I couldn't decide what I wanted...to dive in, experience Jax in all the ways I hungered for...or bow quietly away, before I could get hurt.

He broke the kiss first, but not before I felt the evidence of his desire through both our jeans. I bit my lip, crawling into the cab of his truck.

Jax climbed in a second later, after trying to discreetly adjust his jeans. He closed the door while keeping his eyes on me, drinking me in.

"You are gorgeous," he said lowly, his voice almost dazed. He leaned forward to kiss me again. I was already a mess from that first kiss, my heart pounding frantically in my chest and a sweet ache between my thighs.

He pulled away before things could get even more out of hand, before I could completely forget all of my reservations as to why a part of me wanted to hold back in the first place. He shook his head as if he needed to clear his mind before he could focus on driving.

I took advantage of that moment to hungrily assess Jax again. His forearm muscles strained ever so slightly as he shrugged out of his jacket, casting it aside before he merged onto the road.

"So, what's the plan?" I inquired, getting comfortable. "Where are we going? What are we doing?"

"We're going for a hike,"" Jax answered, tearing his eyes off the road momentarily to meet mine. I almost melted at the look in those warm brown eyes.

"Where?" I asked, my interest peaking. I was glad he wasn't taking me hunting or fishing. I wasn't ready for either of those activities.

"To a little spot I know," Jax said mysteriously, not quite answering my question.

"Jax," I took a deep breath, trying to calm the anxiety that swept over me at his rebuff. I knew he was just trying to be romantic. It wasn't his fault that my past reared it's ugly head making me paranoid and on edge.

"It's called the Pinhey Forest," Jax explained, hearing the alarm in my voice. He reached over, gently squeezing my hand in quiet reassurance. He understood, without me having to explain myself. I relaxed against the seat, the feel of his warm, large hand over mine.

I tried to pay attention to where we were headed, but with so many turns...I lost track of where we were. Still, I felt safe, despite my earlier panic over him not answering my question.

We pulled into a parking lot and found parking. The lot was mostly empty, with a few vehicles parked randomly throughout it. I put my cowl scarf back on and jumped down from the cab. I joined Jax as he was pulling a bag from the back seat.

"Are you ready?" Jax asked, grinning at me as he swung the bag over his shoulders.

"Yup. Did you need me to carry anything?" I offered, eying the bag skeptically.

"Nope, got everything here," Jax answered, gesturing to the North Face hiking bag.

He nodded to a trail to the right of the parking lot, and I followed him as we started our hike. It was a beautiful, sunny September day with just a little chill in the breeze. The forest around us was breathtakingly beautiful, with all the fall colours and the sound of birds.

"I can't believe you have never been camping before," Jax said, ruefully shaking his head over my earlier confession.

"Wait, are we camping tonight?" I paused, my hand on a branch to keep it from slapping me in the face as I walked by. I wasn't prepared for camping. Jax was carrying gear though...he *probably* could have a tent somewhere in that massive bag of his.

"No," Jax laughed, looking back at me. "I figured we would

start off slow. Besides, it gets really cold at night. You probably want your first camping experience to be in the summer."

"True..." I trailed off, continuing to follow him over the uneven pathway. Out of all the footwear I owned, the boots I had chosen were the best suited for this hike...and even *they* sucked. Twenty-minutes in, my feet were aching. I could feel every pebble and stone against my heels. If hiking was going to be a regular thing, I would have to invest in better footwear. I inwardly cringed as I stepped in a mud puddle, soaking my boots in gunk. Despite their shiny appearance, they were not very absorbent. "I do want to camp, though. I think it'd be fun."

"It is fun," Jax nodded, smiling as he took my hand to aid me up a steep hill. "How do you like hiking so far?" he asked, glancing down at my feet as if he knew how horrible the boots I wore were to walk in.

"I like it," I answered, carefully hopping over a puddle. "Next time, I think I'll get some hiking boots though. These ones kind of suck."

"Yeah, I should have thought of that," Jax frowned apologetically.

Thirty minutes later, I was almost sweating and my stomach was rumbling from the excursion. I was distracted, thinking about how hungry I was and how tired my feet were, we finally came to a stop. Or rather, Jax did. I walked into his back.

"Ummpf," I muttered, catching myself before I could fall on my ass. I glared at his back, irritated by the lack of communication. Of course, I wouldn't say anything...I knew it was my fault for not paying attention.

Jax grinned at me, swinging the bag off of his shoulders and setting it down in front of his feet. He fished out a large blanket and spread it out on the hard ground while I took a look around.

Jax had chosen a scenic spot by the pond. The red, yellow, orange and brown hues of fall reflected against the water like a mirror, a scene that could inspire a painting. The water was peaceful and undisturbed. I took a deep breath, welcoming the cool air to my lungs as I drew it in.

Jax watched me looking around, a smile on his face.

"Is this an okay spot?" he asked, pulling out a cooler. I didn't answer at first, I was too busy taking in my surroundings.

It was the perfect escape.

"Yes," I said, my eyes flickering back to his face. He was grinning at me, sitting down on the blanket with the cooler opened. I dropped down beside him, accepting the wrapped sandwich he offered. "Hey...did you con Mark into making us lunch?"

"I sure did," Jax confessed, winking. "I'll be honest...I'm not much of a cook and I didn't want you to end up puking in the bush or something." He pulled out the thermos, offering it to me. I opened the lid, pausing as the fragrance of hot cocoa assaulted my senses.

I hadn't drank hot chocolate since Iain. The realization sunk in as my memories brought me back to his kitchen table, watching as he stirred a pot on the stove. I shook my head, forcing myself back to the present.

"I didn't make that either, if you're hesitant. I cheated and bought it from *The Bean*," Jax confessed, bemused.

I smiled, taking a tentative sip of it. It wasn't as good as Iain's homemade hot chocolate, but then and again...nothing could beat that.

"It's good," I murmured, handing it back. "I'm not really a fan of hot chocolate though..." I said, half lying. I wasn't a fan of hot chocolate *except* for Iain's homemade kind. My heart thudded painfully in my chest, the memories making it ache with longing and sadness. I went to reach for the necklace, remembering that I had left it on top of my dresser. For a moment, a strange, hollow feeling in the pit of my stomach washed over me.

You wanted this, I reminded myself, looking at Jax. The ache in my chest eased as I took in his warm brown eyes. And I did want this, I did want him.

"Who took you camping?" I asked, laying back on the blanket.

"My grandpa," Jax replied fondly, crumpling up his empty sandwich wrapper and shoving it into the soft cooler it had come from. He took my garbage as well, shoving everything back into the bag. Then he stretched out beside me on the blanket, gesturing for me to come closer.

"Really?" I asked, not at all surprised. Jax moved about the forest as if he had been born in it. It was clear that he knew nature.

"Yup," Jax added, a look of remembrance crossing his features. "My grandpa did all kinds of fun stuff with me. He taught me how to fish, how to survive in a forest, and how to hunt."

From the little bit Jax shared about his family, I ached to learn more. My dire mood slipped away, and was replaced with curiosity about the man who laid beside me.

"Tell me more about your Grandpa?" I suggested, nestling closer to him. Our body's were turned towards each other, ever so slightly. Jax's eyes roamed my face, as if he was internally deciding whether or not he should reveal his past to me. Where we on that level yet? I drew in my lip, biting down in apprehension as the minutes ticked by without Jax making any move. His raised his hand, allowing his fingers to brush my cheek bone. My breath hitched, and my eye lids fluttered despite my attempts at controlling myself.

"He was silent, he wasn't overly affectionate but he wasn't...like my dad," Jax finally said. I frowned, catching more meaning behind his vague words than Jax had intended. "He would take me camping in the summer, hunting in the fall, and every Sunday in the summer...he would take me fishing. The only conversation he made was to teach me. Those were the best days of my childhood."

"He sounds like a great man," I remarked, gently playing with the zipper of Jax's coat.

"He was," Jax said, smiling. "He died when I was twelve, of a heart attack," Jax shifted, as if uncomfortable with the topic. I edged closer, resting my head on top of his outstretched arm and snuggling up to his side.

"I'm sorry to hear that," I murmured, feeling sad for him. I had lost my dad at a young age, but I hadn't really *known* him. I didn't have beautiful, painful memories to contend with. I just had a...void. "Jax..."

"Yeah?"

"Why don't you see your family often?" I asked him, knowing my question was bold. I felt bad for asking, but I also felt as if we were both stuck in an odd limbo. Neither of us would make the move to question the other about our individual pasts, and I knew that I couldn't move forward with Jax until I knew him a little more. I had my assumptions about Jax's childhood, but I needed to hear his story from him.

"My father was an abusive piece of shit," Jax said, his voice hard. "My mother was weak, and didn't stop it. When my Grandpa died, I lost the only protection I inadvertently had from my father."

I shot up, quickly twisting my body so I was sitting with my legs crossed and looking at him. Jax's answer both surprised and disgusted me. "Jax, I'm so sorry. I shouldn't have asked."

"It's alright," Jax's eyes softened, and he leaned up on his elbows to look at me.

"Is that why you want to open the gym?" I questioned gently, praying that my questions weren't harming him. He seemed okay, though. His features had softened considerably and he was even smiling at me a little.

"Yeah, I guess you could say I was the 'troubled youth' in question, not that long ago," he answered. "What about you?"

"What do you mean?" I tried to dodge his questions, knowing that it wasn't fair. I looked out towards the lake, nervously playing with my long braid.

"I'm not stupid, I know you were thinking about something that made you sad. What was it?"

I hesitated, wondering how much...if anything...I should tell Jax. "Back home," I answered, straying from the truth a little bit. I was thinking of Iain, and my past with him...but all that was in North Bay.

"Have you been home since you graduated high school?" Jax questioned, still propped up on his elbows.

"No."

"Interesting," Jax grinned thoughtfully, his eyes fixed on mine. I felt as if he was reading into my soul. It was a vulnerable, tantalizing experience. "Let me guess...a high school relationship that turned sour? You're escaping it and don't want to return?"

It unnerved me just how close Jax was to the truth. I shrugged, trying to remain calm as I met his playful gaze with a steady one of my own. "Something like that. Plus, I don't *really* like my step-father and my mother and I annoy each other at the best of times."

Jax nodded, accepting my answer and pushing himself up

so he was in a sitting position, his legs outstretched beside me. His face was close to mine. The wind was making strands of his long hair dance across both of our faces. The playfulness melted away from his warm brown eyes, the heat of desire absorbing it. His hand enclosed on the nape of my neck, pulling me gently towards him. I rested my hand against his chest, sighing before his lips touched mine.

Fire ignited within in, I moaned when he playfully tugged on my lower lip. He pulled me down on top of him, his hands running up the length of my back as he deepened the kiss. I moved against him in response, unable to stop my body's reaction to him. His body was both familiar and unfamiliar, a new territory that I hadn't yet explored yet somehow...just *knew*. It was as natural as breathing.

Jax's desire was evident against my pelvis, awaking me from the spell his touch and kiss had put me under. I pulled away, resting my head against his shoulder. I knew that I wouldn't be able to reign in my hormones if he continued to kiss me as he was. My better judgment was already long gone, and finally unwrapping all that was Jax was at the front of my mind. It sounded like an amazing idea to me, but we were in the middle of a forest and the temperature was beginning to drop.

The picnic had taken up a good half hour or so, then our conversation had eaten up another hour. The sun was sitting very low over the tree-line. I studied the horizon, taking deep breaths to try and steady the torrent of desire and attraction that had overcome me.

Jax was staring down at me inquisitively, thousands of unasked questions deep within his warm brown eyes.

"Ready to go?" he asked. I smiled, sitting up. I kept my eyes on his face, my heart pounding in my chest. The increased tempo could have been from our searing make-out session, or from the fear that he seemed to just know things about me, instinctively.

"Ya. I bet watching the sun set would be incredible, but I don't really feel like stumbling around in the woods. Plus, I don't know how good you are at navigating through the dark. I know I suck," I remarked as Jax stood up. He laughed and offered me his hand, pulling me up to stand in front of him. He gently squeezed my ass, letting out a primitive groan of regret before he released me.

I helped him pack up, folding the blanket and handing it to him so he could stuff that into his bag, along with the cooler he'd already tucked inside. He swung the bag over his shoulders. He took a moment to brush his hair behind his ears with his hands, and I was again struck by how attractive he was. It made perfect sense that my body was sent into overdrive whenever he touched me.

Surprisingly, it didn't take as long as the hike in. Probably because I wasn't starving, and it was mostly downhill. I almost slipped several times, the tread in my boots proving to be just as useless as the rest of them. Each time, Jax caught me, his strong hand a sturdy reassurance on my arm.

"I promise, I'm not *usually* this klutzy," I laughed after the third time it happened. "It's the boots."

"Definitely the boots," Jax nodded in agreement, staring down at my feet. "But you look hot, and the klutzy you is kind of endearing."

"Thanks," I rolled my eyes, relieved when I saw the trail widen and vehicles in the near distance. We had finally gotten back to the parking lot.

"So, with the right boots...would you hike with me again?"

"Probably not," I said, laughing at Jax's disappointed frown. "I'm kidding. Yes, with the right boots...I'll hike again. I enjoy walking, and I liked hiking. I just hate my boots."

"Fair enough," Jax reached into his jean pockets, fishing out his truck keys. I shivered, the temperature was starting to drop. Thankful that I would soon be in the warmth of the cab, I thought about the afternoon we just had. Despite the minor, heavy disappearance down memory lane, it had been a remarkable date. I wasn't ready for it to end.

On the drive home, Jax kept conversation steady while he talked about the things he had done since leaving British Columbia.

"First I traveled to the UK, backpacked for a bit," Jax said, keeping his eyes on the road. "I worked in various villages for a year, with a work visa."

"Really?" I raised my eyebrows, impressed. I had never traveled anywhere before, unless you counted Ontario...which I certainly didn't. It didn't hold the same appeal as back-packing the UK.

"Yeah," he took his eyes off the road for a moment to smile at me.

"How did you manage that?"

"My Grandpa left me an inheritance." Jax answered, almost stiffly.

"I'm sorry," I muttered. I was silent for a moment, looking out the window. "When did you get the Harley?"

"What?" Jax asked, sounding confused and bemused.

"Your pictures on Facebook," I felt a little embarrassed to admit I'd been snooping on his page.

"Oh," Jax laughed. "Yeah, I got that when I was in Europe. I sold it before I came home, though. Would have cost more to get it here than it did to buy the damn thing."

"Oh?"

"Ya. Besides, I didn't need a motorcycle and a truck. The truck seemed more appropriate for Ontario weather," Jax shrugged.

"Makes sense," I remarked, noting his practical nature.

We were a few blocks away from my apartment, and I felt a growing sense of sadness over the fact that we would soon be parting ways. I wasn't ready to end the night. I looked at Jax, reading the desire and longing on his features that echoed mine.

"Do you want me to drop you off at home?" Jax asked. I knew he'd do whatever I told him to. He respected my space, my need for time...I almost didn't have to tell him when I'd had too much or when I needed more. He just...got it.

I bit my lip, focusing on the fact that I didn't want the night to end so soon. I didn't want to rush things with us either...but still. "Maybe you could show me your place?" I hedged, wondering if it would be a better choice for alone time than my apartment. I didn't particular want to share Jax with anyone else.

Jax grinned, still looking at me as he started up his truck. "That could be arranged."

He drove down a couple streets I didn't recognize, pulling up to a blue two-story house. It didn't exactly look like student housing to me, although I wasn't entirely sure what I had expected after the offhand comments Jax had made about his living arrangements. Maybe I expected to see discarded beer cans? Or perhaps, every light on and music pumping, the window panes pulsing with vibrations? Instead, I looked up at a modest, well-kept house with a sparse dying garden out front, the flowers wilted from the cold snap of autumn.

He parked in the driveway and turned off the truck.

"I'll warn you," he said, searching my face for any reservations. "It's student housing. Luckily, none of us really like each other so it's not like they'll interrupt...anything. But it can be loud, and it's probably messy."

"It's okay," I shrugged, hoping my face didn't betray my

nervousness at the thought of being alone with him near a bed. Jax smiled, opening his door. I opened mine too, pausing for a moment to collect myself and steady my breathing.

My heart was thudding, drumming against my chest in an erratic tempo to the impending evening. No interruptions, just him and I...

I took another deep, steadying breath, hopping down from the cab. Jax was there, waiting for me. He closed the door with his right hand, his left hand pressed against the side of his truck, trapping me between his arms in a cage of strong limbs. My back was pressed against his truck, the metal cold against my back. His lips found mine, tasting and teasing.

My pulse jumped, with desire and a smidgen of anxiety. I didn't usually like being caged in, but I found my anxiety wasn't from that dislike, as I actually enjoyed the position Jax had gotten me into. My anxiety streamed from my fears of what would come next.

Sex was the easy part, it always was. It was easy to turn your mind off and focus on the sensations of pleasure. It was the aftermath that scared me. Excluding my tragic introduction to sexual relations, I hadn't slept with many people. There was Rhys, but only a handful of times. Then there was Iain. I had dove straight in, offering myself without thinking of the consequences. He could have used me once and been done with it...but he hadn't.

Both relationships hadn't ended well. In fact, both Rhys and Iain had ended up in jail. Rhys from driving intoxicated and killing Lauren, and Iain because of our relationship.

I used to think of myself as the kind of girl who went for what she wanted, and I had been that girl...until I watched the man I had fallen in love with get prosecuted. If I hadn't acted on my desires, Iain wouldn't have lost everything.

Sure, I wouldn't have fallen in love with him, but he would

still have his teaching license. He wouldn't have a tainted name, and his face and silence wouldn't be haunting me now.

I raised my head, looking up into the depths of Jax's irises. The brown had almost completely disappeared, giving way to the liquid gold that usually just danced around his pupils. It was surreal, unearthly.

"Do you want to go in?" Jax asked, stepping back and giving me space to think clearly again, his devilish smile challenging me while his eyes underlined the acceptance of whatever decision came to pass.

"Yeah, sure," I shrugged, forcing my reservations to the back of my mind. I would deal with them later. I had been careful with Jax. I had made him wait several weeks and I knew that if I asked him to, he would wait longer.

This was about me, though. My needs. My desires for him were a thirst I knew I couldn't quench unless I gave in to them.

Taking my hand, he led me up the narrow walkway and stairs to the blue house. He produced a key, unlocking the door for us. It was quiet in the hallway, which seemed unusual to me. It was a Saturday night, after all. I would have figured all student houses became party zones on Saturday night, but we didn't see anyone at all as Jax led me up the stairs.

It was dark there as well, the only light creeping out from the door cracks of a couple rooms. Jax stopped at the fourth door, producing yet another key. He pushed the door opened, flicking on the light to his bedroom.

The walls were painted a boring off-white colour. He had put up a couple of posters in an attempt to make the space more his. Floating shelves lined the wall to my right, with a black desk and a laptop computer underneath them. His shelves had various trophies and books lining them, and to the right of them was a large poster of a woman dressed in a white sports bra and tight black shorts, her arms crossed and red fight gloves on her hands as she scowled. Her blond hair was pulled back into a messy pony tail.

"That's 'Rowdy' Rhonda," Jax explained with a wicked grin. "She's a UFC Fighter."

"Nice," I raised an eyebrow, shaking my head. There were more posters of female UFC Fighters decorating the walls. His comforter was black with thick, dark gray stripes, and it wasn't made.

"Sorry," he shrugged. He closed his bedroom door and leaned against it, watching me assess his bedroom. "I told you it would be messy." Aside from his unmade bed, there wasn't a mess to be seen. No dirty clothes littered the floor, no old food wrappers or empty pop bottles.

"It's cleaner than mine," I confessed, thinking about the pile of dirty clothes I had left by my bedroom door. I walked back towards him, my assessment complete.

"Really? I find that hard to believe."

"Guess I'll have to show you sometime," I shrugged, stepping closer towards him. Heart beating frantically, I pressed myself against him and wound my hands around the back of his neck. He leaned down, gently pressing his lips to mine as his arms snaked around to the small of my back.

The kiss started out as gentle, I could tell that Jax was holding back. He didn't want to frighten me. I deepened the kiss, pressing my body against his and allowing my hands to drop down from the back of his neck to his chest.

I touched him, I teased him until I felt him release the restraint he had on himself. He groaned, his hands gripping my hips as he directed me back towards his bed. I fell onto it with a soft thud, our kiss only breaking momentarily so I could pull Jax's shirt off over his head.

His chest was just as defined as his shirts hinted. He stood before me, tall and magnificent, allowing me a moment to drink in just how in shape he really was. No wonder women fell all over themselves when he was around, no wonder *I* fell all over myself. My eyes roamed the hard, lean muscles of his abs, counting eight defined muscles, and dropped down to his lower abdomen. I had never seen the legendary V muscle in the flesh before, but I now understood the hype.

Jax had one tattoo that started on his left pectoral muscle and stretched all the way around his arm, so that when his arm was resting at his side, the pattern continued. It was beautiful, and I couldn't help but wonder what the strange design meant.

"It's a homage to my Hawaiian heritage," Jax explained. "My mother used to show me photos of her family. Her grand-father had the same one...only it was down traditionally instead of with modern ink."

"What's a traditional Hawaiian tattoo?" I asked, intrigued.

"They used ash and soot to make the ink, and they would cut the skin open and pour it in," he explained, the corner of his lip lifting in half of a smile. I touched it gently, almost pulling my hand away when it made contact with his hot skin.

Drawing in a breath sharply, I dropped my hand and tugged the waistline of Jax's jeans, pulling him towards me. I fell, my back resting against his comfortable bed, and watched as he shimmed out of his jeans and crawled towards me. My heart was pounding in my chest, but instead of scared...I just felt a burning need. I gave in to the intense wave of that need.

I foolishly had thought that nobody would compare to Iain, but...well. I was wrong.

Jax evoked pleasure I hadn't even known existed. He read me with ease, knowing instinctively just what to do to make me wither with pleasure. He erased every thought from my mind until all I could think, feel, and breathe was him.

Afterwards, Jax held me in his arms, my head resting on his beautiful Hawaiian tattoo. I fought exhaustion, willing myself to not close my eyes. The hypnotic feel of his hand tracing patterns against my skin made my lids feel heavy.

Sleepovers were not something I just jumped into, or at least...they weren't supposed to be. I had no desire to turn into one of those girls that dove right in, practically picking out wedding venues and naming future children.

At the end of the day, I definitely didn't want to be the girl that couldn't separate amazing sex from intimacy and just assumed that my happily ever after would be with a certain guy simply because he had gotten a few orgasms out of me.

I wasn't exactly sure how sleepovers coincided with all of that, but I still felt there was something more intimate about sleeping beside someone. I wasn't sure if I was ready for that level of intimacy...or if I would ever be ready.

Despite my attempts at staying awake, I was so exhausted from our hike and the activities that followed. I drifted off to sleep almost without realizing.

The sun was beginning to rise, illuminating Jax's bedroom with the pale light of dawn. I opened my eyes and blinked, disoriented as "Rowdy Rhonda's" poster came into view. I felt Jax's warm body still pressed against mine, and the memories of the night before came back to me in a flood. Warmth pooled in my belly, and I turned my face to look at him.

Jax was snoring softly, a small smile on his thick lips. I watched him sleep, trying to divulge how I was feeling.

The inner workings of my mind often confused me. I had conflicting thoughts about breaking my own rules so soon, but it was hard to be angry at myself with Jax's warm body so close to mine.

As I thought about it, I realized that I didn't regret sleeping over. In fact, I was glad I had. I hadn't slept better in years. My mind was clear and alert, and I felt well rested.

However, I was *definitely* going to be late for work.

I shifted, trying to free myself from Jax's embrace so I could get dressed. His arm was heavy though, and he opened his eyes as I attempted to wiggle down and out.

"What you doing?" he asked with amusement, his voice groggy with sleep.

"Trying to get up...I'm going to be late for work," I answered, still trying to fight with his heavy arm.

"Oh, right," Jax said, yawning as he lifted his arm and stretched. I stood up, quickly pulling my shirt on over my head. In the dawn of morning with Jax's eyes focused on me, I suddenly felt self-conscious. I wasn't regretting our night together, but I was apprehensive about how things would change...as they undoubtedly would.

"Are you sure you want to leave so quickly?" Jax asked playfully, gently grabbing me by my waist as I bent over to pick up my jeans from his side of the bed. He effortlessly tugged me on top of him, my shirt doing nothing to protect me from the evidence of his arousal.

My own pulse increased in response, and I leaned down to give him a tormenting kiss. My hand roamed down, stroking him teasingly. I broke the kiss, leaning up slightly to watch the pleasure and desire dance across his handsome features.

"I have to work," I answered, releasing him with regret. He moaned, almost laughing as I got back to my task of getting dressed.

"Fair enough, I'll drive you," Jax offered, sitting up and stretching again.

As it turns out, I was late for work. Nearly an hour late for work. Jax had offered to drive me all the way, but I had to change into my uniform so I sent him home. I figured that it would be safer to not show up with him.

I walked into *The Bean*, seeing Jamie working purposefully behind the counter. "Here you go honey, have an amazing day," he was saying to a customer as he handed her a paper bag and her change. He smiled at her as she walked away, his eyes finally landing on me as I sheepishly stood off to the side.

I had never missed a day of work or been a minute late since I started working at *The Bean*. I was accountable and dependable.

Jamie knew this, Mark knew it, and I knew it. But Jamie was still wearing a look of stern reproach that made me feel immensely guilty, as if I had let him down. I suppose I had.

"I'm sorry, I -" I started to explain, but Jamie's laughter cut me off.

"Oh don't worry about it honey," Jamie smiled with a wave of his hand. "Mark told me you had a date yesterday, I figured you'd be a little late this morning. Consider this a free pass, since you've never been a second late before. Keep in mind you only get one. Next time, you're fired."

I raised an eyebrow at him, turning my head slightly as I tried to figure out if he was kidding or not. It was hard to tell. While Jamie was a very caring, exuberant person, I knew he took his business *very* seriously and only employed dependable workers. He had a reputation to uphold for having the best coffee, the best food, and the hardest working staff. Jamie wouldn't let someone walk all over the schedule. In my time working there, I had witnessed one girl lose her job over her inability to follow it.

"I'm sorry," I said again, slipping into the back to drop my purse and jacket off in the small cubby in Jamie's office.

CHAPTER
NINE

I ended up at Brianna's stupid party because Crimson was desperately excited about it, and I couldn't say no to her bouncing red curls. Plus, she made me feel guilty.

It turned out that Crimson had never been to a bona-fide party before. She insisted that it was an experience she had to have, and that it would be a fun way for us to spend Saturday night. I ended up giving in to her just so she'd stop pleading, her sob story expertly wearing down my resolve.

I took my time getting ready after my shift, but all too soon I found myself standing on the porch with Crimson, Jenna and Luca, allowing Jax to knock on our behalf. Crimson's boyfriend was running late, but Crimson had told us he would just meet us inside. I had tried to argue that we should wait for him, but nobody bought my excuses to delay.

Jenna stood beside me, holding Lucas' hand and almost trembling with nervousness. She bounced on her shiny red heels, looking sexy as hell in her skinny jeans and halter top.

I couldn't help but feel anxious and nervous. The last party I had been to had been one at the beginning of 12th grade. It was the very party that I'd walked into a room and found Andrew Cooper sexually assaulting Jenna.

I knew I could have told Jax the real reason why I didn't want to attend this party, but I remained silent. It wasn't my story to tell, it was Jenna's, and she was standing on the porch with us, not complaining at all. I knew she was nervous...parties always made her nervous since that night...but she also refused to live in fear.

When I told her about the party a couple nights before, she asked if it would be okay for her and Lucas to go. I swear, I looked at her like she had grown an extra head.

"I don't want to live in fear anymore," she had answered my unasked question. "And...I've never been to a University party. If we go in a big group, we'll be okay. Plus, there's no way we *wouldn't* feel safe with Jax around," she added, laughing.

She was right, Jax had an aura of safety and protection about him. Even still, I didn't have a good track record with parties. Aside from the horror of that night with Jenna, the last party I had attended before that one had not been any better.

That party had ended with my best friend dying on the side of the road. It was impossible to not think about Lauren every time I put myself into the party setting. Most of my heavy partying days had been with Lauren by my side.

I think I had good reasons for the anxiety I was feeling, the anxiety that welled up in the pit of my belly...posed like coiled snakes, waiting to strike out.

I took a deep steadying breath as the door opened. Jenna's hand found mine for a quick, reassuring squeeze. I looked at her when she released my hand, and she was smiling at me. I knew she knew where my thoughts had gone, and I was grateful to her for pulling me back.

Brianna leaned drunkenly against the door, blinking slowly as she stared at Jax. "Oh my God! You showed up *Jax*!" she slurred before running at him for a hug. She didn't even acknowledge the rest of us. Jax untangled himself from her sloppy embrace as quickly as possible, casting a bemused look over his shoulder at me.

"Hey Brianna! You look great," Crimson said, smiling with genuine warmth.

"Thanks," Brianna's voice held no warmth. She fixated her gaze back on Jax before flickering to the rest of our group. "Who are they?"

"Jenna and Lucas," Jax replied, bemused.

"Where is your *girlfriend*?" she added, looking hopeful at the prospect that Jax's girlfriend hadn't shown up.

Unfortunately, I was there. I was standing behind him, blocked by his large size. I stepped aside, smiling sarcastically at her while I wrapped my arms around Jax's waist. "Oh, I'm here, against my will." I muttered.

"I thought you said you weren't together?" Brianna pouted, looking up at Jax as if he had lied to her and seriously hurt her feelings. I bet she only had *one* feeling...self-righteousness.

Jax shrugged, his arm instinctively enclosing around my shoulders. "We weren't together at the time. We are now."

"Interesting. Well, come in...I guess," Brianna pursed her lips with disdain. She stood aside to let the five of us pass. Jenna exchanged a look with me, her eyebrows raised as she mouthed *'what a bitch'*. Brianna's cold blue eyes swept over our group once more, narrowing in on Crimson. "I don't see *your* boyfriend anywhere Crimson, are you sure he exists?"

"Wow, that was bitchy," I frowned at her, but Crimson kept a gentle smile on her face.

"I'm sorry, what was that?" Crimson asked, tilting her head sideways.

"Never mind," Brianna rolled her eyes, walking into the foyer. Jax and I followed suit, exchanging a glance with one another. I could tell he was seriously regretting coming to the party. I knew he expected it to be a chill event, probably toss back a beer or two and maybe dance a little with me.

Parties involved alcohol though, and alcohol, especially when mixed with catty women, involved drama. I had sensed that from the beginning. How could I not, with Brianna involved? I didn't know her, but I knew her type.

"We'll leave if this sucks," Jax said, loud enough for Jenna, Lucas and I to hear. Crimson had already followed Brianna to the kitchen, presumingly to grab herself a drink.

"It's going to," I promised him, rolling my eyes. "Let's just go now."

"Oh come on Harlow," Jenna interrupted, zeroing her gaze in on me. "We just got here. Let's dance a little, *try* to have some fun instead of acting like a perpetual 40 year old."

I snorted. "A perpetual 40 year old? That's fresh."

"Besides, Crimson looks so happy to be here..." Jenna added, gesturing her head towards Crimson. She was walking back from the kitchen, clenching a red solo cup in her hand and grinning from ear to ear like a kid at Disney Land.

"Give it time," I sighed deeply, following her gaze and watching Crimson as she mingled. She did look happy, but it would only be a matter of time before someone here said something cruel to her and she caught it. That someone was likely going to be Brianna. Her scowling, dark mood and bitchy comments when we first walked in aside, she seemed like the exact kind of girl that Crimson didn't know how to handle. Double edged words, two-faced.

"Dance with me," Jax whispered, his breath hot on my earlobe. He dragged me out to the makeshift dance floor. I went willingly, biting my lip slightly. Out of the corner of my eye, I watched Jenna's wide smile as Lucas led her to the dance floor.

Jax's moves had me forgetting all about everything else though. My heart drummed nervously along to the beat of Miley's latest single. I couldn't even scoff at the fact that I was dancing to *Miley Cyrus*, not with the way Jax moved against me. His moves on the dance floor were skilled and erotic, telling the familiar tale of how skilled he was in *other* areas.

"You know Jax, if you wanted to grind up against me...I totally would have been fine with that. You didn't *need* to take me to a lame party to do this," I remarked, loving the feel of his body against me. It was lethal, the way he moved his hips and pelvis against mine. He gripped my hips with his hands, leading me in the rhythmic grinding.

"I know," Jax grinned. "It would have been so much easier to do that...but it was more of a challenge to get you to come tonight. And, to be honest...I didn't want Crimson to have to come alone."

He gestured to over where Crimson was standing with Brianna and Alissa. Brianna was ignoring her, scowling in our direction, but Alissa was smiling at something Crimson had said. Crimson was holding a red cup, drinking tentatively from it every so often.

"I know," I grumbled. I couldn't be mad at him when I felt the same way. Crimson was...innocent. She was caring, bubbly, and a little overbearing most of the time...but I still found myself wanting to protect her, to make sure that nobody made her feel bad.

"Plus," Jax added, placing his hand against the small of my back and drawing me closer to him. "I wanted to feel you grind up against me, tease you through your clothes, and drive you wild."

His words set my skin on fire, and he made good of his promise, torturing me through his moves and touches.

The song ended, and a slower one came on. Jax raised his

hand, using the pad of his thumb to trace my jaw line, starting just below my ear lobe. He paused on my lips, his thumb lingering there. As if in a trance, he leaned towards me and kissed me. I kissed him back slowly, enjoying the minty taste of him. I don't know how long we kissed, swaying gently to *Give Me Love* by Ed Sheeran. We only stopped when a tentative tap on my shoulder reminded us both that we were in a very public place. Smiling against his lips, I pulled away to face the person who had tapped my shoulder.

Crimson grinned at us. "Guys, I'd like you to meet my boyfriend!"

Still smiling at the lingering tingles Jax's kiss left upon my lips, I looked at the tall, lanky guy standing to her left.

I felt the air leave my lungs in a whoosh as I stared into the face of a person I hadn't seen in five years, a person I never thought I would see again.

Cole Carmichael stared back at me, just as stunned as I was. He paled, his jaw opened and his eyes widened as if he had seen a ghost. I suppose, in a way, he had.

The demons of my past reared their ugly head up at me as I stared at the face of my first boyfriend. Cole hadn't really changed in five years. He had lost the chubbiness in his cheeks, and had gotten taller. His pale green eyes and even the way he wore his hair remained unchanged. I shook as that night rushed back at me in tattered images, my stomach rolling with disgust and rage.

"You!" I flew at him in a fit of rage. I felt the sting of my knuckles coming into contact with his jaw, and my fists kept flying at him, pounding every inch I could get at while I screamed at him. "You ruined me!" I screeched, tears of anger pouring down my face, my eyes narrow slits of anger.

I felt strong arms pulling me off, and Jax's voice in my ear. "Relax, breathe," he repeated. I saw Jenna rushing over, concern apparent on her face. The entire room was silent, everyone turned to watch the drama unfold. The music had been silenced at some point during my attack.

"What the hell, Harlow!?" Crimson exclaimed, utterly shocked. She had both her hands on Cole's arms, comforting him while she stared at me with confusion.

"I'm sorry," Cole started to talk.

"I don't want to fucking hear it," I shot back, raising my finger threateningly at him. I stepped forward, but was held in place by Jax's arm. "You drugged me, you and your friends. You ruined me, you took a part of me that I will never get back!" Jax's grip around my waist tightened as his muscles tensed.

Cole's shoulders slumped in defeat at my words. Jenna looked back and forth from Cole to me, understanding crossing her face. She put her hand on Jax's shoulder.

"Get her out of here," she instructed gently. "I'll be right behind you guys."

I pulled away from Jax, storming out of the house. I could feel the eyes of everyone on me, and I couldn't stop shaking. Tears poured down my cheeks without constraint. I knew I would regret flying off the handle later, but I couldn't even process anything over the roaring of my blood in my ears.

Jax caught up with me as I raced down the walkway. He gently tugged on my arm, pulling me back towards him. I crashed into his chest, allowing him to hold me and comfort me while the tears fell.

He held me, stroking my back and hair, saying nothing for the longest time. Not until my tears slowed and my hysteria had ebbed.

"Harlow," he pulled me away so that he could look at me. "What just happened?"

I took a deep, steadying breath. I couldn't meet Jax's eyes, I was afraid to, so I looked over his shoulder. "That asshole and his friends drugged me and raped me when I was fifteen. I guess I've never forgiven them or come to terms with it." I laughed bitterly, wiping away the tears desperately from my cheeks. I felt his hands tighten around my arms, and I finally looked at him.

His jaw was clenched in anger. His brown eyes had darkened, and he rolled his neck as if trying to reign it all in.

Before he could say anything, Jenna and Lucas were flying down the walkway towards us.

"Time to go," Jenna said, taking one look at Jax and I. She probably feared that he would turn around and go inside, after Cole. I had never seen him look so menacing, but Jax was a fighter, a defender.

Brianna and Alissa's house was located a couple blocks away from our apartment, so we had walked over. I didn't bother asking if Crimson was coming, I frankly didn't care anymore. She had chosen to stay there with *him*, so she was on her own.

Jax held my hand the whole walk home, but I felt numb and exhausted from my emotional outburst. By the time we were walking into the apartment, the embarrassment had set in. Jenna bit her lip, studying the both of us.

"Lucas and I will be in my room if you need anything Harlow, but I think the two of you really need to talk..." Jenna sent me a look, trying to communicate with me. I nodded, watching the two of them disappear down the hallway.

The silence seemed to stretch on forever. I heard Jax sigh and walk over to me. He put his arms around me, pulling me against his chest again. "Harlow, talk to me. Don't shut me out, please?" he pleaded against my stiff posture. I forced myself to relax, breathing in his scent and closing my eyes.

"I'm sorry I went completely postal back there," I apologized. I was desperately trying to get control of myself again. I

144

felt vulnerable and weak, and stupid. Of course...I had planned on telling Jax about my past...eventually, at the right time and in the right way. Normally, I could have that conversation and remain composed and in control. Of course...I hadn't had to face Cole in *years*.

I broke away from Jax's embrace, walking over to the couch. I sat down, keeping my eyes trained on the Ikea coffee table. "Cole was my first boyfriend. He was one of the popular guys, a part of the basketball team. Everybody loved him, everybody thought he was so amazing. When he asked me out, I was ecstatic. We dated for a couple of weeks, but I wasn't ready for sex. I told him that, and I thought he respected it. Then one night, after a winning basketball game, I met up at Cole's house for a little after party. It wasn't anything big, just a small gathering to celebrate the win. I was the only girl there, only I didn't think there was anything wrong with it...I had hung out with them all before. Cole got me a drink. I drank it. It was roofied, and I blacked out. I faded in and out of consciousness, but I remember the pain. I remember...when there wasn't darkness...crying and begging them to stop."

Jax walked over, sinking down beside me. I couldn't raise my eyes to meet his.

"After that...night, rumors started to fly around the school about me...about how I'd slept with the whole team and Cole broke up with me because I was such a whore. The whole school believed it. I ended up switching schools because I got tired of nobody talking to me, of everyone judging me, of walking up to my locker and seeing "SLUT" written in lipstick on it."

"Harlow," I could hear the anguish in Jax's voice. He pulled me into his arms, and I rested my head against his shoulder. "It's not your fault."

I laughed, almost bitterly. "I know that. It's my fault for not reporting it though. I should have gone to the police. I should have told *somebody*, anybody. But I didn't. I couldn't. I was ashamed. My biggest regret is not going to the police about it."

Jax didn't know what to say to that. What could he say?

We sat in silence, Jax's fingers tracing warm circles on my shoulder. My eyes grew heavy from his warmth and comfort, I was emotionally spent from the night. I drifted off to sleep, lulled by his nearness.

I woke up to the sound of Jenna and Lucas speaking in hushed tones, saying their goodbyes. I waited until Jenna closed the door and retreated to her bedroom to stretch and pull away from Jax.

I thought he had fallen asleep too, he had been so silent, but Jax was staring at me, wide awake.

I bit my lip, running my hand through my hair. I still felt vulnerable.

"Don't," Jax told me, catching my chin with his hand. He forced me to look at him. "What happened tonight doesn't change how I feel about you," he said, his voice full of sincerity. His eyes searched mine, making sure that I understood.

I bit my lip, knowing that there was much more to my history than that, knowing that some of my secrets would make Jax run.

"I have more skeletons than that," I sighed heavily, feeling the weight of my own secrets.

His lips brushed against mine, gently at first. Then when I didn't pull away or tense, he deepened the kiss. His hands tangled in my hair, the gentle tug coaxing an almost inhumane sound out of my throat. He pulled away, resting his forehead against mine.

"Your skeletons don't scare me," he said softly.

Jax left around two in the morning. I went to bed, but tossed and turned, unable to shut my mind off enough to get a decent amount of sleep. When my alarm went off at seven, I had barely slept at all...except for in Jax's arms on the couch.

I knew I had to keep busy, to keep from shutting down and retreating. I wouldn't give Cole the power. I had changed a lot since then, I wasn't the same scared little girl. I hadn't let my feelings of what happened to me stop me from moving forward in so long...I suppose I had Lauren to thank for that.

After the thing with Cole and the basketball team, and after enduring weeks of shame at my old school and spiraling into a deep depression, I begged my mom to let me switch schools. I chose Trafalgar's, mostly because it was an all-girls school but also because it was removed enough from my old school that nobody would know what happened. Nobody would know who I was.

I met Lauren on my first day there. I was sitting by myself at a picnic table at lunch, with my journal in front of me. My journal had been my only friend for the last several months, I spilled all of my secrets within it's pages, and I felt less alone for doing so.

Lauren saw me sitting by myself, and walked up to me with purpose. She was wearing the same school uniform, the tartan kilt, the navy blue Blazer with the Trafalgar crest, the monogrammed white blouse and the navy knee-high socks. She wore black dress shoes and looked exactly like the model on Trafalgar's brochure, what with her beautiful smile, bright green eyes and white blond hair.

"You're new here," she had said, sitting down across from me.

"Yeah...and your point?" I had responded, my voice guarded as I met her gaze with a steely edge. I had let the girls at my previous school walk all over me, and it wasn't my intent to allow the ones here to do the same. I closed my journal, pulling it away from her sights.

Lauren had just smiled and tossed back her head, laughing at my response. She looked back at me. "I'm not going to bite."

I raised an eyebrow at her, sizing her up. She looked like trouble, she acted like trouble, but I could also see beneath her facade that she was kind at heart. There was warmth, understanding and compassion in her bright green eyes.

"Why did you transfer?" she asked, tilting her head with curiosity.

"I wanted to," I shrugged.

"Nobody *wants* to transfer to an all-girls school, unless you're like...a lesbian or something," she laughed again. "Are you a lesbian?"

"No," I frowned, unsure of how to react to this interrogation.

"You don't have to tell me now, but one day you'll want to. My name is Lauren by the way. What's yours?"

"Harlow."

"Well, it's nice to meet you Harlow. Let me show you the ropes," Lauren said, standing up and staring at me, as if waiting for me to join.

After that day, we were pretty much inseparable. Lauren taught me how to have fun again, how to not live in the horrors of the past and embrace the day. She just understood me, and my past, without prying. She made me feel accepted.

I knew that Lauren had a difficult childhood too, although I was never privy to what happened to her. I just knew it from how she carried herself, as if she'd seen the horrors of the world and had learned worldly knowledge.

Seeing Cole again brought me back to that unpleasant time in my life, and worser still...it reminded me that Lauren was gone.

I knew that the only way I was going to get over it, was to keep living and keep moving forward. The sting of Lauren's loss and the shock of seeing that particular demon from my past couldn't overrun all the good things I had going for me *now*.

Despite my pep talk, a part of me still wanted to call in sick for my shift at *The Bean*. If I did that, then I knew that Lucas would have to go in, and he would tell Jenna and she would get all concerned about me, so I forced myself out of bed and into the shower. I tossed my long, nearly dried hair up into a sock bun on the top of my head. I applied enough makeup to cover up the fact that I hadn't slept well, and I threw my jacket on.

I could hear Jenna's soft snores coming from down the hall. Walking softly so that I wouldn't wake her and prompt her interrogation, I left our apartment. I locked up behind me, rolling my shoulders to try and work out the tension I was carrying.

Unease prickled my skin as I walked down the street to work. As far as I knew, they hadn't caught the guy that was loose on the streets harassing women. There had been another attempt a couple nights ago, but the victim had gotten away.

I couldn't help but wonder if it was *Cole* doing it. It seemed like a major coincidence for him to show up in Ottawa when there was a rapist on the loose.

The sun was just beginning to raise, and most of it's rays were hidden by the tall buildings that surrounded me. It was still dark in a lot of places. I walked on the edge of the side-walk, keeping my eyes focused on my surroundings. I didn't see anyone around, but the feeling of unease was still there and strong. I nearly sighed with relief when I approached the shop door to *The Bean*.

We didn't open until 9am on Sunday, so I had to knock against the glass of the door. I stared at the *closed* sign while I waited for Jamie to come around to let me in.

"Good morning Sunshine!" Jamie exclaimed, a wide grin on his face.

"Morning," I grumbled, keeping my eyes down as I walked into the staff room to ditch my jacket and purse. I returned to the front to start setting up the coffee and espresso machines, Jamie's watchful eyes on my back.

He let me work in silence for half an hour before he approached me.

"Girl, you need to tell me what's up. You look, no offense, like utter crap." He leaned against the counter, crossing his arms and zeroing in on me with his miss nothing stare.

"We're going to be opening soon," I reminded him, trying to distract him away from targeting on me.

"We have another half hour until open," Jamie waved away my concerns. "Mark is stocking up the front with delicious goodies that would undoubtedly go to my hips, and you've already prepped the machines. Spill."

"I had a bad night, okay?" I huffed, aggravated. At this particular moment, I almost missed my previous bosses, who didn't bother to invest themselves in employees lives. Upon thinking that, I felt guilty. Jamie was kind, loving, and he cared. I shouldn't hold that against him just because I was in a terrible mood. "I'm sorry," I sighed. "I got an unwanted blast from the past."

"An ex-boyfriend?" Jamie's eyebrows raised up to his hairline, eager for the gossip. I knew he wouldn't tell anyone, that he just wanted to know because Jamie simply wanted to know everything and anything he could learn of other people.

"It's not like that," I shook my head. "Kind of but sort of, not really. It's more complicated and I don't want to get into it...I'll be okay, just that coupled with my inability to get a decent night of sleep has me on edge."

"I can see that. Girl, you need a magic remedy," Jamie

paused in thought, tapping his chin with his index finger. "I have *just* the solution!" I didn't trust the way his eyes lit up.

"Oh yeah? What's that?"

"You need to get laid!" Jamie declared, nodding as if it was his mission to help me out.

I exhaled, my lips perking at the corners. Of *course* that would be his magic remedy.

I really didn't think that sex was the solution to this particular problem, but I also didn't want to confess *why*. As if having old wounds reopened in front of the new guy that I liked and flying off the handle wasn't bad enough, now I was missing my dead friend even more than usual. Those weren't exactly mood setters.

Still...Jax's company was more therapeutic on my soul than I cared to admit. "Ya, maybe."

"Lucky for you, you have that delicious piece of eye candy," Jamie nodded, as if satisfied that the world would be all right.

"Ya," I sighed, wanting to just end the conversation. I bit my lip, thinking about Jax again. It was impossible to forget how incredible he had made me feel, and I longed for it now...but I didn't want to use sex as a band-aid. I had gotten into that habit once before, and I hadn't actually solved any of my issues that way.

"You're holding back from him," Jamie observed. "Why are you holding back?" his observation and the question that followed caught me completely off guard. I forgot how intuitive he was.

"I...I don't know," I frowned. I didn't want to spill all my secrets to my boss, but Jamie was relentless, and you just *wanted* to talk to him. He was just one of those people that you could open up entirely to and he wouldn't judge you, he would understand. "I guess I'm not completely over my ex. Maybe."

"The 'blast from the past'?"

"No, a different ex," I sighed, thinking of Iain.

"One way to get over someone is to throw yourself into someone else!" Mark chirped, startling me as he came around with a tray of fresh scones. He smiled lovingly at Jamie. "Isn't that right?"

Jamie rolled his eyes, smiling at his partner. "It is one way. Memories don't compete with what's in front of you. Especially if what's in front of you is sexy, incredible, and willing to be there."

Jamie's words were imprinted in my mind for the remainder of my shift. I served coffees and fetched scones until nearly my shift ended at three. I said goodbye to everyone, then made my way home.

Jenna was hanging out in the living room when I walked in, painting her toenails a bright shade of red. She looked up as I closed the door.

"Hey," she said, smiling at me. "I ordered pizza for lunch, I was hungry," she added, looking guilty at the box on the island. I shrugged, walking over to grab a slice of cold pizza. I had skipped out on two meals, and my stomach was growling in protest.

"Good, I'm hungry," I said, taking a massive bite. Jenna shuffled over on the couch to make room for me, and I sat down beside her, inwardly sighing. I knew the look on her face. I knew that avoiding this conversation was impossible.

"About last night," Jenna started, carefully closing the lid on her nail polish. She turned to look at me, concern in her cornflower blue eyes. "Are you...okay?" I could tell she was having a hard time finding the right words to ask the questions she had.

"Yeah, I'm fine Jenna...really. I am," I told her, meeting her eyes and imploring her to believe me. "It just was a shock, you know? And it brought back some memories that I've been repressing. And it kind of made me miss Lauren."

Jenna nodded, understanding the little I confided in her. After three years of friendship, Jenna was intuitive and able to understand me. I didn't have to give her lengthly explanations for everything on my mind, she was there for me even if I didn't say a word.

"I'm more embarrassed for how I acted. I was going to tell Jax about everything...maybe...when I was ready...but that's definitely not how I wanted to do it." I sighed, leaning back against the couch. "I'm worried he'll look at me with pity."

"I told Lucas about senior year," Jenna said, crossing her arms. "I told him everything...including the...what happened after."

"Really?! Jenna that's great," I was happy for my friend. I knew her secret was a burden on her as well, and that she secretly worried men would get weirded out by the fact that she gave birth to the baby. She hadn't told anybody who didn't already know about.

"He was sympathetic, empathetic...but he didn't pity me. Do you know why?" Jenna asked, looking at me intently. "Because it wasn't my fault, and what happened wasn't your fault either."

"I know," I couldn't help but smile. It was the same speech I had given her countless times in our twelfth grade year. Jenna hesitated, as if she had something she wanted to say but wasn't sure if she should. "It's okay, spill it."

"Has Crimson texted you at all?" Jenna asked.

"I'm not sure," I admitted. "I haven't checked my phone today. I worked. I left it at home." The truth was, I was avoiding checking my phone. Jenna nodded, biting down on her lip. "What?"

"Just...go easy on her. You don't know her story. You can't

blame her for something her boyfriend did. She probably didn't even know about it, and she definitely didn't hear half of what you said."

"I know..." I sighed. It wasn't fair to be angry at Crimson. But maybe if she had told me a little about her boyfriend before having us meet, I could have realized who he was and told her that there was no chance in hell I wanted to be around him. Then and again, how was she to know?

TEN

On Monday morning, I met Jax outside the lecture hall before our Psychology seminar. He had gotten us both a cup of coffee, and I smiled my thanks at him as I accepted it. My heart was pounding with nervousness. I wasn't exactly looking forward to seeing Crimson, or Brianna for that matter. The look on Brianna's face as I left the party pissed me off. She was *thrilled* by my pain, enjoying it. Probably hoping that my outburst put a stop to what was happening between Jax and I.

It hadn't, of course. True to Jax's word, this particular skeleton of mine didn't bother him in the way I thought it would. It pissed him off and likely made him want to add Cole and those other guys to his secret hit list, but it didn't change how he saw me. I could tell that in the way he looked at me with unmasked desire as I approached. The ache in my chest lessened as he gently pulled me towards him to kiss me.

His tongue sent a familiar surge of desire welling up from the lower depths of my belly. I pulled away, biting down on my lip. My head was still all mixed up from Saturday. Part of me wanted to drag Jax to his truck and have my way with him again, but another part of me was terrified that what had happened would taint what we had between us.

Sex was always a complicated subject for me. My past muddled it up *a lot*, and as much as I liked to pretend I was impervious to the sexual assaults I had endured in my life time, I wasn't. It affected my ability to connect with the men I was with. Or it had, anyway. Iain had been...different. I had been the seducer. Looking back, it was clear that I was using sex to tie me to him, to something that I thought was good. I had risked it all for Iain, and I had suffered the consequences. So had he.

Sex with Jax had felt like a natural progression of how things were supposed to be, but that was before my skeletons came out to play...and even if he *did* say he wasn't bothered by it, I still was. I was bothered that I hadn't gotten to tell Jax in my own time and my own way about my past.

It was hard to separate yourself from sexual assault victim to sexual being. With my skeletons safely locked up, I hadn't had to think about that at all.

I looked at the lecture hall door, knowing that Crimson was likely already sitting inside, saving us seats like she had been doing every day for the past several weeks.

Jax caught a strand of my long hair as it danced in the late September wind. The action drew my eyes away from the doors and to him. He was smiling down at me, his gold rimmed eyes melting like heated caramel chocolate as he gazed at me. "Morning, beautiful. How was work yesterday?"

"Interesting..." I trailed off, thinking about Jamie's words again. I shook my head to clear it. I couldn't believe how distracted I was. "How was your day?"

"Good, worked at the garage," Jax shrugged. I knew he

moonlighted as a mechanic when he wasn't working at the gym teaching MMA classes to kids.

I bit my lip, looking at the door again. I had put this off as long as I could, not responding to any of Crimson's text messages. I was going to, but I just didn't know what to say. "It's okay" didn't seem right, especially when I wasn't okay with a friend dating a guy who did such a horrific thing to me. Of course, I didn't know for sure if Crimson was still with him. For all I knew, they broke up that night after she found out his dirty little secret.

Somehow, I doubted that. Crimson hadn't spoken much about her boyfriend prior to us meeting him (and prior to *me* discovering exactly who he was), but I knew she was stupidly in love with him by the way her face sort of glazed over when she did mention him.

Jax opened the door and I followed him in. I allowed him to lead us to free seats that were thankfully nowhere near Crimson. I knew we would have to have a chat sooner rather than later, but I wanted to avoid it right before Professor Pedersen's lecture. It was going to be hard enough to focus as it was. I finally glanced around when I settled into my seat, scooping out Crimson's red hair on the other side of the room. She was sitting with Brianna and Alissa, trying to make eye contact with me.

I couldn't hear what they were saying, but Brianna was smirking while she spoke to Alissa, her eyes kept sweeping over to me. From the look on her face, I could tell that Brianna had *nothing* good to say about me.

I turned to face the front of the classroom, glowering.

I gave up on trying to focus on Professor Pedersen's lecture halfway through class. Instead, I sat and waited for the inevitable. As soon as Professor Pedersen dismissed us, Crimson was in front of me.

"I saved you guys seats," she said, her eyes wide with uncertainty and hurt.

I blinked at her, unsure of how to respond to that.

"Sorry, we didn't see," Jax's lie came easily, unless he hadn't actually seen her, which was possible. He had been pretty focused on watching me...

"Oh, well," Crimson shuffled from foot to foot, staring at her toes. She looked up at me, meeting my eyes. "I'm sorry about the party, Harlow. I...I didn't know about that." She looked at the floor, unable to hold her gaze. Shame flickered across her features, paling her.

"It's not your fault," I told her, because it wasn't. I adjusted the strap of my messenger bag, clenching it to keep control of my emotions.

"After you left, I talked to Cole and he told me everything," Crimson's eyes welled with tears as she looked back up to meet my eyes again. "I'm so sorry."

"Again, not your fault," I said, my patience wearing thin. I had to force myself to not snap out at her in aggravation. If there was one thing I couldn't stand, it was someone else taking on my pain and pitying me. Jax squeezed my arm, providing silent comfort to me.

"Cole's changed since then Harlow. I know he regrets what he did to you. I know him better than I know anyone and I know he's never forgiven himself and never will. You *have* to give him a second chance!" Crimson pleaded, her eyes wide and her hands reaching out to grab my free one.

I pulled my hand away from her grasp, as if her hands were on fire.

"Excuse me?" I stepped back, giving myself space from her as I glowered at her. "I don't have to do *shit*. I don't have to talk to him, I don't have to get to know him, and I certainly don't have to give him a second chance." I spoke loud enough that there was no way she wouldn't have heard me.

My body was vibrating with anger. I couldn't believe the audacity Crimson had to stand there and basically tell me to *forgive* Cole. My stomach rolled with disgust.

"I just meant-" Crimson went as red as her name and hair, embarrassed.

"That's enough," Jax said, firmly but gently. He looked pointedly to the front of the room, where Professor Pedersen was observing the three of us. The lecture hall had all but cleared out.

I lurched out of Jax's grasp and stormed off, not bothering to see if he was following me.

Of course, he did. He was right behind me the moment I pushed open the doors to the lecture hall. The fresh cool air was a welcoming slap against my face. I had been so angry and anxious that the lecture hall had felt like a oven to me.

"That went about as well as I thought it would," I grumbled, sparing him a quick look. I sighed at the concerned expression on his face. "I'm fine Jax. I just...I don't need Crimson making me feel guilty for not wanting to hear his side. I'm sorry, but I just don't give a shit what he has to say."

Jax nodded, putting his hands in his pockets. "I understand," he said, and he did understand. I let out a sigh of relief, glad that I didn't have to argue my reasoning.

Throughout the rest of the day, I had time to reflect upon my fleeting friendship with Crimson. As far as I was concerned, it was over. Friends, even new friends and potential friends, did *not* ask friends to forgive their rapist boyfriends. I wouldn't be able to get past that.

I was a little sad about it, Crimson was the first friend I had made in my two years at University. She was the first person I had opened up to since befriending Jenna in twelfth grade. I wasn't counting Jax, because I was dating him. He was more than friend. Still, Jenna could no longer say that I didn't *try* to let people in, because I did.

It just often wasn't worth it for me.

I chewed on my lip, staring blankly at the front of the classroom as my Fundamentals of Oral Communication professor lectured important speech cues. I numbly took notes, barely absorbing any of the things he was saying. I couldn't focus on a damn thing, and I was beginning to panic about it.

I may not have let anyone in over the last two years, but I was focused and driven, always getting my assignments completed on time. After meeting Jax, I started losing my concentration more and more. Luckily, my marks weren't drastically affected by my lapse in concentration...but if I wasn't careful, they would be.

Of course, everything else wasn't helping either. The Crimson drama, the maybe sighting of Andrew at the music festival two weekends ago...

Frowning, I made a mental note to call Officer Mike Turner after class. I hadn't heard anything back from him, and frankly...I was getting tired of waiting. How long did it take a police officer to check up on someone?

I DROPPED my messenger bag down at the entrance, kicking it aside so that it wouldn't be in the way when Jenna got home. Our apartment was eerily silent. I felt the compulsive urge to check every room, just to make sure it was empty. I felt foolish when I completed the search, finding nothing amiss.

I retreated to my bedroom, sifting my phone out of my jean pocket. I tossed it on the bed and sat down beside it, staring at my phone as I debated on what to do next.

I really didn't *want* to call Mike Turner again, not after the first less than warm reception my call had wielded. But I had a terrible feeling in the pit of my stomach, and I knew I couldn't rest easy until I heard from him about exactly *where* Andrew Cooper was.

I didn't exactly have an obsessive personality, but I had a difficult time letting things go. I didn't want my suspicious to cloud my feelings of safety I had been wrapped in since our move to Ottawa. For the past two years...I'd felt numb, but safe. I hadn't been watching over my shoulder, like I had done for so long in North Bay.

Now though, that feeling of safety was gone. The sensation of being watched was strong, and becoming increasingly difficult to ignore. I don't know if I had Cole's return or the two possible Andrew Cooper sightings to thank for that, but I needed to figure out who was the threat. Cole was the obvious choice...and yet, my intuition was telling me it *wasn't* Cole.

Sighing deeply, I picked up the phone and dialed Mike Turner's phone number. It rang three times before going to voice mail, almost as if he'd seen my number and hit ignore. Gritting my teeth, I tapped my foot as I waited for his voice-mail message recording to end. "Hi Officer Turner. I'm sure you know who it is...I'm just calling to see if you were able to track down Andrew Cooper or not? Please get back to me and let me know..." I paused, searching for anything else to add. "Okay, thanks. Bye." I hung up, feeling like a major idiot.

I dropped the phone back onto my bed and buried my head in my hands, exhaling loudly.

"Everything okay?" Jenna's voice completely startled me. I jumped up, my heart racing.

"Jesus Jenna!" I frowned, more angry at myself for being startled than her for startling me.

"Sorry," Jenna apologized, leaning against the door way. I

bit my lip, wondering how much she had heard. Studying her, I noted how sad her eyes looked.

"Everything okay?" I asked, hesitating.

"No, not really," Jenna sighed. She bit her lip, looking away. "I...I got another letter."

"Oh," I awkwardly stepped towards her, wanting to offer her some kind of comfort but knowing that I sucked at physical contact. "Did you -?"

"Read it?" Jenna asked, her eyes flicking back over to me. Her expression broke my heart. It was one of unmasked pain and overwhelming sadness. "No," she laughed bitterly, looking away. "I put it in the box."

"It's good that you're saving them. One of these days, you're going to want to read them..." I trailed off, wondering if what I had chosen to say was comforting or not.

The letter Jenna was referring to was one from the adoption agency, an update on her birth daughter's life and new family.

I still remember the day that Jenna received the first update letter. It was shortly after the baby's first Christmas, and it was filled with a heartwarming letter from the Fetcher family. It was penned by Sarah, expressing how much gratitude and joy she was filled with over getting to love and raise her daughter. They named her Jayden, and included pictures of her. Newborn photos, and a family portrait under the Christmas tree.

Jenna had cried then, grasping the photos of her birth daughter. The smile she wore was one of thankfulness, thankful that her daughter had a loving family, and pain...pain from how she was conceived.

I remember picking up the photo of baby Jayden with her parents. I held it, staring at Sarah's face, finding similarities to Iain in her Caribbean blue eyes and blond hair.

It was like a strange twilight zone. Jenna's birth daughter

was now the daughter of Iain's sister Sarah and her husband, she was now forever a part of the Bentley family...a part of Iain. I couldn't help but wonder if baby Jayden saw her uncle often.

Sometimes, I wondered if I had been used by Iain. When he found out that my best friend was expecting, did he see an opportunity for his sister? Did he get the ball rolling on adoption, lining up the ducks so that his sister and her husband would get to be the adoptive parents? Was it all intended?

One of the only secrets I had ever kept from Jenna was that Sarah was Iain's sister. At first, I hadn't wanted her to doubt her decision to chose Sarah and her husband. I knew, just by looking at Sarah, that she was going to be the best mother to the baby, that who her brother was didn't matter. I knew that Iain would love and protect his niece.

I didn't want to confuse or hurt Jenna, either. I worried that she would have thought *I* planned it all out that way. I hadn't even known until that day I had run into Iain at the hospital, and he had been so excited for his sister. Before I could get a chance to tell Jenna, Iain was arrested and my world flipped upside down.

Even though two years had passed, I couldn't bring myself to tell Jenna the truth. I didn't know how. Speaking about it hurt me too, because the seed of doubt planted by Iain's silence had me wondering if he used me to get a baby for his sister. The seed of doubt had flowered, growing with the guilt I felt over it.

I tried to comfort myself with the fact that Jayden was loved, safe, and had everything she could ever need or want, but the secret was still an ugly one to have.

"Looks like a Ben, Jerry and Ryan night," I remarked. A small smile tugged the corners of Jenna's lips up.

"Maybe Chinese food too?" she inquired hopefully.

"Okay, I'll order. But pajamas are a requirement," I told her.

An hour later, Jenna and I sat cross legged on the couch in our PJs, our Chinese food fest spread out on the coffee table in front of us and a Ryan Gosling movie playing. It was one we had seen a billion times before, so we barely paid attention to the dialog on screen.

"I feel guilty," Jenna confessed, setting her carton of Chinese food down on the coffee table so she could draw her knees up to her chest and hug them. She stared blindly at the TV, not meeting my eyes.

"Why would you feel guilty?" I asked. I personally thought that Jenna made the best decision she could have made, given the circumstances. I admired and respected her so much. I definitely wouldn't have been strong enough to carry on a pregnancy like that.

"I abandoned my daughter, I knew I couldn't look at her every day..." a single tear escaped down Jenna's cheek, and she brushed it away with frustration.

"You didn't abandon her," I corrected, setting my own carton down on the table and shifting my body to face Jenna. "You found her a loving home, with loving parents. She is cherished every single day."

"That's why I feel so guilty, because *someone else* is making her feel loved and cherished. Because *I couldn't*. I do love her...you can't grow something inside you and have no feelings towards it, but...there's a lot of ugliness there and I feel guilty for that ugliness. I don't want to hear how awesome she's doing. I'm glad she's doing awesome, but it just rips at the hole in my chest because I failed her and every day I am reminded that I failed her."

"You didn't fail her," I said firmly. "You gave her life, you gave her a chance."

"I just wish things had been different, you know? My arms feel empty, but I could never bring myself to hold her. I knew it would rip me apart even more than it does now if I held her at the hospital. I was afraid I wouldn't be able to let her go, and I *needed* to let her go."

"I don't think you'll ever let her go," I said sadly. "It's not something that you *can* let go, you just have to acknowledge that you did the right thing. You do feel like you did the right thing, right?"

"Of course," Jenna brushed at her wet cheeks away. "The alternative would have been...it wouldn't have brought that couple into her life, that's for sure. And they do seem to love her."

Guilt rolled in my stomach as I thought about Sarah, and in turn...Iain. I knew beyond a reasonable doubt that Jayden was loved by that family. The guilt came from my secret keeping. Would Jenna feel different about everything if she knew?

Before I could open my mouth to tell her that *yes, they loved her*, my cell phone rang. I grabbed it, answering without looking at the screen, thinking that Mike Turner was *finally* calling me back.

"Hello?"

"Harlow! Honey, I've been trying to get in touch with you for a week now!" my mom's voice tethered somewhere between whiny and annoyed.

"Hi Mom," I winced, rolling my eyes at Jenna in apology for the interruption. "I'm sorry, I've just been really busy with work and school." I wasn't actively avoiding answering her calls...I just wasn't actively trying to take them. Usually when she called, she spent a fair bit of time talking about how she wished I would come home to visit more.

"I figured," Mom sighed, almost sadly. "Larry and I were just wondering if you would be able to make it out to Thanksgiving dinner? I spoke to the Burke's, I know Jenna will be coming home. She's bringing her boyfriend!" She sounded deeply thrilled for Jenna, and I knew that she was. My mom had been privy of what happened to Jenna, as I had played such a key roll in the court proceedings.

"Yeah, um...I don't know if I'm working yet," I answered, twirling a strand of my hair on my finger.

"You're not," Jenna said firmly. "Lucas talked to Jamie and Mark. They're going to handle the store."

I covered the microphone with my hand, sending Jenna a deadly glare that communicated my complete disdain at her interruption. Of course, I already knew that, but I still wasn't planning on going home.

"Oh that's perfect!" Mom exclaimed, hearing Jenna before I had time to silence her. Mom's voice lowered and shook. I think she guessed my hesitation at coming home. "I promise honey, it won't be like...like the last time."

Mom was referring to the first and only time I came home for the holidays. Things had been wrought with tension between Larry and I. I still hadn't forgiven him for the whole Iain thing. I knew it wasn't *really* his fault, Larry hadn't taken the photos. It wasn't Larry who mailed them to the police station. It was Larry who had to clean up the massive scandal surrounding one of his top schools. It was Larry who had to track down the leaked photos of Iain and I, just to get me off of the Internet.

Technically, I had a lot of reasons to thank Larry, but his hatred of Iain and his undeniable belief that 'Iain got what he deserved' clouded my judgment. Iain was not a monster, but Larry acted like he was.

"I'll see Mom," I frowned, my thoughts drifting away from them and to someone completely different...Jax. From what little he told me about his family and life, I knew that he would be spending Thanksgiving alone.

"Okay," Mom sighed, resigned. She knew I would either

come, or I wouldn't...but that no amount of pleading with me would change my mind. She knew how stubborn I could be.

"I love you Mom, I'll call you later, okay? Jenna and I are just watching a movie."

"Love you too honey," Mom was trying to hide her sadness with cheer, but I could see through her act.

The line went dead, and I tossed my phone down on the coffee table, frowning at Jenna.

"What?" she asked innocently. "You should come! It's just Thanksgiving. I'm sure you could endure one dinner with your folks."

Jenna knew about my relationship struggles with my mom and Larry, but she was forever trying to get me to fix things with them. Family was important to Jenna, but she luckily had a way easier relationship with her parents. They had stood by her unquestionably after she confessed to them that the Chief of Police's son raped her and got her pregnant. They bought the best lawyer that money could buy and pressed charges, not resting until their daughter saw *some* kind of justice. They stood by her when she made the difficult decision to give up her baby.

When the whole thing with Cole and his friends went down, I couldn't tell anyone. Mom had heard through the grapevine that I was promiscuous and sleeping around. Instead of talking to me about it, she believed them. Ashamed and hurt, I had put even more distance between the two of us. She had tried to redeem herself ever since, keeping the secret of Iain and I when she discovered the photos I had foolishly taken on our first trip together, but there was still that distance between us, and I didn't know how to move past it. I didn't know how to forgive her for all the hurt and anger I felt.

Plus, I blamed Larry for Iain's harsh sentence. He had all but gone on a witch hunt, and allowed the towns people to as well. Had Larry not raised such a stink about it, I was absolutely certain that Iain wouldn't have been charged.

I hated that town, I hated going back to it. It was aggravating that the entire town could turn a blind eye to the Carl Cooper's corruption and the vile excuse for a human being his son was for *years,* then prosecute Iain simply because we had been involved with each other, a completely consensual relationship.

"What about Jax?" I asked, twisting my hair up into a bun and clipping it back. I needed to draw my own thoughts away from home, away from Iain, before the anger surfaced again.

"Invite him," Jenna encouraged, her eyes bright with excitement. "Maybe if your mom and Larry saw you date...other guys...will help."

"Maybe," I mused, thinking that it probably would. It shouldn't have mattered, of course, but they were constantly waiting for Iain to walk back into my life. That wasn't going to happen, and I needed to prove not only to them, but to myself as well, that I had moved on.

Even if I hadn't *exactly* moved past everything that happened.

We watched the rest of the movie in relative silence, both Jenna and I lost in our own thoughts.

I had never invited a guy I was dating home to meet my parents. I *wanted* to invite Iain, I wanted him to meet my parents as my boyfriend. I wanted them to like him, but I knew that the likelihood of that happening was *very* slim. My English teacher couldn't exactly show up for a Sunday roast, especially not when the Superintendent was my step-father.

I chewed my lips, wondering if I really *wanted* to invite Jax home. He had already seen some of my fractured parts, did I really want him to see my family dynamics? What if Larry or my mom gave something away? What if we ran into someone who made a comment about Iain? I wasn't ready to talk about Iain. I wasn't even sure if I was really over him. Sometimes, I thought I was. Being around Jax, getting lost in his touches and kisses...it almost seemed like I truly was over Iain.

But then, when Jax and I weren't together...when I was home alone, Iain would return to my thoughts. I could push him away from my mind all I wanted, I could distract myself with the incredible way that Jax made me feel...but was I over Iain?

CHAPTER
ELEVEN

Thanksgiving was approaching, and I had yet to make up my mind on whether or not I was going to be going home for the holiday. I dodged my mom's phone calls, telling her I still wasn't sure...that I had group work I was trying to finish, but that if I couldn't finish it in time...I would have to miss out.

The truth was, I didn't know if I could get up the balls to ask Jax. Funny, when I usually prided myself on being blunt and strong-willed.

I had a lot of time to mull over everything during my night shift that Thursday. At my insistence, Jamie had started to allow me to work the late evening shift again. I had lost too many hours on his new schedule, and I flat out told Jamie that if my hours didn't return to normal, I was going to have to find a new job. I needed the cash, and even if they hadn't caught the guy behind the attacks, I still had bills to pay.

Jamie gave in to my demands, installing more security cameras as an added measure. I bit my lip at this false attempt at safety - *if* I was going to get attacked, it wouldn't be inside the coffee shop.

Once Jax heard that my schedule would be returning to normal, he insisted on walking me home during those shifts. It worked out, since Jax was done work just before I closed up shop, and he would sit and wait for me.

Part of me resented the fact that I needed a chaperon, but the other part was relieved to have his company. Spending time with Jax was never a burden, and it got a little lonely the last hour before close. The customers were infrequent, and time seemed to pass by quicker with him around. We were able to work on our half of the group assignment, too. Our section was to focus on the psychological aspect of verbal child abuse. Crimson, Brianna and Alissa were working on the psychological aspect of physical abuse and neglect.

It was a heavy topic, one that Jax wasn't entirely comfortable with. I suppose he felt the same way about the topic that I felt about sexual assault. It's hard to disconnect yourself from something you've experienced first hand, and I knew that Jax had definitely experienced abuse as a child at the hands of his father.

I was shinning up the appliances and thinking about Jax and his childhood and how it all tied in to inviting him home from dinner, when the door chimed. I looked up, half expecting it to be Jax. My blood froze as I stared at Cole.

"What are you doing here?" my tone instantly went as cold as my blood. I glared at him, not caring that he was a customer and I was supposed to serve him. Not a chance in hell.

Cole looked desperate. His pale green eyes were blood shot and red, as if he had gone weeks without sleep. His hair looked dirty, and he seriously looked like someone put him through the ringer. *Good*, I thought nastily.

"I just need to talk to you, please," he pleaded, his hands on top of the counter. I backed away, distancing myself from him.

"I am not interested in hearing *anything* you have to say," I answered, crossing my arms. "You need to leave now, before I call the police."

"Please Harlow! You don't understand, I never met to hurt you! I can't live with this guilt anymore." Cole begged, imploring me to understand. I didn't, I couldn't. I wouldn't.

"Oh, that's fresh," I sneered, feeling the anger surge up through my veins. "You didn't 'mean' to drug me. You didn't 'mean' to force yourself on me. You didn't 'mean' to let your friends all have a go. Must have just been an accident, huh?"

"It wasn't like that," Cole started, attempting to explain himself. I held my hand up, silencing him.

"There is nothing you can say that will ever make me forgive you. You put my safety at jeopardy. You knew I wasn't ready to have sex, and you drugged me and did it anyway. Worse still? You let your friends do it too. You let *everyone* call me names and think I was a massive slut. You are a monster, you don't deserve my forgiveness or understanding. You deserve to suffer for this, every single day. Go rot in hell, and get out of this store."

Cole listened to my verbal attack with his head down, accepting the lashing I was given him. When I had finished speaking, he looked up. His eyes were dead, as if all hope had left him. The expression chilled me worse than encountering him to begin with. "I'm sorry Harlow. For all the pain I've inflicted on you." he said simply, before turning around and leaving the store.

I was still trying to catch my breath when the door chimed again. This time, it *was* Jax. From the look on his face and the way his fists were clenched tight to his sides, he had seen Cole leaving.

"Are you okay?" he demanded, approaching me quickly, his eyes assessing my face. His hand gently traced my jaw line, as if touching me would reassure him that I was okay. Even though I was shaking from the encounter, I suddenly felt fine in his presence.

"Yeah, I'm fine," I said, waving away his concern. Jax nodded, his jaw tense. "He apparently came to apologize and tell me that 'I don't understand'".

"What did you say?"

"I told him to get the hell out. I won't listen to any apologizes, Jax. There's no excuse for what he did." I turned around, crossing my arms in an attempt to warm myself against the chill of the memory of the emptiness in Cole's eyes. I went back to work, getting Jax a coffee that I knew he'd want.

Jax parked himself at his usual table, close enough to the counter that we could still talk and see each other. With the store dead, we had plenty of time to talk.

"We'll have to meet up with the rest of the group soon," Jax warned me as I finished shutting off the last of the machines. I nodded, turning off the lights.

"I know, another thing to look forward to," I said sarcastically, rolling my eyes. I definitely wasn't looking forward to dealing with Crimson again, especially when it would definitely get back to her that I had been mean to poor Cole again.

We still hadn't really talked to each other. I sat as far away from her as I could, and she didn't dare try and talk to me about anything outside of our mutual group project. Even that had been awkward. I knew a full group meeting was inevitable, but I still wasn't looking forward to it. At least Jax and I had finished our half of the project...

"We should set it up after the Thanksgiving break," Jax said, yawning.

"Speaking of..." I trailed off, pausing for a moment so I

could lock up the store behind me. I punched in the alarm code. I started to walk, knowing that Jax was following closely behind me, waiting for me to finish my sentence. I adjusted my scarf, sending him a playful smile. I knew my delay was driving him nuts.

"Yes..." Jax grinned, motioning for me to continue. I took a deep breath, drawing in the chilly early October air, and reached out to hold Jax's hand. *It's now or never*, I thought, trying to give myself a little pep talk.

"Do you want to come to North Bay for Thanksgiving dinner with me?" I finally asked, looking up at him tentatively.

"Hmm..." Jax considered, puffing out his cheeks and exhaling. "Well..." I waited several more seconds, raising my eyebrows with impatience.

"Well what?" I asked, nudging him hard with my hip. He barely felt the impact, and certainly didn't stumble.

"I guess I could go," he finally said, grinning down at me gleefully. "I'm curious to meet your mom and step-dad."

"We're planning on leaving Sunday morning. As much as I don't want to have to spend the night at my parent's house, it looks like I can't avoid it. We'll be leaving Monday morning. You'll have to sleep in the guest room. Larry is *very* religious."

"I wouldn't have dared tried to sleep anywhere else," Jax assured me, pulling me towards him to kiss me on my forehead. "As much as I'd love to spend another night holding you, I don't think it would set a good first impression with your folks."

"Probably not," I shrugged. "But you're a step up in their eyes, so who knows?"

Jax laughed. "I'm a step up? Me with my long Metal-head hair and juiced out muscles? That's sad."

"Not really," I thought about Iain's profession...and age. "Wait, you don't do steroids, do you?!" I demanded, my eyes widening with surprise. Jax was deeply offended by my question, he actually stopped walking.

"No, I do not...thank you very much," he answered.

"Good, they make your junk shrink, and I happen to like yours the way it is," I laughed, pulling him towards my building.

"ARE YOU READY YET HARLOW?" Jenna's voice rang down our apartment hallway as I paced around my bedroom, packing my overnight bag. I knew Jax and Lucas were downstairs were waiting on us, but I was in the middle of having a panic attack about the whole thing.

It had been a stupid idea to say I would go home for Thanksgiving, and an even stupider idea to invite Jax. What had I been thinking?

As if Jenna could sense the coiled thoughts whirling around in my head, or hear my panted breathing, she appeared in my doorway with a sympathetic look on her face.

"I can't do this," I hissed, waving my hands toward the half packed overnight bag. "I don't want to go back there right now."

I hadn't been back, not since my last painful dinner the first year of University. I never *wanted* to go back. Sure, I had some good memories there...but most of those good memories were encased with bad ones. Bad experiences that tainted the good things that had happened...mainly Iain.

I didn't want to go back and be thrown right into those memories, and I definitely didn't want to have Jax there to witness the possible destruction.

"Harlow, relax," Jenna said, her voice soothing and gentle. She approached me slowly, as if afraid I would startle.

"What if..." I trailed off, thinking of all the possibilities at once and unable to grasp even just one to use as an example. I glanced over to my dresser, where the necklace Iain had given me still rested. I hadn't put it back on. Every so often, I had walk over and pick it up...just to look at it again, but putting it back on felt like a step backwards. I didn't want to go back, but I was about to head straight to where it all began.

"Relax, breathe," Jenna told me, gently squeezing my shoulders with her hands. "It's going to be fine. Your mom and Larry are not dumb enough to screw this up. You haven't been back and they know why, trust me. They will not screw it up."

"I'm not worried about them so much as me," I confessed, sitting down on my bed beside my half packed overnight bag. In fact, I was positive Mom and Larry wouldn't whisper a word about Iain. They wanted to forget about him, and they were ecstatic that I had finally moved on...or at least was trying to move on. My hand absently sought out the necklace I no longer wore.

"Don't let memories consume you," Jenna advised, a pained look crossing her features. It was as if she was speaking to the both of us. Going back to North Bay wasn't easy for Jenna, either, but she did it because that was where her family was. She wasn't going to let the demons of her past dictate where she would go.

My demons in that town were a broken heart and wounded pride. Drawing strength from Jenna, I stood up. I wouldn't let them dictate where I would go either.

"Okay," I said slowly, resuming the task of packing. "Okay," I repeated, more to myself. It didn't take me long to finish tossing the necessitates in my overnight bag, and before I knew it, we were in Jax's truck and on the highway headed to North Bay.

The drive to North Bay was a long one, nearly five hours.

With Lucas and Jenna in the back seat, and me up front with Jax, it didn't seem as long. We listened to music, talked about random topics from the latest trends (square beards and people photographing their food and posting it to social media) and passed the time laughing over the silly stories Jax shared about his time visiting Amsterdam.

Soon enough, we were waving goodbye to Jenna and Lucas as they walked up to Jenna's house. Jax reversed his truck, pulling carefully back out onto the crowded street. Seemed like everybody was home for Thanksgiving.

My old street was no different. An abundance of cars lined the street, making maneuvering his truck a slight challenge. Or it would have been, had I been the one driving. As it was, Jax showed no sign of being stressed. He pulled into the driveway I directed him.

It was nearly 4pm, and I knew Mom would already have dinner pretty much almost finished. The porch light was on. Mom's car was missing from it's usual spot, likely parked in the garage so that there would be enough space in the driveway for Jax to park his truck.

"Are you alright?" Jax questioned when I didn't immediately move to get out of the truck. He didn't seem nervous at all to be meeting my parents.

"Have you done this before?" I asked him, wondering if I was the only one anxious about the whole thing.

"Yeah, once or twice," Jax shrugged. "What...you've never brought a guy home before?"

"Nope," I said, shrugging at him. "First time for everything, right?" I added over my shoulder before I climbed out of the cab.

I waited for Jax to join me, nervously worrying my lip. I had absolutely no idea how this whole 'meeting my parents' thing was going to play out. I had lectured my mom a billion times on how not to embarrass me, but I still wasn't overly confident that she would pull through. And Larry...his over zealous personality was *a lot* to handle.

Jax took my hand and gently tugged, leading me up towards my own front porch. I didn't really know what to do, since I didn't actually live there anymore. Just walking in seemed wrong, especially with a new guest. Ringing the doorbell seemed too impersonal. Instead, I knocked tentatively on the door.

My mother was threw open the door with fervor. "Harlow! Honey! It's so good to see you!" she exclaimed, her voice breaking slightly. She pulled me into her arms for a massive hug. Her hands stroked the back of my head, like she used to do when I was a small child. I could feel her shaking with emotion, and when I looked at her, I was surprised to see her eyes were damp with unshed tears.

"Aw, Mom, don't do that..." I said, feeling uncomfortable. I knew she missed me, and that having me away at University was strange for her.

It had been the longest that we had gone without seeing each other since the day I was born. I hadn't realized just how difficult that was for her. Seeing her standing in front of me, a wide smile on her face as she struggled to keep her tears from flowing freely, well...it opened my eyes to what she must have been going through while I was busy isolating myself and putting the miles between me and this town...and her.

"I'm just so happy to see you," she said, trying to wave away both my discomfort and her emotional reaction. Her eyes rested on Jax, and she smiled. "You must be Jax, it's so nice to meet you!"

"Yup, I am. Thank you for having me, Mrs. Stevenson," Jax said politely, extending his hand to shake hers.

"Call me Lisa," Mom said warmly, clasping his large hand

with both of her dainty ones. "Larry! Harlow and Jax are here!" she called over her shoulder, presumingly to where Larry was. "He's turned the basement into a 'man cave', now I can scarcely get him out of it!" she explained to us, rolling her eyes.

We heard the tell-tale sound of footsteps on a stairwell, and the basement door opened to reveal my step-father.

Larry had lost some weight since the last time I had seen him. He was balding a little more, the remaining hair had turned gray. He was still rocking a thick mustache and the tweed pants and button up shirt.

He kept his distance from me, putting his hands in his pocket as he nodded in welcome. "We're glad you could make it home, Harlow," he said formally. I nodded, tucking a strand of hair behind my ear.

"This is Jax," Mom said, gesturing to him as if he was difficult to detect behind me.

Larry was silent for a moment, assessing Jax with his dark eyes. "Welcome to our home. Lisa's made up the guest room for you to stay in, Jax. If you want to put your bags in it."

"We'll do that later," I said, gently putting my hand on Jax's arm. I had insisted on leaving our bags in the truck so we could escape if things got weird. Jax could sense where I was coming from, and he gave me a reassuring smile.

"Well, come inside," Mom said, standing aside.

The house hadn't changed much from the days when I lived there. Mom and Larry had a very traditional way of decorating, and everything remained the same. I sank down on to the couch, Jax sitting beside me.

"Can I get you two anything to drink?" Mom asked, looking back and forth from Jax to I.

"Water would be good," Jax said, while I mumbled an incoherent no.

Mom nodded at Jax, smiling tightly as she disappeared into

the kitchen to grab the water. Larry sat down in his arm chair, pressing the palms of his hands down against the arm rests as he inspected Jax critically. I knew he was taking in Jax's tall and broad stature, and the long hair. Jax's hair, while longer than what Larry thought was traditionally appropriate for a male, was never unruly or uncooperative. Not a strand was ever out of place, I was pretty sure Jax could be stuck in a hurricane and once the winds died down, his hair would return to it's usual perfection.

"So, tell us about yourself," Larry broke the silence when Mom returned with a glass of water for Jax and a brandy for Larry. He accepted it and smiled his thanks to her before returning his stern gaze to Jax. "Is Jax short for something?"

Jax grinned, as if caught doing something embarrassing. "Yeah, it's short for Ajax."

"I didn't know that," I remarked, looking at him with amusement. He shrugged without apology.

"I don't often admit it," he winked at me.

"How old are you?" Larry's question prompted me to freeze. My eyes widened as I looked back and forth from Larry to my mom and held my breath.

"Larry," Mom said sharply, but Jax smiled.

"It's alright, I'm twenty-five," Jax answered, entertained. Larry nodded once in approval before moving on with his interrogation.

"Where did you grow up?" he asked.

"Lake Cowichan, British Columbia," Jax seemed unaffected by Larry's questions. He probably knew what to expect, after all...he'd done this before.

"Does your family still live there?" Larry continued, swishing the amber liquid in his tumbler slowly, never taking his eyes off of Jax's face.

"Yes Sir, they do," Jax stiffened ever so slightly, but relaxed again when Larry moved on.

"What are you in University for?"

"I'm almost done my final year. I'll be graduating with a Bachelors of Science in Psychology. After that, I hope to get funding to open a Mixed Martial Arts Gym that specializes in helping troubled youth."

Larry's eyebrows arched, he was impressed with Jax's answer.

"Honey, why don't you come help me in the kitchen?" Mom suggested, smiling at me as if to say *this might take a while.*

"Yeah, sure," I muttered, standing up and abandoning Jax to Larry's clutches. He didn't seem bothered by it in the slightest. I followed my mom into the kitchen. The scents of a deliciously cooked meal made my taste buds dance with anticipation. Everything was already prepared, and Mom's kitchen was spotless. She was never one to leave a mess, even in the middle of the chaos of cooking a huge dinner.

She walked over to the counter and picked up the dish towel, absently wiping at the already gleaming counter top.

"I've missed you a lot, Harlow," she said, her back to me.

"I know...I've missed you too Mom," I replied, feeling guilty.

"I understand why you left, and why you haven't been back," Mom continued, pausing so she could take a deep breath as she turned to face me. "I just hope you know that you are always welcome here, and that I - *we* - love you very much."

"I know. I've just been...busy," my excuse was weak, and we both knew it.

"Well, you're here now. That's all that matters." Mom stepped forward, putting her arms around me for another hug. I was still at first, but then my arms tentatively wrapped around her too.

My mom and I had never really had a relationship like that, where we could just hug each other out of the blue. When I was a kid, sure, but when I got older...I think she was afraid to try to hug me.

I was an unpredictable, unpleasant teenager. I felt bad for it now, for hurting her and lashing out at her, but I couldn't change my past.

"I'm sorry," I whispered, my head against her shoulder. She knew what I was apologizing for. The years of punishing her, for lashing out at her when I should have tried to let her in.

"It's okay, baby," Mom said softly, rubbing my upper back as she had when I was a child. She released me, stepping back to look at me. "Jax seems sweet," she smiled.

"Yeah, he is," I said. "I...I like him a lot."

"That's good honey," Mom hesitated, looking as if she had something she wanted to ask me. She shook her head, deciding against it. Instead, she smiled at me again. "I hope you're being safe."

I knew she was talking about sex. I rolled my eyes, exasperated. "Yes Mom, I've got it under control."

"Good, because I don't want any grand-babies until you're done university and married."

"Really Mom?" I raised my eyebrow, trying not to smile at her. I definitely thought it was *way* too soon to be thinking in terms like that, but I suppose mothers thought differently. They probably saw grand-babies everywhere.

"Really Harlow," Mom turned towards the counter and picked up a dish of beans. "Let's get the food to the table."

CHAPTER
TWELVE

"See? I told you it wouldn't be terrible!" Jenna said from the back seat on our drive home Monday morning. I rolled my eyes, smiling.

"Yeah, I guess not. What did you think?" I asked Jax, curious. I still didn't know what other questions Larry had asked, or if anything else was even said after Mom and I went into the kitchen.

"They're nice," Jax shrugged, looking at me for a moment and smiling. He returned to staring at the highway.

"Detailed," I remarked, shaking my head as Jax smirked in response. I turned my body so I could look into the back seat. "What about you, Lucas? How was meeting Jenna's parents?"

"It was interesting," Lucas confessed, earning a smack in the chest from Jenna.

"He did fine, they liked him," Jenna told me, almost proud. I knew that her parents approval was very important to Jenna. "Oh! And guess who I ran into?"

"Who?"

"Callie," Jenna pursed her lips. "I had to run to the convenience store to get cigars for my Grandpa, and she was there."

"How was that?"

"Oh, alright," Jenna said slowly, glancing at her nails as if there was something extremely interesting on them. "She's pregnant."

"Oh?"

"Yeah, says it's Riley's baby," Jenna looked up, giving a small, forced smile. "I congratulated her."

"That's good of you. It's a good thing I didn't run into her, punching her in her teeth wouldn't have been very appropriate."

"Who's Callie and why would you want to punch her in the teeth?" Jax asked, intrigued by our conversation.

"Callie is one of Jenna's old high school friends. She's a massive bitch, and I don't like her," I replied, thinking about all of the times Callie and her comrade in arms, Tara, had made Jenna feel like shit. They had called her a slut and spread rumors that she was making up the charges against Andrew because Andrew didn't want to be with her. All because Callie had a thing for Andrew.

I was also undeniably positive that Callie was one of the alleged victims that came forward after Iain's arrest to claim that he made unwanted advances on them too. She was an attention seeker, and I knew she wouldn't miss up an opportunity to cause drama.

We had nearly reached Ottawa city limits, and I was thankful. I couldn't wait to get back into my own apartment and relax. I'd been anxious the entire time we had been there. Nothing had happened, and things had gone about as smoothly as they could have, but being home was still difficult.

When it was time for bed that night, I had finally gone into my bedroom. Everything was as I left it, and I knew without looking that the photos from my trip to Niagara Falls would still be in the locked box under my bed. Everything reminded me of *him*, just as I feared it would. Only...the pain of remembrance was slight.

I tossed and turned all night, unable to fall asleep. I couldn't stop dissecting everything. I couldn't help but think about Jax, asleep in the guest room down the hall, and yet wonder where Iain was. I wondered what he was doing, and if he was okay. I didn't know how I still felt about Iain, but any time I thought about saying goodbye to Jax, my heart furiously rejected that idea.

By morning, I had figured out that I cared deeply about Jax, and that I wanted to be with him, and I didn't want a ghost of someone I used to know...and maybe didn't even know all that well...holding me back from truly falling.

The problem was...how did I say goodbye to the ghost of the past? How did I move forward with my future?

A large part of me felt that I had to tell Jax about Iain. I had to explain to him what was truly holding me back. He had a right to know. Another part of me argued that it was redundant, I was with Jax and we had a good thing going. Hearing about past loves would only ruin that. I certainly didn't want to think about Jax with another girl, meeting her family and making her laugh.

"Don't forget, we have to meet Brianna, Alissa and Crimson at noon," Jax reminded me, drawing me back from my complicated thoughts. "Professor Pedersen is expecting the first draft of our reports by Friday to check on our progress."

"Ugh, fine," I sighed, my lip curling in disdain. Jax reached across the seat, taking my hand from my lap.

"We'll get it over with quick," he winked at me. "I could think of a hundred better things to do today than hang out with them," he added with promise.

"Ew, guys...we're still here," Jenna snorted.

"Not for long," I retorted, watching our apartment building quickly approach. "We'll see you later," I told Jenna, nodding a goodbye at Lucas. We didn't have much time before we were had to meet with Crimson, Brianna and Alissa, but Jax's earlier promise had me long for some alone time. I watched as Jenna and Lucas grabbed their bags and jumped out of Jax's truck. They walked up to the apartment, holding hands and smiling at each other.

"So we've got an hour to kill before we have to meet them," Jax said, putting his truck in drive. "What do you want to do?"

"Could we go back to your place?" I asked coyly. Even though Jax rented a room and shared the living area, his room was completely off limits to any of the other house dwellers, meaning we wouldn't be interrupted.

"Hell yes," Jax grinned, revving the engine.

Jax's house was nearly empty, everyone had gone home for the holiday and had yet to return. I heard the sound of one person fleeing up the stairs when we came in, but by the time we made it up to the landing where Jax's room was, the person had vanished.

Jax didn't seem bothered by it, so I let it go. He unlocked his room, standing aside to let me in. Everything looked the way it had the last time I had been in his room. I turned to face Jax, and opened my mouth to speak.

My head was telling me to talk about this weekend, to talk about our relationship and maybe tell him about Iain, but my heart and body were both vigorously telling me something entirely different.

Fueled by the way Jax was watching me with unmasked desire, my blood heated and my mind quickly shut off. I pulled him towards me, our lips meeting with fevered intensity. His hands tugged at my shirt, pulling it up over my head. I stood back, allowing him the space to take his own shirt off. My hands explored his chest again, trying to commit to memory the exact curve and dip of each muscle.

While I was busy exploring him, Jax's hands were roaming my torso, igniting my skin as he traced my waistline. His hands drew patterns upward, until he was expertly unclasping my bra while he kissed my neck. I shrugged out of it, tossing it carelessly to the side. Jax's head dipped forward, his mouth dusting kisses from my collarbone to my breast.

I moaned, my head falling backwards and my hair spilling behind my shoulders.

"You're stunning," Jax told me, effortlessly picking me up. My legs went around his hips. I felt like there was truly no where else that I would rather be.

Our first time together had been more rushed, I had been so desperate to just have him in me. This time, Jax was taking his time. He was intent on getting to know me in ways he hadn't yet. It was as if our bodies were speaking a different language, one that they were fluent in.

"Jax," I pleaded as he pulled my jeans and the lace underwear I wore off. He tossed them carelessly to the ground. It hardly seemed fair that I was completely undressed and he was still wearing his jeans. I withered, trying to shimmy myself up so that I could help rectify that problem.

"Not yet," he grinned, lowering his head between my legs.

———

Jax and I were a little bit late for our meet up with Crimson, Brianna and Alissa. The chosen venue was The Buzz Restaurant, and I could see Brianna and Alissa waiting at a table. We approached them, Jax holding my hand. Brianna looked at the contact and pursed her lips. I had absolutely no doubt that she was hoping the drama that happened at her party would put an end to Jax and I.

"Where's Crimson?" I asked, sitting down across from Alissa. Jax dropped down into the chair beside me, his hand absently finding my thigh under the table. He gave me a reassuring squeeze, letting me know he was right there with me. He knew I was still angry with Crimson for what she had said in the Psychology hall that day.

"Oh? You didn't hear?" Brianna's expression could almost be described as delightful. "Crimson's boyfriend tried to offed himself. He probably got sick of listening to her excessive babbling," Brianna added, smirking cruelly as if she found it hilarious. She probably did.

"Brianna, that was really mean," Alissa scolded, frowning at her friend.

"Sorry," Brianna said without meaning. She shrugged as if it couldn't be helped.

I felt the air leave my lungs in a whoosh. "What do you mean?"

"I mean, he tried to kill himself," Brianna rolled her eyes, as if she found me completely obtuse and had absolutely no time to explain things. "We've already done our part in the project, so let's hear yours." Brianna sighed, bored.

I didn't need to ask why Cole would try and kill himself. The harsh things I had said to him the other night came rushing back to me. The colour completely drained from my face. I could feel Jax's hand squeezing my thigh again, trying to comfort me. It was a strange situation.

"But he's okay?" Jax asked, giving Brianna a no-nonsense look.

"Yeah, he's fine. Crimson found him in time and got him to the hospital," Alissa explained. "He's at The Ottawa Hospital. She's there now with him, from what her text message said."

Jax took a deep breath. "Don't you think it's imperative that we wait for Crimson to be here? This assignment isn't due for another two weeks. It seems kind of inconsiderate to meet without her, given what she's going through right now."

Brianna sighed dramatically. "Alright, pretty boy. We'll postpone the group meeting."

"Um, yeah," I muttered, pulling out our notes to hand to Brianna and Alissa. They read it over while Jax looked at me.

"Let's meet up in another week," I suggested, challenging Brianna by looking at her through narrowed eyes. "When Crimson can be here." I was practically daring her to say something else about Crimson. She looked as if she was about to take the bait, but Alissa nudged her sharply.

"Sounds fair," Alissa nodded, she gave Brianna another warning look. "I hope she's okay."

Jax stood up, looking down at me. I wordlessly grabbing my bag and nodded to Alissa, narrowed my eyes at Brianna again, before I followed Jax outside.

"What are you thinking?" Jax asked once we had gotten back outside and were walking to his truck.

"That I should go..." I trailed off. I knew that aside from myself and Jax, Crimson only really talked to Brianna and Alissa. By the looks of things, neither girl was going to show up and offer support to Crimson during this difficult time. Plus, something was telling me that I should go.

If the guy was going to kill himself over it, maybe he did have something to say that I needed to hear. Attackers who felt absolutely no remorse did not track you down to apologize, then try to commit suicide. Something just wasn't sitting well with me...

"I'll drive you," Jax offered. I nodded my thanks, relieved to have him near me. He reached out for my hand.

I didn't know where the hospital was, but Jax seemed to. We drove in silence, with me locked in my own head.

I didn't know if going to see Crimson at the hospital was a good idea or a bad idea. I wasn't sure if facing Cole right now was a good idea. I wanted to look at him and demand to know why he thought he had a right to check out early.

If I was being honest with myself, I was doing it of guilt. I felt guilty that I hadn't listened to Cole, and that he had tried to kill himself as a result. There was a time that I really cared about him, that I was enthralled with him. Of course, that time had *long* since passed...but still.

Plus, I had a request to make of him. If he *really* wanted forgiveness from me, he was going to have to do something brave and selfless...and I wasn't all that sure if he had it in him.

"Do you want me to come with you?" Jax asked, parking his truck and waiting for me to respond.

"Yeah...if you don't mind," I answered, chewing on my lip. What I was going to ask Cole was heavy, really heavy.

We walked into the hospital. Jax took my hand without question, encasing me with warmth. I loved that I didn't have to explain myself to him. Any other guy would demand to know why I was going to visit the girlfriend of my rapist in the hospital. Not Jax, he just understood.

We walked around, not really knowing where to look for them. Jax approached the information desk. "Hi," he said, smiling at the young nurse behind the counter. "Could you tell us what floor Cole Carmichael is on?"

The nurse, dazzled by Jax, blinked a few times before she quickly got to typing on her computer. "What are your names?" she asked, not looking up.

"Jax Walker and Harlow Jones," Jax answered.

After a moment, the nurse looked back at him and smiled

apologetically. "I'm sorry honey, he's got a restricted visitors list."

"Darn," Jax sighed, scratching his head. "Well we're here to pick up Cole's girlfriend, she hasn't slept in days...I just can't remember what floor she said he was on, and she isn't answering her phone."

The nurse seemed to be thrown off by Jax's dashing smile. "Sorry, I can't give you that information. Why don't you try the cafeteria?" She gestured to the corridor to the left of the information desk.

Jax smiled at her. "Thank you so much for your help."

I shot him a bemused look. I'd never actually seen a guy attempt to work his looks to get information from someone before. Usually, females were guilty of that.

"Nice," I remarked. We made our way down the corridor, following the signs towards the cafeteria. I gave Jax a wan smile as he reached for my hand.

We didn't have to look long for her, the tell-tale shock of Crimson's hair against the off-white walls of the hospital drew my eyes almost immediately to her. She was heading back from the cafeteria, a cup of coffee in her hand.

Her red hair was a tangled mess of knots, as if she hadn't brushed it in days. Her eyes were red rimmed from crying, and her nose was irritated, probably from blowing it too much. She was wearing clothes that looked wrinkled and had a few tiny old coffee stains. She obviously had been at the hospital for a few days.

I felt bad, it was no way to spend Thanksgiving weekend.

"What are you doing here?" Crimson's voice sounded nasally, raw from crying. I shifted from foot to foot, uncomfortable.

"We wanted to make sure you were okay," I answered,

looking at Jax. He had his hands in pockets, and his jaw was tense, but he looked at Crimson with warmth and compassion.

"Oh yeah, I'm grand," Crimson said, her voice dripping with sarcasm. I almost laughed. It was so different from her bubbly, vibrant regular self. She saw me biting back a smile, and her lips perked up slightly.

"I heard about...what happened," I said, lifting my hands slightly before I dropped them at my sides again. I had no idea what to do with them. Part of me wanted to hug this girl, who was clearly suffering, but I wasn't the huggy type. I didn't really 'do' the whole hug thing, at least not with people I wasn't close to. Given my recent history with Crimson...

She sighed deeply. "I'll be okay, I guess. It's just a shock. I didn't realize Cole was hurting that bad...like, I knew he felt bad about everything...but..."

"Do you think Cole would talk to me for a minute? I think I'm ready to hear him out," I said, my voice wavering. Jax's hand found mine and squeezed gently.

"You don't have to do this," he whispered.

"I know I don't have to," I told him, keeping my voice even. "But I'm more than what happened to me. I won't let it take control of me anymore...I need closure."

Jax nodded, understanding. Crimson watched our exchange with sad eyes.

"Yeah, that's not possible right now," she replied sadly. "He's in a medically induced coma. They pumped his stomach. He took his entire bottle of Effexor and had a major seizure in the ambulance. He's had five more since..."

"Oh," I muttered.

"Yeah," Crimson said, drawing in a shaky breath. The bags under her eyes hinted at how exhausted she must be.

"Do you need a lift home?" Jax asked, his expression gentle.

"No, I'm waiting for Cole's parents to get here. They were

in Whistler for Thanksgiving," Crimson answered, distracted. "I appreciate you guys coming by, but honestly...I would kind of like to be alone right now."

"We understand," I told her, hesitating. "And Crimson...if you need anything, let me know, okay?"

"I will," Crimson assured me, heading down the hallway towards the banks of elevators.

Jax and I walked back to his truck in a heavy blanket of silence.

"I don't know what you're thinking," Jax commented, reaching into his jacket pocket to grab his keys. He kept his eyes trained on my face, imploring me to look at him. "But you should not feel guilty about what happened. You had every right to say what you did. Cole's actions are Cole's alone."

"I know," I said, and I did know it. I wasn't just agreeing with him to shut him up. I lingered for a moment, wondering if I should fill Jax in on the dark things I was thinking. "I just figured..."

"What?" he asked, gently guiding my chin up so that he could look into my eyes.

"If he truly feels remorse for what happened...why doesn't he turn himself in? Why doesn't he give a statement?"

Jax drew in a deep breath, considering my words as he studied my face. "That's why you wanted to come tonight."

"Yeah," I dropping my gaze. I was uncomfortable with the confession. I didn't want to seem like a cold-hearted bitch, which...I suppose I kind of was, considering I was prepared to walk into Cole's room and demand that he turn himself in. "When he came by my work the other night...I didn't truly believe he was sorry for it. I still don't want to hear his *why*, not really anyway. I realize now that I want to see justice...I want to see something done."

I had been asking "why" for years, and then when Cole back

up in my life, I realized that I didn't really need a reason why my first boyfriend had betrayed me like that. I needed closure, the kind of closure I could only get from seeing those that hurt me suffer legal repercussions, or any kind of repercussions.

My memories of the night had always been foggy, due to the Rohypnol in my system, but I knew without a doubt the whole thing had been premeditated. Who brings roofies to a party for any other reason?

It angered me to think that Iain had severed time for being with me, *with my consent*, while Cole and the other guys at that party suffered no repercussions for the horrible things they had done to me.

A constant, reoccurring fear of mine is that they continued to do that to other girls, girls like Jenna. I could have stopped it back then, or at least reported it. It was too late now, unless I had a witness willing to testify.

Cole could be that witness. If he truly felt remorse for his actions and truly wanted me to forgive him, he could give a statement.

The only problem was, Cole was in a coma. I had no idea if he would even wake up for it, and if he did...if he would even *want* to turn himself and his old friends in.

THE NEXT DAY, Jax was waiting for me outside of my Social Criticism class. He took me into his arms, holding me close to him. "How are you doing?"

"I'm actually okay," I answered honestly. It was a waiting game to see when Cole would come out of the coma, or if he would...I had no idea what his medical state was. I was hoping that Crimson would be in class so we could talk about it.

"Good," Jax said, exhaling deeply. He gently caught my chin with his hand and lifted my face so I was looking into his eyes. "If you want to talk about things...I'm here, okay?"

"I know," I smiled with appreciation. "But like I said, I'm honestly okay. I can't really do anything until Cole wakes up anyway. I can't get his statement when he's in a coma." Jax nodded in agreement.

I loved that about he was willing to just be there for me...for whatever I needed. I love that he wouldn't press, either, and he hadn't. He knew I had secrets, and he knew that in my own time...I would come to him with them. I got the sense that he would allow me all the time in the world if I needed it.

I knew I was going to have to tell him about Iain sooner rather than later, but I didn't want to heap too much onto his shoulders at once. He was already trying to help me deal with the whole Cole thing.

"Well, I've got to get to class...but I'll see you later, okay?" Jax raised his eyebrows at me in question.

"I work until 9, but you'll probably show up anyway," I said.

"Yup, need my night-time coffee fix," Jax agreed with humor. He kissed me quickly on the lips. "I'll see you tonight," he added, backing away and heading towards the Political Science building.

My next class was Gender Studies, a class that I shared with Crimson. For the first time ever...I was hoping she would be in class and willing to talk to me. Before our falling out, I could never get her to *stop* talking, so me hoping she would talk to me was a completely unlikely event.

I glanced around the classroom, looking for her red hair. I spotted her towards the back of the classroom. She had showered recently, and had attempted to tame her hair a little by pulling it back in a messy pony tail.

She slumped over in her seat, her expression one of quiet sadness. The regular exuberance she vibrated with was absent. I made my way through the desks, weaving around other students' legs and bags, and sat down in the desk beside her.

"Hey," I said softly. Crimson made no move that she had heard me. I shook my head, feeling foolish. Of course she hadn't heard me...I hadn't spoken loudly enough and she wasn't looking at me. It was easy to forget Crimson was partially deaf, especially with her dainty hearing aids. I knew a lot of the time, she read lips to understand what people were saying. I would have to speak up if I wanted her to hear me. "Hi," I said again, louder this time.

"Hi," Crimson said, seeming surprised that I was sitting beside her. She sat up a little, still picking at the small hole in the center of her desk.

"How are you doing?" I asked, instantly regretting my question as Crimson winced. "Right, stupid question." I added. She gave me a small smile, but otherwise said nothing.

I sat back in my chair, thinking. I didn't know how I was going to get through to Crimson and let her know that I was there for her. I frowned thoughtfully, trying to remember how I had bridged the gap with Jenna.

"How is he doing?" I asked, trying to bite back my personal agenda. This wasn't just about my end goal, about seeing justice for what had happened to me. This was also about a girl who's boyfriend tried to kill himself, and how alone she must feel right now.

"Stable," Crimson responded. She looked at me. "He's still in the coma. His seizures are starting to slow...it's all a waiting game. It could be three days, it could be seven." She shrugged, wiping a tear from her eye. "Then they have to test to see if he suffered any brain damage from the seizures."

"I'm sorry," I told her again, my grand plan to seek justice deflating at the mention of brain damage. If Cole suffered brain damage, then he wouldn't be able to testify...and I would not be able to get justice. It was a selfish thought and I knew it, but I was only human.

"Don't apologize," Crimson muttered, her gaze falling back to that spot on her desk. "It's not your fault that he did what he did."

"You know you can talk to me about it, Crimson," I told her honestly. "I can't imagine how painful it must be for you...and regardless of what happened between...him and I...you're a sweet girl, and I don't want you feeling like you're alone."

"I am alone," Crimson answered, raising her eyes to meet mine again.

CHAPTER
THIRTEEN

Cole woke up from his medically induced coma on day seven. Crimson had missed the Psychology seminar, so I text messaged her to see if everything was okay. I'd been talking to her every day, taking time to ask how both she and Cole were doing...and not just because I needed Cole to wake up so I could talk to him, but because I generally cared about Crimson's feelings.

The way she had told me she was all alone, with such a lonesome, broken look in her eye had broken my heart. It was still important to me to talk to Cole about confessing, but I could wait.

At first, she was hesitant of my intentions. It made me feel a little guilty to know they weren't entirely innocent. Slowly, she warmed up to the idea that I cared about what she was feeling, because I did care.

On the day that Cole woke up, Jax and I were sitting on a bench on Tabaret Lawn, sipping hot apple cider during a recess between classes. Between both of our hectic class and work schedules, it was getting harder and harder to find time together, but Jax always thought of the most creative ways to see me, even just fleeting. Our little in between class dates were a regular, familiar thing that enveloped me in light, happy feelings.

The cold crisp late October air was a refreshing welcome from the stuffy lecture halls and classrooms. With Jax's warm body beside me, I felt at peace...even when I read the text from Crimson.

"Cole's awake," I told him, nestling closer to his embrace. We would have to part ways soon, and even though I knew I would see him again soon...I still wasn't in any rush for our time together to end.

"Any sign of brain damage?" Jax asked, his voice hard and the arm around my shoulders tensing slightly. Jax understood, but he still didn't like Cole, or rather...what Cole had done. I knew it made Jax angry, but he never put that anger on me, or even showed it aside from the tensing of taut muscles.

"Crimson says that he seems alert and alright, but they'll do more tests later," I answered, slipping my phone back into my pocket.

"She'll probably want a few days with him," Jax remarked.

"I know." My phone notification dinged again. I grabbed it out of my pocket, frowning as I read the message. "Um. Crimson says that Cole wants to talk to me...soon."

Jax knew how important this little quest was to me, so he stood up. "We'll go now then." he said.

"Don't you have an assignment due?" I asked, arching an eyebrow.

"Ah, right," Jax countered, frowning.

"Don't worry," I assured him. "I'll walk over. Nothings really happening in my Sociology class anyway today. Just a lecture that I can snag from the bulletin board."

"Are you sure?" Jax didn't seem thrilled with my suggestion. I'm sure the idea of having his girlfriend go off to talk to her attacker without him wasn't an enduring one. I wrapped my arms around his neck, hoping to provide reassurance.

"It'll be okay," I whispered, my face close to his. The wind tossed our hair around each other, I ignored the tickling sensation as I leaned forward to kiss him softly on the lips.

"I don't know..." Jax took a deep breath, his eyes searching my face. I brought my hand up to touch his strong jawline, my fingers brushing against the tight beard he was now sporting.

"I'm not afraid of him," I told him, holding his gaze so that he would know I was completely honest. I wasn't afraid of Cole Carmichael. He was weak and cowardly, and I knew from our last few encounters that he couldn't hurt me anymore.

Jax smiled, the unmasked love and affection for me that showed on his face was making my heart stutter in my chest. "I believe that," his lips found mine again, and he kissed me tenderly. "Text me though, okay? I still don't like the idea of you walking around alone. I'll meet you there to drive you home."

"It's day time," I pointed out, my brow arching with slight aggravation. I didn't like being perceived as helpless or weak, and while I wasn't a fan of walking places alone...I definitely wasn't going to surrender to the notion that women couldn't walk from point A to point B without a chaperon. They should be able to.

"They still haven't caught the guy that's been attacking women, and two more have come forth," Jax pointed out, the voice of reason. I knew he didn't mean to make me feel helpless. "Which is why I keep telling you, get your sexy rear to the gym. I'll teach you some self-defense. For *my* peace of mind," Jax added, his gold bordered eyes pleading with me. When he looked at me like that, I wanted to give in to whatever demands he had. It was a good thing Jax wasn't in the habit of making demands.

I knew he was right, the predator was still out there. It wouldn't hurt to have a couple self-defense lessons under my belt. I had been putting it off for weeks now, and it was something that I knew Jenna would benefit from.

"He doesn't attack during the day," I countered, standing up and adjusting my bag strap so it rested more comfortably on my shoulder.

I had finally heard back from Officer Mike Turner, by way of a voice message telling me that Andrew Cooper's last known where abouts had been in Sudbury. It alarmed me that he had moved back to Ontario, but I couldn't find any just cause in freaking out about it. Officer Turner assured me that Andrew was nowhere near Ottawa. Still, someone else was there out...and it definitely wasn't Cole. The two new incidents had occurred when Cole was in his medically induced coma.

"I know, but again...it's mostly for my peace of mind," Jax stood up too, his hands gripping my waist as he pulled me towards him. He kissed me deeply, channeling all his desire into it. When Jax kissed me, I had never felt more cherished. Jax just had a way of making me feel as if I was the most intriguing, beautiful girl on earth.

"I'll see you later," I promised, reluctantly pulling away from his embrace. I felt the cold more without his hands on me. Jax grinned as I turned around. He remained at the bench for a moment longer, watching me walk away, before he headed to his class.

I couldn't shake Jax's concern, and even though it was early afternoon, my skin prickled with the sensation that I was being watched. I didn't see anything amiss around me, students were walking all over campus. Still, that prickly sensation grew. I ended up fishing my phone out of my pocket to call a cab. My nerves were on fire, I obsessively checked around me as I wanted for the cab to pull up.

I breathed a sigh of relief when I saw the black car pull to a stop in front of me. I hopped in quickly, already feeling safer and less exposed. I told myself I was just letting Jax's concerns get to me. Shaking my head, I fired out directions to the Ottawa Hospital.

The drive took 15 minutes during rush hour. The cab driver pulled up in front of the hospital, and I grumbled as I handed him the last of my cash. Cabs were so bloody expensive.

Crimson had texted me the floor and room number. Cole was on the 8th floor, in room 305. I headed toward the bank of elevators, not bothering to stop at the information desk. The ride up to the 8th floor seemed to take forever. My stomach churned with nervousness. It seemed to surreal to be going to visit this particular monster of my past in a hospital, to hear him out and ask him a favor. If I had been told that two years ago that I would be doing this, I would have laughed hysterically.

I had absolutely *no* intention of ever seeing Cole Carmichael again.

The elevator doors opened to the 8th floor, and I stepped out into the hall, my hands shaking. Crimson was waiting near the elevators, I'd told her I was on my way.

"Hey," I said, inspecting her warily.

Crimson looked relieved, but also hesitant.

"Hi," she tried to smile. "I won't lie, I'm not sure if this is a good idea...Cole is, well. Cole isn't himself."

I nodded. Of *course* Cole wasn't himself, he had just woken up from a medically induced coma after trying to take his own life.

I followed Crimson down the hallway as she led the way past the nursing station, toward Cole's room.

Cole was in a small room, the privacy curtains opened to reveal his hospital bed. Cole's eyes were closed, he was resting. His skin looked pale and moist, and he had large bags under his eyes. His arms were resting on top of the hospital blanket, and I noticed for the first time that his arms were marred from the wrist up with faint pale scars.

My mind had painted Cole in such a twisted, evil, monstrous light that I failed to realize until that very moment that he had been a boy. I didn't know what prompted him to do what he had done, and that didn't matter. What mattered is I had given him a major platform in my mind and fears.

In that moment, I let it go. I released the hold that Cole had had on me. I still didn't forgive him for it, but I let go of the hatred that twisted me up inside. Cole was a cowardly person, and he suffered from his decision to hurt me. That much was obvious.

I stood towards the back of the room, scarcely breathing. Crimson approached his bed and gently took his hand.

"Cole," she said softly. "Harlow is here."

Cole's eyes fluttered open. He looked at me with shame and regret.

"I'm sorry Harlow, for what I did to you. I really am. I don't deserve to live." Cole's voice was scratchy and raw, likely from the tubes he'd had in his throat for nearly a week.

I crossed my arms, my eyes narrowing at him. "You think you can just check out? You did a horrific thing, and you think that your punishment should be the easy way out. That's a cowardly move."

Crimson's eyes widened, she had caught the majority of what I had said. "Harlow!" she scolded, outraged.

"It's fine," Cole told her, squeezing her hand. A tear escaped the corner of his eye. "She's right. I am a coward."

"No, no you're not," Crimson argued, stroking his strawlike hair in a soothing matter, as if he was was a child that needed comforting.

"Crimson, I...I let it happen," Cole reminded her. Crimson's gaze desperately darted to me.

"She doesn't know the whole thing," she replied, her voice breaking. "She couldn't know."

"Know what?" I demanded, my foot tapping angrily on the floor. "What are you talking about?"

Cole looked as if he was choking on something. He looked from Crimson with pleading eyes to me, panic and heartbreak clear on his face.

"He never raped you, Harlow," Crimson exclaimed. "Yeah, he threw the party. But it was Casey who drugged you."

The cloudy memories from that night swirled around in my head. I still remembered Cole on top of me, Cole with his hands down my pants. I glared at him, my heart pounding.

"Casey told me that all girls say no, that you have to help them relax. He said that he would fix you a drink, with vodka, and you'd let go of being scared and..."

"And you *believed* that?!" I yelled, shaking with anger.

Cole looked at me with regret and shame. "I didn't know what to believe. I..." he trailed off, unable to continue.

"She will never understand if you don't tell her," Crimson said, gently touching his face. Cole closed his eyes, turning his face into her hand. He started to sob, making huge ugly gulping sounds.

"I can't," he sputtered.

My blood was boiling, but I controlled my breathing. This wasn't going to go anywhere if I didn't get it together.

"Cole, just tell me. I think I deserve to know what happened that night...and why."

Cole opened his eyes, studying me hopelessly. After a

moment, he took a shaky breath. "I didn't know any better, because that's what...that's how I was introduced to...that."

What he was saying didn't make any sense. I stared at Crimson, waiting for clarification. He nodded at her, giving her permission. Obviously, she knew the tale. My eyes narrowed at her. I felt betrayed by her all over again.

"I'm sorry Harlow, it wasn't my place to say...I tried to tell you to talk to him...I knew you needed to hear it. I just," Crimson shrugged helplessly. The emotions in the hospital room were running extremely high. She inhaled sharply. "Cole is a victim, too."

"A victim?" I raised my eyebrows.

"I was inexperienced, and I looked to Casey and the other guys for guidance. They made me believe that all girls were nervous about it, and that they had to drink a little to relax. We were all drunk...I didn't know that Casey drugged your drink. You and me...we started kissing and fooling around. I stuck my hand down your pants and you were...moaning and stuff, and I thought that was right. But you wouldn't look at me, and your eyes kept rolling into the back of your head, and I realized that something wasn't right. So I got up asked Casey what he did. He said you were just drunk, and to just do it. I couldn't... Casey started laughing at me. I tried to punch him, but he blocked it and punched me in the guts. Logan and Gavin held me while Casey went over to the couch where you were. Casey...did things, and when I struggled...Logan and Gavin took turns punching me."

I felt dizzy. Cole's words were calling back more of that suppressed night.

"Was it...was it only Casey?" I whispered, my voice shaking.

Cole nodded painfully. "Yeah."

"Why didn't you say anything? Why didn't you tell on them?" I demanded, my eyes wet with unshed tears.

"I was afraid. It was my word against theirs...and they had pictures of me..."

"Doing what?"

Cole closed his eyes tightly, as if he couldn't stand to look at me. "Of me with my hands down your pants. And you look unconscious. Casey told me if I told anyone, he'd show the pictures. It looked like it was me. He said there was no evidence of what really happened."

I nodded stiffly. That made sense, I guess. "What about the rumors?"

"Casey started them. He told everyone that you hooked up with all of us at once, and that's why we broke up. After they left, I got you home. I couldn't even look at you, I was so ashamed of myself."

I remembered that part. I remembered feeling sore and disoriented, and having Cole struggle to carry me back to my apartment. I remembered how he wouldn't look at me, how his arms shook. I didn't clue in on what happened until I woke up the next morning, covered in dry blood and vomit.

"Do you have any idea what it feels like to wake up bloody and violated?" I demanded, stepping towards his bed threateningly. "To believe the rumors you hear about yourself, because there's no other explanation? To have the ENTIRE school turn on you and say such horrible things to you?"

"No," Cole said, bowing his head. "I never forgave myself for any of it. It was my fault. My fault for putting you in that situation. It's like you said, I'm a monster. I could have told someone, I could have done something...and I didn't."

"You are weak," I agreed heatedly. Crimson was sobbing quietly beside him.

I looked away from them both, the tears pouring down my cheeks freely. It was some what of a relief to find out that that it hadn't been the "entire" basketball team, but the memory of

Casey's twisted face made me feel no better about it. My stomach churned with disgust. I turned around, intending to leave without saying another word.

"I'm sorry," Cole said again, his voice wavering. I paused in the doorway of his room and looked back at him.

"If you're truly sorry Cole? Truly sorry? I want you to come forward. I want you to turn them in. Casey, for what he did, and the rest of them for letting it happen."

I stumbled out of the hospital, my cheeks still wet with tears. I didn't even care that complete strangers were staring at me with pity. I walked blindly towards the street, barely paying any attention to my surroundings at all.

Suddenly, Jax was there, jogging up to me. His face was full of concern and worry. His large arms wrapped around me, pulling me tightly to his chest.

My sobs were muffled in the material of his jacket, his large hand cupping the back of my head as he held me.

That night, I told Jax what Cole had revealed to me while we laid together in my bed. My head was resting against Jax's chest, my left leg through over his legs with his arm around me.

"I just don't know what to do," I confessed, sighing. "He's right...there's no proof and it's his word against theirs." I lifted my head up, reading Jax's face.

"Maybe the other guys will testify against this Casey asshole," Jax told me, his hand stroking my back over my oversized sleep t-shirt. His shoulders moved as he shrugged. "I doubt they'll all still friends."

"Who knows," I relented, my eyes fluttering, heavy with fatigue. I felt so drained, and Jax felt so warm and comfortable. "Spend the night?" I asked him, nestling closer into his arms. Ever since the first time I'd accidentally fallen asleep in his arms, I had been careful to not have a repeat. I didn't want Jax to think I was the kind of girl who would move her toothbrush in after a couple of hookups.

"Thought you'd never ask," Jax said through his smile. He kissed my forehead. Jax's scent of amber, sandalwood and spice lifted me into a deep, peaceful sleep.

FOURTEEN

The next few weeks passed by in rapid procession. At first, interacting with Crimson was challenging. She didn't exactly receive my request of Cole very well, but neither of us mentioned it. I knew Cole was still recovering from his suicide attempt. Crimson told me he was an inpatient at the hospital on suicide watch.

It would likely be a while before he got back to me about my request, and I had to be okay with that. Pressuring him wouldn't help speed anything up, and I was starting to think that there would never be any legal repercussion for Casey. I couldn't even remember the guy's last name, and Cole was right - it *was* his word against theirs. Who knew if Casey still had the photos?

There was no time to worry about it, my heavy coarse load demanded my attention. Preparing for finals and finishing up the major group assignments took all of my concentration, and before I knew it...my world was blanketed in snow and frigid temperatures. Christmas break was upon us.

I wouldn't find out what my final marks were in each of my

classes for at least a week, but I was relieved to no longer have to deal with Brianna and Alissa on a semi-regular basis. Group work with them had been a headache like no other.

Jax was desperate to take my mind off of University and the Cole thing. I had finally surrendered to the self-defense classes. Jenna and I were subjected to the torment of physical exertion each Sunday night. We had learned how to get out of potential holds, where to kick and how much force to apply to hits. In addition to self-defense, Jax showed us a couple of basic MMA moves.

After four sessions, I could understand how having a Mixed Martial Arts gym would help troubled youth. It was a great outlet, and very therapeutic. I left each session with tender muscles and a clear head. Plus, watching Jax in action did strange things to my blood.

He didn't stop there, though, He continued to take me out on fun dates. Which is why I found myself at the Rideau Canal Skateway, lacing up rental skates on a Friday night. Jax stood in front of me, already laced up in his skates. He was wearing a pair of jeans, his thick black winter coat, a black Timberland winter cap and thick gloves.

I wore my new red North Face coat, the black cowl scarf, a thick beanie, and warm mittens, which rested on the bench beside me as I attempted to tie my skates up.

"Ugh, these are impossible," I grumbled, frowning. I had never been skating before, and I was admittedly having trouble with the laces. Jax smiled, shaking his head. He pealed off his own gloves and crouched down, expertly tying my laces tightly up within seconds. "That's annoying," I told him, narrowing my eyes at him.

"What's annoying?" he asked innocently as he stood up.

"How good you are at everything," I rolled my eyes, attempting to stand up. My feet slid apart, and I fell backwards onto the bench smartly. "This is a terrible idea, for the record."

Jax chuckled at me as he helped me up into a standing position. I wobbled, unfamiliar with the ice and the skates. Jax slowly glided backwards, his hands clasped to my arms securely. He held my gaze, those warm brown eyes with the golden rim looking straight into my soul. I smiled, my apprehensive mood melting away. Sure, I might fall on my ass a thousand times, but Jax would be there to pick me up.

I was starting to appreciate that. Before, I hated the idea of someone rescuing me, of needing someone. I had rejected that notion with venom, especially after Iain. Now, I was learning that it wasn't such a terrible thing, to have someone who wanted to be the arms that caught you when you fell. To want them there.

It wasn't like Jax wanted to do all the rescuing, either. He was teaching me to face my fears, to approach uncertainty regardless of the outcome. He was even giving me tools to rescue and defend myself, by way of the self-defense classes.

Jax pulled me closer to him, still anchoring me safely in his arms. He kissed me softly, his warm lips tasting mine.

My heart raced, simply from the way he was looking at me, holding me, and kissing me. Jax could convey all his feelings by simply being. He didn't hide anything from me.

But I was still hiding something from him. A lot of things, really. Mainly, my true feelings for him...how deeply I had fallen for him in such a short time. How those feelings overwhelmed and scared me. *Why* they overwhelmed and scared me, and how the ghost of my past still crept into my thoughts when he shouldn't.

"I'm going to let go now," Jax said, his voice drawing me back to the present. He slowly skated back a little, keeping his hands near mine in case he needed to grab them. "Take turns moving your feet forward, slowly and carefully...that's it. See? It's not so hard."

We skated for a while, holding hands. My moves were choppy and slow, unsteady on the slippery ice. Making conversation was difficult to do when I had to put so much concentration into not falling on my ass. Plus, the beauty of the Rideau Canal left me speechless. The canal was illuminated with purple and blue lights, giving a soft, romantic glow to all the skaters. Snow was falling at a leisurely pace.

I watched as a couple glided past us effortlessly. The girl twirled in a circle, laughing as ice shavings danced around her skates. They looked like professionals.

"I doubt I'll ever be able to do that," I warned him, feeling unsteady on my feet.

"Maybe by next year," Jax grinned. "You're not doing too bad for your first time."

As if he had jinxed me, I slipped and fell down onto the hard ice.

"Okay, I'm done now," I said after he helped me up. I gingerly rubbed my behind. "Can we go back to my place now? Maybe snuggle up under my *warm* blankets? Naked, perhaps?"

"Not fair," Jax said, mock pouting at me. "I wanted to do a romantic date night, and you're luring me to your bed like an evil temptress." Even as he spoke, he was directing us back to the benches where we had left our boots.

"Is that a yes?" I asked, innocently batting my lashes. He winked at me, gently helping me sit down on the bench before he dropped down beside me.

"That's a hell yes," he answered, leaning towards me to kiss me.

A few days later I had a rare day off work. Jenna and I decided to head to the St. Laurent Centre to do some Christmas shopping.

"I honestly have no idea what to get Jax," I complained, aimlessly searching through another department store. *Nothing* had caught my eye all day. He hadn't given me any ideas at all.

"Maybe you need to get him something that *isn't* in a mall," Jenna recommended. She was loaded down with shopping bags. Jenna took her Christmas shopping *very* seriously. "He likes that MMA stuff, right?"

"Yeah..."

"Get him tickets to one of those UFC fights everyone's always talking about," Jenna suggested, shrugging.

"Oh my God, you're a genius," I told her, grinning as she disappeared into H&M. I found her at the sales rack, holding up a pair of crocodile print leather jeans. She snickered at me.

"I actually think these would look really hot on you," she told me, trying to hand them to me.

"Um, no thanks," I laughed, shoving her hand away. "I don't do crocodile print."

Jenna's laughter dropped away as she squinted towards the front of the store in disbelief. I turned around, my breath whooshing from my lungs as I caught sight of the familiar dirty blond hair and piercing Caribbean blue eyes of my twelfth grade English teacher.

Iain stared at me in shock, the pair of jeans he was holding dropped back down to the table he had picked them up from. He had lost a little weight, but it was still undeniably him. His hair was a little longer, and he had a slight hint of stubble across his jaw. His eyes locked with mine, and I felt a small shiver of desire, as if the past two years hadn't happened...as if we had never parted ways.

Jenna touched my arm, a frown on her face. "Harlow, I don't think -"

"I need to talk to him," I muttered, avoiding her look. I felt guilty about the attraction I still felt for Iain, when I was with Jax, but I couldn't ignore it. I had spent the last two years longing for him to return, longing for just one minute with him so I could find out what was truly between us. Fantasy, or reality?

Her hand dropped in defeat and she nodded. "I'll...be here," she said. I walked towards him, taking a deep, calming breath as I did. It was as if the entire world around us melted away, leaving us momentarily suspended in time, staring at each other from across a table of jeans.

"Hi," I said softly. He blinked as if he still didn't believe I was standing right there, his Adam's apple bobbing as he swallowed hard.

"Hi," he finally choked out. He cleared his throat, offering me an uncertain smile, his blue eyes drinking in my face. I wondered if he was thirsting for details of this moment, just like I was.

"Can we talk?" I asked him, tilting my head. My heart was pounding in my chest. It was hard to ignore the attraction that snapped and sizzled between us, even with Jax's face appearing in my mind.

"Yeah, sure," Iain put his hands in his faded jean pockets, gesturing with his head towards a vacant mall bench outside of H&M. With Jenna watching with a careful eye, I accompanied him to the bench.

I put a respectable amount of distance between us, mainly to protect myself. I wasn't sure what would happen if we touched. He still smelt like an enticing combination of books and forest. I hugged myself with my arms as I stared at him, trying to hold in the broken pieces that his silence had left.

"Why?" I whispered, my voice wavering with pain, my eyes desperately searching his for an answer.

Iain looked at me, tormented, not surprised at all by my first question. "I couldn't talk to you Harlow," he confessed, looking away from me. "I wanted to...I just couldn't."

"Because of your sentence?" I asked, needing to understand.

"A little bit, but also because...jail changes you Harlow," Iain explained, slouching over and holding his head in his hands. He sounded older, although he barely looked older. Exhaustion and regret warred in his voice. His face was still as handsome as it had always been, the stubble across his jaw line just adding to his physical appeal.

I couldn't think of a reply to that. I sat on the bench, my arms crossed and my foot tapping nervously. "What about now? Why couldn't you talk to me now?"

"I'm a shell of the man I once was," Iain told me, speaking to the ground. "I'm not the same."

"I'm sorry," I whispered, feeling the tears well up in my eyes. "It's all my fault." I looked away, feeling an overwhelming amount of grief and pain.

"No, hey, no," Iain argued. He lifted his hands, gently cupping my face as he brushed away the tears from my cheeks with the pads of his thumbs. "I should have known better. I did know better. I just couldn't stay away...you were always my weakness, Harlow. Even now."

I drew in a breath, the sting of his sentence cutting deep. It was the truth though, and I had been aware of it for quite some time now. We both had known better, we both had known it was dangerous and foolish, but I had pressed. We had both been too weak to say no to desire.

"Harlow, I don't regret it...I don't regret you," he continued, his hands still cupping my face tenderly. He gave me a weak smile. "Who knows, maybe one day..." he trailed off, letting the sentence hang between us.

I shook my head, thinking about Jax as more tears spilled out. Guilt consumed me. Iain had endured jail time for being with me, and while I still had strong feelings for Iain...I had also fallen hard for Jax. I never thought it was possible to love two people at once, to literally feel torn over them both.

"I didn't know if I would ever see you again," I whispered, pulling away from his touch. I instantly felt empty with the warmth of his hands gone.

"I'm sorry," Iain apologized. I could hear the heartbreak in his own voice. "I never meant to hurt you, Harlow. Not then, not after, and not now. I love you."

I stood up quickly, furiously brushing the tears from my cheeks as I spotted Jenna leaving the store. "I have to go."

Iain said nothing more. He sat on the mall bench, watching as I walked away, my shoulders shaking as I sobbed into my hands.

THE NEXT EVENING, I hopped in the shower while I waited for Jax to get off work. Jenna and Lucas would be gone for a while, leaving Jax and I alone in the apartment. I knew I had to tell him.

I took my time in the shower, lathering the shampoo into my long hair and letting the hot water heat my chilled soul. I couldn't stop thinking guilty about Iain, about the shiver of desire I had felt when our eyes locked across the store. I had no idea what I was going to tell Jax, I had no idea what he would think of me. *I* didn't know what I thought about me. I didn't even know what I wanted...or who.

Time, I thought. *I need time.*

When the water ran cold, I turned off the shower and stepped out. I wrapped a towel around my waist and left the bathroom, making my way down the short hallway to my bedroom.

I flicked on my bedroom light, and then froze. A heavy weight of ice cold fear settled in the pit of my stomach as I looked into the sneering face of Andrew Cooper.

He was sitting on the end of my bed, twirling a hunting knife in his fingers. He was almost unrecognizable, his dark curls had been sheared off. His cheeks were more angular, his classic boy next door looks faded to reveal the twisted rage and hatred from within.

"I've been waiting *a long time* for this," he told me, his voice hard and cruel. I let out a terrified scream and attempted to flee from my room. Andrew chased me, his hand grasping my long wet hair. He yanked back with force, my eyes watered as I was propelled backward into his chest. He yanked my head to the side so that the steel of his hunting knife kissed the artery in my throat. "Oh, you're not going anywhere," he whispered, licking my ear.

He dragged me back towards my bedroom and tossed me toward my bed. I fell onto the mattress, struggling to keep the towel around me as Andrew looked on with a bemused expression in his cold eyes.

He was so different from the last time I saw him. Gone was the carefree, untouchable attitude of a spoiled boy who always got his way. In its place was a twisted creature whom I knew was capable of even more terrible things than he had ever done before.

My heart was pounding with fear and dread. All of the self-defense classes hadn't prepared me for this.

"My boyfriend will be here soon!" I spat at him, trying to back away as he approached me.

"Jax? Nah, he's not coming," Andrew grinned maliciously, caressing the tip of his hunting knife.

"What did you do to him?" I demanded, my voice shaking with dread.

"Oh, nothing," Andrew shrugged innocently, the wicked grin still on his thin lips. "But his truck...yeah. He won't be driving anywhere. Now...where were we?" He studied me for a moment, as if thinking. "Oh, right. Back to how I've waited a *very* long time for this."

"For what?" My pulse was roaring in my ears, and my stomach churned with disgust and fear, but I held his gaze. I knew I had to keep him talking, to keep him distracted.

"You are the reason that my father rots away in jail and my family name is forever tarnished," Andrew chuckled, shaking his head ruefully. He tapped the hunting knife in his left hand. "All the trouble you caused me...you're going to pay."

"You did that to yourself," I argued, my voice wavering.

"Perhaps," Andrew sneered, his eyes roaming my barely concealed body hungrily. "I had a good thing going though, and you came to town and ruined it. And I haven't even had the pleasure of fucking you. Seems a bit unfair, no?"

While Andrew talked, I desperately searched my room with my eyes for something I could use as a weapon. Unless I could beat him unconscious with my laptop, I had nothing.

"First," Andrew told me, undoing the button on his jeans. "I'm going to fuck you. Then," he continued, lifting up the hunting knife tenderly. "I'm going to fuck you with this."

I gulped, drawing my legs up tight against my chest. I had never been more afraid in my life. He moved quickly, ripping the towel from my feeble hands and throwing it aside.

"Jax seems to enjoy your sweet little cunt, I wonder how he'll like it once I've ripped it apart?" Andrew asked with a twisted laugh, his vile words making my skin crawl.

He moved quickly, and I struggled. I kneed him hard, connecting with the sensitive spot between his legs.

Andrew swore, cracking the butt of the hunting knife down on my left cheek. My vision blurred with searing pain. I felt the warmth of blood trickling down my cheek, into my ear. I felt him struggling with his pants, trying to free himself of them. I closed my eyes, tears escaping freely down my cheeks.

Before he could free himself, the door to my bedroom flew open. I felt a lightness as Andrew was lifted from my body and thrown against the wall by an enraged Jax.

Andrew jumped up, the knife gone from his hands. Jax advanced on him, the rage evident on his face. Andrew rushed at Jax, head-butting him in the stomach. They stumbled backwards, but Jax was stronger from years of MMA training. He shoved Andrew and punched him hard enough to crack a rib. Andrew fell back from the impact.

"Harlow, run!" Jax instructed, turning his head momentarily to look at me desperately.

"Look out!" I screamed, seeing Andrew flying at Jax with the knife. Jax raised his left arm, blocking the attack and punched Andrew in the jaw with such a force that the sickening crunch of his jaw bones breaking could be heard over the sound of my panicked hyperventilating.

Andrew fell back again, this time hitting his head off of my dresser. He slumped to the floor, unconscious.

I whimpered, trembling. Jax picked up the towel, offering it to me so that I could cover up my body. He lifted me up, carrying me out of the bedroom just as the police were spilling into the apartment.

Jax was pale, his eyes searched mine desperately. "Are you okay? Did he...?"

"No," I trembled, unable to stop shaking. "You came in time." Tears of relief were pouring down my face and his. He lifted his left hand shakily to my face, wiping the blood from my cheek. I looked down, there was so much blood. My head started to swirl when I realized that Jax was bleeding profusely from a massive gash in his forearm. I saw the white of his bone.

"Jax, you're bleeding," I muttered, before the darkness consumed me.

I woke up in a hospital bed some time later. The moment my eyes opened, Jenna was on me, crying hysterically. "Oh my God Harlow! Are you okay?"

"I'm fine...I think," I answered her. Speaking alerted me to the sensation of tightness on my cheek point. I tentatively reached up, feeling tape.

"You needed stitches," Jenna explained, tears still pouring down her face. I dropped my hand, nodding.

"Where is Jax? Is he okay?" I asked, suddenly remembering all the blood. My head swirled again.

"Yeah, he's in the hall...giving his statement," Jenna's voice shook. "I called your parents, and mine. They're all on their way right now."

I couldn't even be angry at her. I would have done the same if the roles were reversed.

Jenna sat down in the chair beside my bed, she was shaking. "I thought I saw him, I could have sworn it was him. I should have done something to the police before...before this."

"I thought I did too," I told her, trying to comfort her. "I called Officer Mike Turner, and he told me that Andrew was nowhere near Ottawa."

"Well, he was wrong," Jenna said bitterly. At that moment, Jax walked into my hospital room. His hair was mused, as if he had been running his hands frantically through it. His left forearm was bandaged tightly.

"They want to talk to you," Jax told Jenna, gesturing

towards the hallway. She nodded as she stood up and squeezed my hand.

"I'll be back," she promised.

Jax sat down in the now vacant chair, smiling at me through the brokenness. His hands cupped around mine.

"How did you know?" I whispered. I still had no idea how Jax ended up getting to the apartment in time. How did he know I was in danger, when I hadn't even known?

"It was my roommate," Jax answered heavily. "I went out to my truck, to head over to your place. All the tires were slashed. I went back to my room, trying to call you. It kept going to voicemail. Then I noticed a weird glint on the poster by my desk...I looked closer, and it was a camera lens. A fucking camera lens." Jax released my hand, running both of his through his hair in aggravation, as if he couldn't believe that it had gone unnoticed. "I pulled on it, and the cords went through the wall into the room beside mine. I fucking broke down the door, and I found all these...pictures of you Harlow, and a video." His voice broke.

"It's not your fault, you didn't know," I told him, trying to comfort him. Jax smiled at me with tired eyes.

"No, I didn't. Because if I had known, I would have killed him sooner."

"He's dead?!" I exclaimed.

"Oh, no," Jax said darkly, as if he wished he was. "He's alive. He's in jail. They are likely going to charge him with breaking and entering, aggravated assault, assault with a weapon, and attempted murder. He's going away for a long time."

I nodded, feeling numb from all the fear.

"I'm sorry I didn't tell you about Andrew Cooper," I apologized. "It's just...it happened to Jenna, I didn't feel it would be right of me to tell her story..."

"She told me," Jax said, sighing heavily. "It's not like you knew he was in town, either. And I didn't even know him by Andrew. He went by Drew. I barely talked to the guy all year. He kept to himself."

Tired of laying down, I pulled myself up into a sitting position, leaning out of the bed to wrap my arms around Jax.

"Thank you," I told him, fresh tears welling up. "I don't know what would have happened to me if you weren't there."

Jax held me close as we both shook.

CHAPTER
FIFTEEN

The police revealed that Jenna and I wouldn't have to worry about Andrew Cooper anymore. He would be charged with one count of breaking and entering, two counts of aggravated assault, two counts of assault with a weapon, and one count of attempted murder. Based on the overwhelming, incriminating evidence found in his room alone, along with his prior record from North Bay, it would be a slam dunk case.

The hospital released me after holding me for observation overnight. The doctors feared that I was in shock, and wouldn't let me go until I had spoken to the psychiatrist.

Speaking to the psychiatrist was painful. She recommended that I see her once a week for at least six months to make sure I didn't develop any systems of Post Traumatic Stress Disorder. I wasn't exactly pleased about it, but at least my student benefits through would cover it.

Lucas handled Jamie and Mark, explaining to them what happened. They called me when I was still in the hospital, and Jamie told me to take as much time as I needed, but I honestly just wanted to get back to work and move past it. No harm, no foul. Shortly after, my hospital room was overrun by my mom, Larry, and Jenna's parents. I could tell the nurses were relieved to be handing me my discharge papers.

The moment we got home, Mom started trying to talk me in to going back to North Bay with them, but I refused. The four of them decided to get a nearby hotel for the next week, just to be close by.

Christmas was in a few short days, and Mom couldn't bare the thought of leaving me so soon. I couldn't bare the thought of enduring another week of having my apartment stuffed to the nines with overly concerned people.

It was bad enough that everyone, excluding me, was obsessing over the blood on the carpet and mattress. While Larry and Mr. Burke went out to pick up dinner, Mrs. Burke, Jenna, and my Mom tried to scrub the blood out. When it was clear that the stain would never fade, they started to talk about ripping up the carpet to ordering me a new mattress. I hadn't even been home from the hospital for a solid day yet, and I was already ready to toss myself out the nearest window.

"You guys are being ridiculous," I grumbled, grabbing the edge of the mattress and tugging it out of Mom's hands. I flipped it over, hiding the stain on the other side. "It's mostly my blood and Jax's anyway."

A loud knock at the door interrupted their argument, but they finally settled for moving the furniture around. I left them to it, intent on answering the door.

I opened it, staring with my mouth agape at Iain Bentley. "Harlow!" he exclaimed, his eyes widening as he took in the taped stitches and massive, ugly bruise on my cheek bone. I glanced behind me, making sure that my mom, Jenna and Mrs. Burke were all still preoccupied in my bedroom. I stepped out into the hallway, closing the door gently behind me.

"What are you doing here?" I demanded, crossing my arms to keep my trembling hands hidden. I hadn't told Iain where I lived, although it wasn't impossible to find out that information if he had access to a phone directory and had clued in that I was living with Jenna, which he probably had.

"I had to see you," Iain said, still staring at my cheek. "What happened to you?" Iain stepped towards me, gently cupping my left cheek and turning my face so he could inspect the wound.

"I'm fine. I just had a run in with the butt of a knife," I tried to shrug it off, turning my face away from his hand.

"What?!" Iain demanded, his eyes hardening at the thought of someone hitting me.

Sighing, I rolled my eyes. "Andrew Cooper paid me a visit. Don't worry, he's been arrested and is sitting in jail. Aside from the fucked up cheek, I'm fine."

Suddenly, Iain was pulling me towards him. I collided into his chest, his arms tightening around me in a hug that stopped my heart. "I almost lost you again," he muttered into my hair. I felt his hot breath on the top of my head, and I felt him losing control.

Iain's hands tangled gently in my hair, tipping my head back to bring my lips to his. He kissed me as if he was starved for me, and he must have been. With tears burning behind my closed eyelids, my body responded naturally, as it would have had it been two years ago, before the arrest, before the silence, and before Jax.

The thought of Jax sent an electrical current through my body. *This is* wrong, I thought, the tears spilling freely from my eyes as I pulled away. It hadn't been quick enough. I had kissed him back, and a the part of that wasn't twisted with guilt over Jax had enjoyed it.

"Iain..." I choked on my words, heartache and confusion

evident on my face. He touched my chin, turning my face to his again as he searched my eyes.

Iain opened his mouth, about to speak, when voices drifted up the stairs. Larry and Mr. Burke turned into the hallway, both of them stopped talking when they saw Iain with his hands on me. Larry's face went from smiling to enraged in mere seconds.

"What in God's holy name is going on out here?" he demanded, pointing at Iain threateningly. "Haven't you put her through enough?" he added, as if every bad thing that had ever happened to me was Iain's fault.

"Calm your tits, Larry," I shot at him. "Iain was just leaving." My voice broke. He pursed his lips, nodding once.

"I'll see you later, then," Iain said to me, his Caribbean blue eyes raw with emotion.

I shook my head, unable to tell him no. I didn't know if I *wanted* to see him again, or if I wanted him to remain in the past. I was angry, confused, and reeling from our kiss.

Iain nodded tightly, understanding. I could tell that it broke him.

I didn't bother waiting around to watch him go. I went back into the apartment, finding Jenna, Mom and Mrs. Burke still obliviously debating the blood stain problem in the kitchen.

"Did you have any idea that she was out in the hallway with that monstrous teacher?" Larry bellowed, slamming the door behind him while Mr. Burke stood awkwardly off to the side. I stiffened, turning very slowly around to glare at Larry. Anger serged in my veins, and it far exceeded his own.

"Don't presume that you can come into my apartment and carry on like that, Larry. I'm a grown woman, capable of my own decisions. Step-father or not, you need to realize that," I told him through the narrowed slits of my eyes.

"What was he doing here?" Mom asked, looking back and forth from Larry to me. She looked as if it were her I had betrayed, not Jax.

"Does it matter?" I retorted, throwing my hands up in aggravation.

"Of course it matters!" Mom said in utter disbelief. "You have a wonderful, caring boyfriend who probably literally saved your life, and you're still sneaking around with that teacher?"

"I am not sneaking around with him!" I practically shouted, my blood boiling. Or at least, I *hadn't* been, and I wouldn't. The kiss had caught me off guard. I hadn't had time to process anything before I was being pounced on for answers.

I couldn't think with everybody staring at me with accusation. I looked at Jenna for help. All of the Burkes looked completely shocked at what was transpiring in front of them.

"She isn't," Jenna backed me. "She didn't even know he was here, until yesterday."

"Then why was he touching you!" Larry roared.

"Because I had my face smashed in with a knife!" I retorted, shouting just as loudly.

Our massive family argument was interrupted by someone knocking at the door. Jenna opened the door. Jax was standing at the threshold.

Jax walked in, carrying a massive bag from Sears in his right hand. His left arm was still tender and bandaged. In addition to the deep gash on his arm, he had been cut on his ribs when the knife cut downward. That cut had also required stitches. The man had literally suffered stab wounds for me. My heart felt as if it was caught in my throat.

Jax could sense the tension in the room, he looked from

Larry's red face to mine, from my mother's tears to the white faces of Jenna, Mrs and Mr. Burke.

"I got you a new bed set," he finally said, breaking the heavy silence.

"Thanks," I said, my voice shaking as I accepted the bag from him and set it down beside the island. I was overly aware of all of the eyes on us, of the thick tension that swirled about in the room. "Do you want to go somewhere?" I asked, sending him a pleading look. My eyes were red from crying, and I was certain my face was all blotchy from anger. Guilt and confusion were eating me up, and I knew I had to talk to him.

Jax looked at me, nodding once.

I grabbed my coat, leading the way out of my suffocating apartment building. I took a shaky breath as we stepped out onto the snowy street. Jax's truck was parked against the curb. I had a desperate urge to get in it and drive somewhere, anywhere with him. Leave it all behind...my parents, the trauma of Andrew, Iain...

As if reading my mind, he pulled his keys out from his jacket pocket and hit unlock. "Are you hungry?" he asked me.

"No, I just need to get out of here for a bit. I don't care where," I answered, my voice raw. I climbed into the cab of the truck.

Jax ended up driving to Nepean Point. He parked the truck and I unbuckled my seat belt. I slid over to face him, and he wrapped his right arm around me, pulling me closer.

"Does it hurt?" I asked, referring to his knife wounds. I knew what I was about to tell him would.

"I've been through worse," he answered, smiling charmingly at me.

"Really?" I raised an eyebrow, skeptical.

"Well...kind of. Breaking bones hurts more than getting stabbed, although both suck," Jax shrugged.

I took a deep breath, watching the sun set over the bridge. We were silent for several minutes, both of us lost in our own heads.

"I feel like I should tell you about twelfth grade," I finally said, breaking the silence. I shifted so that I could turn my body to face him. "Actually, I feel like I should tell you a lot of things," I added, thinking about my recent run in with Iain. My eyes felt hot with fresh tears, and I blinked...furiously trying to keep them at bay.

Jax looked at me curiously, but waited in silence for me to continue. The patient, caring warmth in his eyes got me talking. I told him about Lauren, and Lauren's death. I told him about spiraling into depression, and then moving to North Bay.

I told him about the party, about Jenna and Andrew, and I told him about Iain Bentley. I told him about running into Iain at the mall, and how he had appeared at my door earlier.

"He kissed me Jax," I said, my voice shaking. I couldn't meet his eyes. The whole time that I had been talking, Jax had held my hand, gently tracing his thumb across my palm. At my last admission, this action stilled.

Jax drew in a pained breath. I finally met his eyes.

I thought I would find him angry, but he just looked hurt.

"I can't blame him," Jax said after several moments of agonizing silence. "Did you...kiss him back?"

I let out a choked sob, nodding my head as the tears spilled freely from my eyes. "Only for a moment Jax, I was just shocked that he was there."

Jax inhaled again, as if the action burned his lungs. He turned his gaze away from my face, his jaw clenching and releasing. He had let go of my hand to run his through his hair in aggravation as he processed what I just finished telling him...that I had kissed another man.

"Do you still love him?" Jax looked at me, pained.

"A part of me does, Jax," I admitted, imploring him to understand. "Iain was my first love, and it was a complicated situation...but I do know that I'm in love with you, and I don't want to lose you."

The expression on Jax's face could only be described as tortured. I had yet to tell him about my feelings for him, and it seemed almost unfair to admit them in this circumstance, but I had to tell him.

I held my breath, waiting as my heart pounded frantically in terror. It was a different kind of terror than the terror I had felt when Andrew Cooper attacked me. It was the terror of the very real possibility that I could lose Jax, and the realization that I didn't want to.

"I knew you were holding on to something," Jax finally said, his voice raw with heavy emotion. "I told myself I understood, because I do. It doesn't make it hurt any less, hearing it from you."

I let out a strangled sound, bringing my fist up to my mouth to try and hold in my despair. He heard it, and he looked at me again. He gently raised his hand, cupping the side of my neck and cheek gently. He searched my eyes, the pain evident in his.

"What do you want, Harlow?" he whispered.

"You, I want you," I told him, because I did. I couldn't stand the thought of losing him. He nodded, satisfied with my answer. He leaned in to kiss me, hesitating at first as his lips gently brushed against mine. My stomach flipped with desire and anticipation, my body craving his touch even amidst our relationship-changing conversation.

Jax broke the kiss, keeping his forehead pressed to mine. "I knew you had secrets, and I knew you would tell me in your own time. I can't be mad at you for taking time when I told you to do just that." Jax added, referring to the night after the concert.

"I don't deserve you," I whimpered. He was so understanding, even after I admitted that a part of me still loved Iain and that I had kissed him back.

"You do too," Jax assured me, brushing the tears away with his fingers. "I know I'm a catch, but you're definitely worthy," he added, attempting to lighten the mood.

I shoved at his shoulder, apologizing quickly when he winced slightly at the tug of the stitches on his ribs.

"It's alright, I had that coming," Jax laughed. "Besides," he said, growing serious as his gaze locked onto mine. "It's impossible to learn every single detail about someone in just a few months. I already knew all I need to know."

"Oh yeah? And what was that?" I whispered, conscious of how close we were. He smiled tenderly at me, lifting his right hand to touch my bruised cheek.

"I know that you are an incredibly compassionate, strong person. I know that you are fearless and resilient. I know that you make me think and you make me laugh. I know, Harlow Jones, that I am undeniably in love with you. I didn't need all the details of your past to know those things. I'll fight for you Harlow, but I'm hoping it won't come to that," He leaned forward, his lips gently pressing against mine, igniting my soul and consuming my heart.

ABOUT THE AUTHOR

J.C. Hannigan lives in Ontario, Canada with her husband, their two sons, and their dog. She writes contemporary romance stories with compelling characters and vibrant plots that focus on relationships, mental health, social issues, and other life challenges.

http://jchannigan.com

A NOTE FROM THE AUTHOR

If you enjoyed this story (or if you didn't), please take a moment to post a review on Amazon, Goodreads, your blog, or whichever platform you use. Reviews help other readers find books, and I appreciate any and all reviews!

Sign up for my newsletter to receive exclusive stories, sneak peeks, and updates: https://www.subscribepage.com/jchannigannewsletter

Also, I do have a reader's group on Facebook where I share exclusive sneak peeks and other fun stuff: J.C. Hannigan's FANnigans.

OTHER BOOKS BY J.C. HANNIGAN

The Collide Series

Collide

Consumed

Collateral

The Damaged Series

Damaged Goods

Reckless Abandon

The Rebel Series

Rebel Soul

Rebel Heart

Rebel Song

OTHER BOOKS BY J.C. HANNIGAN

The Forgotten Flounders Series
Off Beat
Off Limit

Standalones
The Key to 19B
Coalescence

www.ingramcontent.com/pod-product-compliance
Lightning Source LLC
Chambersburg PA
CBHW051240250626
47155CB00009B/3101